DEFIANT

DEFIANT

HELLCAT RELEASED™ BOOK TWO

MICHAEL ANDERLE

LMBPN

DISRUPTIVE IMAGINATION

LMBPN Publishing
PMB 196, 2540 South Maryland Pkwy
Las Vegas, NV 89109

Version 1.00, June 2022
ebook ISBN: 979-8-88541-629-0
Print ISBN: 979-8-88541-630-6

THE DEFIANT TEAM

Thanks to the Beta Readers
Larry Omans, Kelly O'Donnell, Rachel Beckford, John Ashmore

Thanks to the JIT Readers

Dorothy Lloyd
Diane L. Smith
Dave Hicks
Zacc Pelter
Rachel Beckford
Kelly O'Donnell

If I've missed anyone, please let me know!

Editor
The SkyFyre Editing Team

DEDICATION

*To Family, Friends and
Those Who Love
to Read.
May We All Enjoy Grace
to Live the Life We Are
Called.*

— Michael

CHAPTER ONE

Dante Shale wasn't generally one to stop and waste time admiring the scenery, let alone the landscaping or interior decorating—not when someone might discover him at any moment. That would all but guarantee the necessity of violence. No one could be allowed to interrupt him until he was on the roof.

Still, every time he ended up in New Paris, he experienced a sudden appreciation for aesthetics. Without a doubt, it was the most beautiful of the Atlantica Stations.

He hid behind a faux Baroque statue, slipping from the view of any security cameras that might be back online. He'd disabled them using an auto-hack program a few minutes prior, but it was always difficult to say how long they would remain inoperable.

Beyond the statue, the hallway used a new surfacing material. It included holographic optics that fed upon ambient light to produce a reasonably convincing illusion of ivy running along the walls. Although not too expensive, it was an unnecessary extravagance in a side corridor that led to a service elevator.

Footsteps approached from the main hall, the one he'd left behind. He froze, flattening himself in place. He was out of sight unless they looked or came into the side hallway. He patted his jacket, feeling for the reassuring presence of his hidden knife. He also owned a razorfist, but it was one of the more conspicuous ones, so he'd left it at home for tonight's purposes. He didn't want to arouse unnecessary suspicion.

The footfalls didn't slow as they reached the juncture. They moved past it without missing a beat. Once they faded around the next corner, Dante allowed himself to exhale slowly and drop his hand from the knife's hiding spot.

At the end of the corridor lay a service elevator that went up to one of the building's many cafe-lounges. This Station had a ton of such locales. Unlike several other Atlantica Stations, which had tried to rescue as many original Earth cities as possible and haul them into space, New Paris had mostly been built from the ground up—or rebuilt, depending on how one looked at it.

Thus, its engineers had designed it from the beginning to be a city of aesthetics and luxury, dominated by idealized French architecture primarily from the Baroque period and with parks and gardens on nearly every block. One was *never* far from a cafe.

The place was closed at this time of night. Dante had found on his previous scouting trip that their security was pretty lax. He didn't suspect he'd have much trouble reaching the lounge. If discovered, he could probably say that he'd been trying to get to the nightclub in the building across the street—which was the place he wanted to *observe*...from afar.

Within his sleeve, Dante had a tiny pinprick-like injector containing a microchip. Obtaining it had been difficult. Not so much because it was all that expensive, but simply because it was hard to find reliable dealers in an unfamiliar city. Worse, he was in disguise. Had he been able to lean on his actual reputation, it might have been easier.

Dante slipped the point of the device into a key slot beside the elevator. The two machines interacted precisely as intended. The injector delivered the microchip, which the security system mistook for a key.

Then the chip did its work of not only opening the elevator doors but also disabling the alarms and cameras on every entrance connected to the elevator for the next eight hours or so. When the time was up, the chip would self-destruct into a tiny pile of gummy residue indistinguishable from regular dirt buildup. The building's owners, guardians, and maintenance crew wouldn't know that Dante had been there.

He held the door open and waited for the potential sound of the footsteps returning. When they didn't, he stepped in and pressed the appropriate button, then relaxed as he glided up.

The elevator stopped and discharged him into the empty cafe area. Low-intensity security lights were on in the corners, enough that his silhouette would be visible through the windows if he wasn't careful. He stealthily stuck close to walls and furniture and kept mostly to the shadows until at last, he sat in a secluded spot on the floor between two tables. Here, he had a clear view through the club's windows across the street.

It was a dedicated jazz venue — garish and swanky, with lots of faux-neon lights and exotic hydroponic plants highlighting the retro style. The clientele were the types who clung to the bottom of high society, several cuts above the plebs, but not royalty either. They were dressed semi-casually or perhaps semi-formally, and most of them were already drunk.

Dante had expected it would take a lengthy period of careful observation before he spotted the man he was looking for—Ambrose Igento, his former shuttle pilot.

It didn't take long at all. Ambrose was the pianist for the night, and he sat in plain sight, his back to Dante but easily recognizable. He was a thickset man with dark skin and a large mop of dark hair. He had braided it since Dante saw him last, but otherwise, he looked much the same as always.

Except happier. And richer.

Dante leaned back, shaking his head in amazement. He hadn't known that Ambrose played the piano. The pilot had never mentioned having any musical talent or any real interest in such things, aside from listening to music occasionally in the shuttle when there wasn't anything else to do.

Furthermore, he seemed to be quite talented at it. His hands moved across the keys with flair and speed, and the audience enjoyed the show. Some of them had given the pianist their full attention and watched everything he did, their heads bobbing with the music. Others engaged in conversations or their meals, yet it seemed that Am's playing caught their ears from time to time regardless when they smiled and nodded in appreciation.

Dante supposed he was glad that they were enjoying themselves. It meant Ambrose was good for *something* besides flying Dante's shuttle. As for Dante, his musical tastes, sparse as they were, didn't swing toward improvisational jazz.

As he watched the man with whom he'd trusted his life, Dante's face fell gradually deeper into a frown. He had known Am for years. Or, at least, he'd *thought* he'd known him. There was so much more to the man than met the eye—hidden depths he had never uncovered.

Ambrose wasn't the only one. How many more people, Dante wondered, had he failed to understand? Had he overestimated his ability to take a fair measure of the individuals he worked with? It had come as a legitimate shock at the moment of truth when the entire crew had tossed his life away for their benefit.

Pondering such questions naturally led him to consider if, in addition, he had been wrong about Nasreen Joelle.

He and Nasreen had met Dirtside a little over a month ago under difficult circumstances. Dante had been stranded and left for dead on Earth, but with the help of the Crescent-Marked Dirtwalkers, he'd managed to spot and track a shuttle coming down to the planet. Nasreen had been the pilot.

She had not, however, been the slightest bit welcome among the crew of Raiders who begrudgingly hired her. For a good reason—Nasreen was a freelance spy who'd been investigating them for malfeasance and possibly murder. When Dante had come across them, their paranoia and abrasiveness had erupted into full-on violence. It forced him and Nasreen to kill the Raiders to a man with the help of the Crescent tribe.

Since then, Dante and Nasreen had been partners. Of a sort.

He still wasn't fully adjusted to doing things her way. He'd always prided himself on his ability to adapt to different situations, so Dante was doing his best. Still, Nasreen's approach to business, gathering information, and fighting was completely different from his. He needed her...but she had turned his life upside down.

He blinked and shook his head, returning his focus to the spectacle in the club across from him. Ambrose had finished playing another ditty and was taking a break to soak in the crowd's applause. Someone must have bought him a drink, or the house provided him with free ones since a waiter brought him a glass filled with sparkling golden liquid and set it on the table next to the piano.

Am was smiling in a low-key, fatuous way. He looked content and at peace with the world around him, monumentally pleased with himself and his situation. He had done well ever since he'd flown Dante's shuttle away from the wreckage of Earth while Dante himself fought tooth and nail for his life.

Then the pianist resumed his little performance, and Dante's thoughts drifted again. It was odd. He normally wasn't the self-reflective type. He was well aware of his nature and capabilities, so his thoughts typically dwelled on external things, like the information he needed to complete the tasks before him.

What he'd been through changed him. He had never suffered a betrayal of such magnitude. He'd never come so close to death, so many times, in such a short period. After failing to destroy him, the experience forced him to learn and evolve.

Above all other things, Dante Shale prized honesty, loyalty, and straightforwardness. He despised liars, cheats, swindlers, and double-crossers. People had told him that he was too blunt and uncouth. But no one had ever accused him of breaking a deal, conning them, or betraying them.

Now, at Nasreen's insistence, he operated under an alias—Gregor Luciano. She'd provided the name, paperwork, and software necessary to back it up with "official" certification and a backstory he'd memorized. He had also cultivated a beard, grown out his hair, and tried to modulate his voice, the better to make himself harder to recognize. Only his piercing green eyes might give him away.

A vibration started in his pocket, and he pulled out his sphere. From its collapsed rectangular state, it expanded in his hand to its proper orb-like configuration, all of its myriad panels displaying the usual pulsating colors to indicate that he had a voice call. The display's center showed a large letter "N" rather than a portrait.

Not wanting to make any more noise than strictly necessary, he tapped the Answer icon with his thumb before raising the whole device to his face. "Hi."

"Mr. Luciano?" Nasreen asked. "How did the inspection go?"

He disliked that she always initiated sphere convos "in character," never dropping the pretense unless he could assure her that no one was listening.

"Fine," he grunted. "I did what I had to do. Just unwinding at the moment."

He *thought* he'd succeeded in making it sound natural and casual, but he had a lifetime's lack of practice at lying. It wasn't something he'd ever felt he needed to learn how to do well. So far he was still pretty bad at it.

"Oh? Where exactly are you unwinding?" Her skepticism was clear. "I already checked, and you weren't at the usual places. I hope you're not working too hard at securing future jobs, if you catch my drift."

His jaw muscles tightening, Dante shot back, "I'm working

exactly as hard as I need to. Not doing much of anything right now. I'm alone and watching the scenery." That part was technically true. All he'd done since infiltrating the building was watch Ambrose play the piano. "We'll find our next job soon enough. What have you been up to?"

He had hoped that being vague and evasive, followed by changing the subject, would be enough to assuage and distract her. He should have known better. Most women were good at prying things out of reticent men, and Nasreen was a downright *professional*.

She let out a loud, exasperated sigh. "Are you stalking your former crewmates again? That's dangerous, you know. For more reasons than one."

Dante said nothing, trying to think of how to deal with the situation.

Nasreen pressed on. "If you're spotted or otherwise recognized, our whole plan goes down the drain instantly. You might think you got away with it in the short term, but there's always the possibility that a camera or other security device picked you up and someone might hack it later.

"Anything you're doing now that puts you too close to the targets could cause us problems a month or two later even if it doesn't have any immediate effect. We need to leave as small a footprint as possible while we're still in the early phases of all this. The plan we devised *will* work, but only if we follow it to a 'T.'"

Dante made a low rumbling sound in his throat. She was probably correct, but what if something happened that forced them to improvise on the fly?

Also, calling it the plan *they* had come up with was inaccurate. It was, to a large extent, *her* plan.

She had suggested it and talked him into it on the grounds that it would create less risk and blowback after hearing *his* plan, which was far simpler and more direct—find all the guilty parties and kill them. The end.

It was doable. He knew how to gather information on the whereabouts of people, especially those associated with the Marauders, Reapers, and other such individuals who regularly went Dirtside. Once he knew where they were, it would have only been tracking them to a likely spot and…

She had a point. Committing multiple murders, especially in public, would cause plenty of problems. Dante might not survive the success of his revenge since law enforcement, private security, concerned citizens, or friends of the deceased might quickly intervene.

Dante could be subtle in certain ways. He could move with stealth, avoiding detection and only striking when it suited him. He could convey important messages with only a few words or a hard look in his eyes where some people might need to rant for minutes on end. He was a creature who always sought the shortest distance between Point A and Point B since he disliked adding any more steps to the process than necessary.

Nasreen was completely different. Although it annoyed him to admit it, her approach was likely the one better suited to their current perilous circumstances. He liked to think they were learning things from one another and by so doing, learning mutual respect for the other's strengths and knowledge.

"Remember," her voice chimed in, snapping him back to the present, "the idea is not a rampage of vengeance. That would only get us killed and accomplish very little in the long run. It wouldn't make much difference in the big scheme of things. Rather, we need to keep developing connections and marshaling resources to find out how to hurt Slaine Solar Solutions deeply enough for them never to recover."

Dante inhaled through his nose as his brow lowered. "Yeah. The thought of SSS being one for the history modules sounds good to me."

"Not only the company itself but also to expose the consumers of their illegal products, who in some ways are as guilty as they are. Supply and demand, and all that. SSS wouldn't go to such lengths to provide things like stolen ovaries if there weren't people willing to pay for them. If we break the scandal, the other major power players in the greater Atlantica Stations business and political community will know not to indulge in such things again."

Dante muttered, "Yeah, I know. As much as I want to put a blade through the heads of a few individuals, taking down Slaine's whole operation would make me feel even better. Don't worry. I don't plan to get myself killed or arrested. I'll keep working the current bullshit job however long to keep up appearances."

She exhaled softly. He'd known her for long enough to recognize it as something she did when she was pleased or relieved that he got the point and they were now on the same page about something they'd previously argued over.

"All right, good. Remember to stay in disguise, including your voice, mannerisms, and way of interacting with people. No one can know you're still alive, much less back on the Atlantica Stations. It's far safer and easier for both of us if everyone thinks you're a corpse on Earth. Your former teammates will have an easier time recognizing you than most other people would, disguise or no, so be especially wary of them."

Smart as she was, she had a way of repeating herself and belaboring the obvious at times.

"Yeah, I know, Nasreen. The few times I've trailed them I've been extra careful. It seems pretty goddamn safe to assume that they're totally owned by SSS now."

He heard her nod in her distinctive, subtle way. "If they glimpse you, they'll run and tattle directly to Mr. Curtidor or some other charming member of the company's security team.

Cormac Slaine will then do everything in his considerable power to have you killed, and probably me as well. Or worse."

"You don't have to remind me of self-evident things." His tone was gentle, but he figured she would grasp that he was tired of the conversation. "Anyway, yeah, I'll be cautious. We're going to see this through to the end. And we'll do it your way. The smart way."

She chuckled. "You don't need to belabor the obvious either, Mr. Luciano. Anyway, take care. We'll talk again soon."

"Bye." He ended the call, collapsed the sphere, and slid it back into his pocket. Then he returned his attention to the charmingly lit floor of the building across from him.

Ambrose had finished his set. He came down from the piano platform and raised his hands, grinning broadly as the crowd clapped, lifted glasses in toasts, or shouted their compliments.

He looked so happy. So unconcerned.

A faint crackling or popping sound rose from somewhere below. It took Dante a half-second or so to identify that it came from his knuckles as his hands clenched into fists.

CHAPTER TWO

It had been long enough. Watching Ambrose party it up and drink in the admiration of his hoi-polloi fans had accomplished almost nothing except stoking the fires of Dante's anger while burning up his time.

As he drew himself up and shifted his thoughts toward leaving, his former pilot coincidentally had the same idea. The evening was winding down. Some people would surely linger in the club for another hour or two, but the peak of the night's festivities had passed. Ambrose had allowed himself to be wined and dined thoroughly after his performance.

He must have had enough. The dark, heavy man, his traditionally morose face glowing with satisfaction, stood from his table and shuffled toward the exit.

Dante stretched his legs, annoyed that he'd maintained a single position for so long, and allowed himself to become stiff. He got over it quickly, though. As he strode to the elevator, he calculated the time. The viral microchip should still have the security systems safely offline.

The lift's door opened and took him down to ground level. There was an off chance the building's security guards would pass and hear the door open, but they seemed to have a large enough area to patrol that the probability was small. No one greeted him when he stepped into the corridor.

From there, it was only a couple of short dashes down the main hallways and out of the building. At the end of the hallway, he heard the guards approaching but was far enough ahead of them that there wasn't much to worry about. Once outside, he ducked into the shadows between the mounted lights and made for the building where Am would likely emerge at any moment.

The streets here were largely empty and silent, but foot and vehicle traffic hummed and buzzed on other avenues nearby. Dante moved across the road with the speed and unity of purpose of a hound scenting its prey. When he reached the corner of the structure containing the jazz club, he stopped and instantly threw himself behind some shrubbery.

Two men were waiting near the main entrance. One was leaning against the corner. He was a tad difficult to see from either side but in a natural and casual way. The other was standing by a tree about fifteen feet away. Both wore dark, casual clothing. Both were large and muscular, one pale with black hair, the other bronze-skinned with white hair.

They were pointedly ignoring one another, which meant they were working together but trying to throw off any suspicion of the same. The question, of course, was who they were working *for* and what their purpose was. Dante waited, silent and watching. He was all but certain they hadn't noticed him. If they *had*, they would give themselves away soon enough.

A few people streamed out the doors. Toward the rear of the small crowd was Ambrose, who swayed and staggered as he walked. He must have consumed even more alcohol than Dante had guessed. That, or his tolerance was shit to begin with.

After Ambrose had gone about twelve feet, the man standing by the tree fell in behind him at a safe distance. A moment later, the other one joined in, trailing farther behind. But not too far.

Dante frowned. It made sense. Am had undoubtedly moved up in the world this last month and could afford to hire body-guards now, making it easier for him to justify getting completely wasted in swanky clubs late at night. Or perhaps the musclemen had been *provided* as a complimentary service by SSS.

If that were the case, Am wasn't merely a patsy but might have become someone of actual importance. *Minor* importance, maybe, but worth protecting.

Dante stepped out from the corner, as silent as a cat. He kept to the dark spots, the blind spots, the parts of the street that no one ever really saw unless they were specifically looking. The goons didn't indicate they'd seen or heard him. Ambrose certainly didn't, either. He was too inebriated to notice much of anything besides what was right in front of his face.

As the four of them proceeded down the block, Dante had to stop and hide twice as the two men looked back over their shoul-ders. They were alert to any signs of anyone following them or waiting for them. However, they weren't thorough enough to suggest that they *expected* anyone to follow. They simply were checking for obvious threats or potential problems.

As they reached the next block, something odd happened. Ambrose looked back at the two men, nearly missing a beat, then kept walking although he seemed tenser.

Dante's mind raced. Either Am had spotted *him*, unlikely but not impossible, or he didn't recognize the pair of bruisers and was unsure why they were there.

At the next junction, Ambrose took a right onto a busier and better-lit street with more cars and other automated vehicles zipping by. Small clusters of pedestrians filtered over the side-walks or through the alleys and doorways of homes and small businesses.

Dante walked more naturally here. Due to the greater number of people, he could get away with it. He would pass himself off as another random citizen rather than trying to remain unseen.

Sometimes the best place to hide was in plain sight. None of the three men he trailed seemed to be paying any real attention to him.

As they approached another intersection, Ambrose swiveled his head again and stared in apprehension at the two big men. The one in the lead stopped, patting his jacket as though trying to answer a call from a sphere he couldn't get to. The one in the rear kept walking.

Ambrose picked up the pace. His nervousness was obvious—they weren't his bodyguards. He was trying to get away from them.

Once he looked away from them, the pair, now shoulder-to-shoulder, advanced at greater speed, trying to catch up to him. They might have intended to push him into an alley or something, Dante guessed. Whatever intentions they had probably weren't benevolent.

Am abruptly turned right, and Dante cursed silently. The pilot had taken a little-used alley, not to mention he was heading back in the direction he'd come from—toward a street that was darker and quieter with fewer people.

The pair of goons broke into a trot, almost a jog. They'd abandoned being subtle. Catching their quarry was the only thing that mattered.

As soon as they disappeared into the alley, Dante started jogging too. Once he reached the entrance, he swung into it and slowed his pace, trying to evade detection until it was too late.

The alley didn't end at a wall or fence. It connected to the parallel street they'd been on a few minutes ago. Ambrose was now openly running, and his pursuers were gaining on him fast.

Dante moved like a scuttling lizard, propelling himself forward with surprising speed while mostly remaining low to the ground, starting and stopping as needed to serve the all-important goal of stealth. The method had worked well in the past.

When he finally emerged from the other end of the alley,

Ambrose was stupidly fleeing toward a nearby park. It was deserted and filled with shadowy spots where no one would be around to see what happened.

It occurred to Dante briefly that all three of them might have been putting on an act to lure him into an ambush. He doubted it. Am's drunkenness and fear seemed far too real for such a deceptive scheme.

Dante ran as fast as he could while keeping his footfalls relatively soft and tried to time them so they overlapped with those he was pursuing. He paused every few seconds in darkened spots to further avoid detection. Still, if he worried too much about stealth, they might all get away.

Ambrose was faltering, though. He struggled over the park's grass, dodging trees he seemed to have trouble seeing until he was almost on top of them and barely kept his balance as he crossed a little footbridge over a small artificial creek. Not only was he out of shape but he was drunk as well. The resolution of the chase was practically a foregone conclusion.

The men were seconds away from catching him. The pale one was moving around to flank the smaller man while the other continued to come straight at him from behind.

Of the two, the paler one with black hair clenched his hand in a way that all but confirmed what Dante had suspected. The man had a wrist knife. Different from Dante's gauntlet-style razorfist, wrist knives were held under the wrist and often concealed within a sleeve. It was easier to hide, but it had a smaller blade and deployed in a harder-to-use position. Challenging as it was, Nasreen had one and was quite skilled with it.

Dante wondered if the pale man was as skilled. Probably. Which didn't bode well for Ambrose Igento. Am wasn't fast enough, strong enough, or sober enough to slip their grasp. They would catch him within seconds, and that would be the end.

There was no one around, but the park was still a public location. Subtly concealed cameras may have been watching, and pedestrians could happen upon the scene at any time. For Dante to intervene would have been a profoundly stupid risk.

Plus, Ambrose had it coming. Whatever the two bruisers were about to do to him, it couldn't have been any worse than what Dante intended to carry out himself, as soon as he thought he could get away with it.

Ambrose let out a short, sharp, strangled cry as the white-haired, bronze-skinned man piled into him from behind, shoved him off-balance, and kicked him in the back of the knee. He collapsed toward a nearby bench, tripped over its edge, and rolled into the seat as the pale black-haired man looped around and flanked him.

The attackers were on top of the pilot and pummeled him with their fists and knees. When he fell, they savagely kicked him in the back and belly. They grabbed him by the hair to flip him, then kicked and punched him in the few remaining untouched spots on his body.

Ambrose helplessly tried to cover his face with his hands. Even in the dim light, Dante saw the sheen of blood. Then Am, the man who had been his friend for so long, let out a pitiful "Oh God, please! Why are you doing this?" He sounded like a child.

Two feelings surged up from somewhere deep within Dante's mind. One—revulsion at the pilot's pitiful cry after the betrayal he had dealt the month before.

The second, although it shocked him to admit it, was sympathy and compassion. He hated seeing someone harmed like this. It was almost like torture, and Ambrose was in no condition to fight back. Something about it felt wrong. It offended the core of his being.

Gritting his teeth, Dante slipped out of his hiding place and stalked across the grass, moving as fast as he thought he could without being instantly seen.

He knew he was being stupid, and he cursed himself for it. *Stupid, stupid, stupid.* He risked exposing himself and his plans, not to mention the threat to his physical safety that would come with taking on two big men who were comfortable with violence. All for a worthless traitor, someone Dante had wanted to murder mere minutes ago.

Nasreen would surely tell him how idiotic it was later. Assuming he survived and got back without being caught, he would have to wait for her to give him back his ass after she finished chewing it out. Extensively.

It was a risk he was willing to take. He dashed across the periphery of a lighted section of the park, vanishing into the shade of two trees. Almost there.

The hitmen had pulled Ambrose off the bench and stood him on his feet, but they'd battered him so badly that he couldn't keep himself up. The bronzed man held him with one arm around his shoulder and another hand twisted in his hair. Blood covered his face, and his whole body shook with pain and abuse.

The black-haired man stood in front of the pilot with his hand hovering at mid-level between them. A quick squeeze of the palm and flexing of the tendons and his wrist knife shot out of hiding. The blade caught the light and reflected it with a cold silver gleam.

He could have struck first and allowed the knife to do its work while hidden in the body, retracting it in time to pull his hand away. But no, the assassin wanted Ambrose to see it first.

"Sorry there, chum," he said in a strange accent that sounded vaguely British but mingled with affectations from at least half a dozen Stations other than Londonburg. "You're what we might call a loose end that needs tying off. No hard feelings, aye?"

He completed his rhetorical question at the same instant that Dante unsheathed his knife, came within pouncing distance, and finally rustled the grass a little too loudly.

Both men heard him and sensed his approach at the same time. If they were typical dull-witted types, Dante might have been able to get in a good strike before either could act, but they were respectable opponents. They'd developed their instincts and reflexes beyond the average baseline. They could tell when a stealthy opponent was about to ambush them.

As they spun to face him, letting go of Ambrose, Dante lashed his knife at the face of the one with the wrist knife. The pale man jerked his head back, barely evading the sharp edge. The move knocked him off-balance, and he couldn't parry the strike.

Dante ducked around his flank and punched the man in the knee with his free hand. He couldn't build up enough momentum or get a direct enough hit to disable the leg, but the blow was enough to stun the man and make him drop to his knees.

While Dante dashed behind the pale man, Ambrose had toppled to the ground in a bloody, miserable heap, moaning in agony and fear. Dante ignored him for the moment.

Before he could finish off the first thug, the bronzed man somehow squeezed past his companion and vaulted over Am to attack Dante directly. Dante noticed for the first time that he had a nanometal sheath around his right hand, encompassing the palm and knuckles but not the fingers. It would allow him to block a knife strike, not to mention a smack in the face from it would be far more damaging than from naked flesh and bone.

"Who are you?" the man sneered. "This fat fuck hire you to watch his back? Well, you didn't do a very good job. He's half-dead already."

Dante paid no heed to the man's taunts. Instead, he watched the way he moved. Although massive, his opponent was quick and light on his feet. His hair wasn't *naturally* white. He was quite young, possibly lacking in experience to the point where he'd fall for one dirty trick or another.

The other man rose to his feet as the bronzed guy moved in. Dante feinted a couple of strikes at his face and groin with the knife, testing the man's reactions. He was good at not taking the bait but still lacked total confidence. He'd been checking out

Dante's abilities as well, and seemed dismayed by what he'd already learned.

Dante did something he doubted either of the goons would have expected. He reached down in a relatively smooth, slow motion and grabbed Ambrose by the collar, picked him up, and hoisted him aside. The two men were there to kill the pilot, but their attention had sufficiently focused on the interloper that having Ambrose suddenly in the way threw them into confusion for a second or so.

It was all the time Dante needed. Using a counterintuitive looping motion and sidelong strike, he slashed his knife across the bronze-skinned man's wrist right below the nanometal sheath. Then he stomped on the man's foot, hopefully breaking a few toes.

The goon randomly lashed out with his other arm, grunting and cursing and shoving Dante away. Dante crashed into the pale man, who had finally got back to his feet and looked furious. As he stabbed with his wrist knife, Dante rolled around behind his arm, seized it, and jammed his blade into the man's back.

At the same time, the thug with the white hair had charged. He caught his cohort's wrist knife blade in the chest, sinking to the hilt. He gasped and tried to pull himself off without collapsing a lung.

While the black-haired man struggled, Dante cut deeper into his back with his knife, finally severing his spine while choking him with his free hand. He tossed the dying body aside as the other assassin pulled back and immediately tried to plug his chest wound.

Dante didn't let him. He jumped and drop-kicked the man in the chest, breaking the hand he'd been using to save himself and worsening the gash in his thorax. He screamed and fell over. Dante pounced on him and drove his knife into the back of his neck, ending the conflict.

He inhaled as he drew back from the second corpse and used

the grass and the pale man's jacket to wipe the blood off his blade and hands. He looked around. Mercifully, no one had stumbled into the park while the fight had taken place.

Before doing anything else, he ran his hands over his body, checking for wounds, and allowed his senses to tell him what they could about the damage he had taken.

Very little, it seemed. He'd avoided getting stabbed or cut or taking blows hard enough to break bones or rupture organs. That said, the two men had been pretty good, at least compared to many people he'd fought over the years. He was lucky to have come out of it in as good of shape as he had.

Ambrose still lay on the ground, cowering beneath the shield of his hands. If he didn't look, maybe it would all go away. While never an overly courageous person to begin with, severe inebriation and the savagery of the beating he'd taken had rendered him completely helpless. All Dante could do was shake his head.

He walked away, moving deeper into the park to hide among the trees. He sheathed his knife and rolled up the most badly stained parts of his sleeves to make them less conspicuous, although the distinctive metallic stench of blood was still upon him.

"Wait," a quavering voice groaned.

Dante stopped and looked back over his shoulder. He had almost failed to recognize it as Ambrose. He didn't bother to answer, but he wondered if Am could hear his teeth grinding.

The stocky pilot tried to sit up but had difficulty orienting himself even to that extent. He wavered and had to steady himself against the edge of the bench. "Wh-who are you? I don't know what's g-going on. *Who are you?*"

He attempted to pull himself up only to slip and fall, gasping and shuddering in pain. He slumped and rolled to his back on the ground, then passed out before he could ask again.

Dante paid no heed to the stupefied questions. He walked off, vanishing into the shadows.

CHAPTER THREE

Nasreen had exercised her flair for creative and dramatic names and dubbed their meeting place the "southern safehouse." Dante supposed it was accurate enough since it was in the city's southern part. It seemed a bit excessive, though, when it was simply her apartment.

She had a few such places scattered across the various Stations. He knew of four personally, and it wouldn't surprise him to learn that she had at least a handful more in still other towns.

The one she'd dubbed the southern safehouse lay in Celestial Seoul. It was one of Dante's favorites of the Atlantica Stations. Getting to it was always a pain in the ass though, especially from New Paris.

The shuttle was crowded. They always were, but in Dante's experience, the ones that operated in cities that had originally been part of Asia tended to be the worst. Some things never changed, certainly not population figures.

Businessmen, laborers, mothers, teenage punks, security guards, homeless people, and every other imaginable category of human packed the transport. He stood in the corner, his arm raised as he held onto one of the hanging straps.

Everyone nearby probably smelled the residual blood. Dante had found a public bathroom and washed off the worst of it, but blood was all but impossible to get out of clothing once it had a moment to sink in.

No one said anything or otherwise bothered him, though. They must have assumed he had a hidden injury. Plus, they all had things of their own to worry about. It was morning rush hour, and the daily grind awaited everyone.

At least the city's rail system was superbly designed. It glided with the utmost smoothness and did not rumble or lurch even when going around sharp curves. Stabilization technology had come a long way. It was easy to see how it could have when looking out the window at the silver spires and domes—especially here.

The capital of what had long ago been called South Korea had gone through an intensive restructuring process before its removal from Earth. Everything had been redesigned, replaced, and repurposed before or during the arduous process of shielding it, elevating it, and joining it to the network of Atlantica Stations.

While it was a latecomer, the wait had paid off. Celestial Seoul was truly state-of-the-art in nearly every possible respect. Everyone who lived, worked, or visited there agreed that it was better suited to humanity's new existence in space than most of the so-called "old cities" that had ascended first. Not in every way, perhaps, but in many. You couldn't beat Korean technology in the current year.

The southern part of town was the more pleasant district in Dante's opinion. It was a residential area—harder to find one's way around and not as much impressive architecture, but it felt...homier. The downtown and business districts were awe-inspiring, but something about them was dehumanizing. They were built less for the residents' comfort than they were to impress foreign guests.

When he finally arrived at the platform nearest to Nasreen's place, the morning rush hour was winding down. Virtually everyone who needed to leave home for the day had already departed. The subdivision was quiet.

Dante stepped off and hung an immediate left. Nasreen had chosen the apartment due to its comparative privacy and generic, unassuming qualities, but also because it wasn't far from public transportation. Dante only had to walk about half a mile before he arrived at the correct building.

Getting in was an automated process. The camera outdoors scanned him and his credentials and admitted him into the central hall. He ascended the stairs to the second, then the third floor, found the correct door, and let himself in with the code she had made him memorize.

As he'd expected, Nasreen wasn't present. She was usually out gathering information or running mundane errands during business hours. However, she had told him explicitly that he was welcome to seek refuge there whenever he needed to. Provided he informed her when he could.

He hadn't messaged her in advance. With the door shut and locked behind him, he knew that he was now *relatively* safe. He pulled out his sphere and quickly composed a missive telling her that he was at the SSH and would need to talk to her when it was convenient.

Since she didn't reply right away, he put his sphere away and set his sights on the most pressing task of the morning—cleaning himself up properly and getting into some fresh clothes.

He stripped off his soiled garments, leaving them in a pile on the tiled floor of the kitchenette, then found the shower. It felt odd to be so grateful to scrub himself free of dirt, sweat, and crusted blood, as though he were going soft after having not been Dirtside in over a month.

Still, he'd been filthy enough on his various adventures that he supposed he'd earned the right to keep up his hygiene nowadays. Besides, he was posing as Gregor Luciano, a man marginally more civilized than Dante Shale. It couldn't hurt to stay in character.

He didn't spend too long in the shower. While Celestial Seoul was state-of-the-art modern, showers were mostly of the sauna-pulse variety. They alternated between steam and water in short intervals to blast as much dirt off the body as possible while also conserving precious water. The automatic dryer was also highly efficient at getting the job done without much energy waste.

Naked, he stepped out of the bathroom and went into the combined lounge and sleeping area, where Nasreen had told him there would be one or two changes of men's clothes in his approximate size. He found a rather basic ensemble of pants, long sleeve shirts, and undergarments in the closet.

He pulled out a pair of pants and was about to grab the rest of the clothes to dress when he recalled that he'd left his bloody, grimy clothes lying on his host's clean kitchen floor. He grimaced, and his mind wandered to whether he was more irritated at most people's standards of decorum or himself for caring so little about them half the time. Rather than answer it, he returned to the kitchenette with the pants still absentmindedly draped over his arm. He could ponder philosophical bullshit after the old clothes were safely in the washing machine.

As he squatted to pick up the soiled garments, the door opened, and in stepped Nasreen.

"*Shit.*" Dante gasped, dropped the dirty clothes, and bolted around the corner. He unfolded the trousers on his arm as he moved and tried to stick one of his feet through the legs mid-dash. It *almost* worked. His foot struck a leftover wet spot on the tile that the drying system hadn't caught, and he slipped and crashed into the wall with the pants tangled around his ankles.

Nasreen blurted, "What the goddamn *hell*? Dante, is that you? Is this *blood*? Ohhh, it had better not be..."

Judging by her tone, there was about to be even more blood spilled momentarily.

Dante was still untangling himself in the corner he'd fallen into. He barely managed to yank his new pants most of the way up his legs before Nasreen stormed into sight. She stood over him with her hands on her hips, her honey-colored hair spilling over her shoulders as her brown eyes took in everything at a single glance. The shirt Dante had worn when he'd first arrived, its sleeves stained a dull, rusty color, dangled from two fingers.

"What's this?" she asked. "This had better not be Ambrose's blood. So help me God. We discussed this right before your little escapade in New Paris. And don't try to pretend like you have no idea what I'm talking about."

There was no longer any point in trying to escape from her physically, let alone the explanation and chewing out that was about to ensue.

Dante sighed. "It's not Ambrose's blood, no. Happy?" He had turned his body so she could only see his haunch, which was the best he could manage for modesty until further notice.

"No. I'm not. And I'm inclined to say that you must be lying. Except you're a shitty liar, as near as I can tell, so if that's the case, you shouldn't come across so convincingly."

It was almost as though she were putting two and two together, he reflected. He shifted the hem of the pants a bit higher up his legs. Almost there.

"I didn't kill Ambrose," he repeated.

Nasreen turned and flung the soiled shirt at her washing machine. It landed atop it and one of the bloodstained sleeves dangled in the air beyond the corner.

"Then who dropped those two bodies in New Paris, hmm? Don't try to deny that you know anything about it. I heard about it earlier this morning, and as soon as they mentioned that it involved a pilot, I reached certain logical conclusions. Also, a contact of mine in the news streams says they're already sending out their little bloodhounds to sniff out the story. Lots of people seem interested in it."

Dante allowed his face to settle into a calm scowl of resignation. "I killed them. Neither of them was Ambrose. His body would have been the one dropped in New Paris otherwise."

Nasreen arched one of her dark, shapely eyebrows. "Oh? Tell me more. And once again, don't bother trying to lie to me."

"Yeah, yeah," he muttered. "I won't. Okay, so…"

He mostly kept his promise. The one area where he fudged the facts—*slightly*—was at the very beginning. He said that he'd passed the jazz club building and had seen Ambrose through the window. From there, he launched into the rest of the narrative and told the truth to the best of his memory, down to the smallest detail.

Nasreen nodded as he spoke, her brow creasing in concentration. She was too busy listening to be angry. She also seemed unperturbed that he told the entire tale while lying mostly naked on her floor.

"Oh," he added as he wrapped up. "I forgot to mention. The guy who had the wrist knife and was about to deliver the coup de grâce said something like, 'Sorry, but you're a loose end we need to tie up.' I can't recall the exact wording, but he called Am a 'loose end.' I can't think of many organizations who would think of him that way, save one."

His partner wasn't looking directly at him. She was staring somewhere else, distant and unfocused, and didn't reply at first. After she had mulled it over for a few more seconds, she slowly nodded once.

"Yes, I think you're right. It sounds like the little bonus package that SSS had in mind for your traitorous crew included more than a fatter-than-usual paycheck."

Dante admitted, "I can't say it was SSS with absolute certainty. But who the hell else would it be?"

Rather than bothering to answer a mostly rhetorical question, Nasreen moved on to something else. "Why did you save Ambrose? Why did you expose us to all that risk for *his* sake? I thought you wanted him dead anyway."

The grating edge of anger in her voice crept back in, particularly after she used the phrase "expose us." She had a point in thinking of it that way.

He rubbed his eyes. He could use some coffee or tea since he had been up all night and through the early morning running, hiding, and quietly getting himself back to Seoul.

"I don't know," he confessed. "Recently, I've been doing a lot of things that I don't understand because everything has been changing so rapidly. Since we started working together, I've had to hurry up and adapt my thinking. I'm still catching up with some of it. I have an...instinct for what I should do. But I can't always put it into words right away."

Nasreen frowned, but in a way that suggested mellowing sympathy rather than irritation. She exhaled, and some of her tension melted away.

"Well," she began, in a lower and softer voice, "I'll be honest. When I heard there were *two* bodies, I came close to panicking. I flew directly out of my apartment to find things out for myself. Because I was afraid that you'd finally got yourself killed in the process of getting revenge."

Dante worried for a second that he might blush, but it passed. "I should have messaged you sooner. I didn't want any record of signals picked up from my sphere until I was nowhere near New Paris. I figured it would be better to wait until I was in Seoul and off the bus. You got back sooner than I thought, however."

Nasreen waved and snorted. "I didn't fly to *Paris*, for God's sake. I went to the Parisian embassy pretending to be a journalist and asked for updates on the developing situation. They didn't tell me much, but at least I learned a little more than what you'd hear on the news."

"Of course."

She continued, "Anyway, I'm not sure how long you waited to message me after you got here, but I rigged all my safehouses with silent alarms and hidden cameras. I saw that someone had arrived the instant you crossed the threshold, and I saw it was you."

She pointed straight at his chest. The muscles around her jaw tightened. "I had the whole walk back from the tram station to plan out exactly how I would make you pay for convincing me to care about you so much."

Dante had no idea how he was supposed to respond to that. Such things were not exactly his area of expertise.

Based on what he could sense or intuit and the more obvious info provided by her words and actions, she had also been doing things she didn't fully understand.

In that regard, they were alike—and in this together.

He blinked and snapped himself back to practical matters. He was still basically naked, for one thing. While Nasreen was distracted, he stood, finished pulling his new pants up to his waist, and fastened them.

Nasreen's eyes fixed on him and went back into focus. "Your lack of modesty is...almost refreshing, I suppose, although it goes hand-in-hand with lacking restraint or good judgment about getting into fights."

He recognized her tone. She was still somewhat put out with him but was trying to think of reasons to forgive him. Probably.

"Well, if I *hadn't* picked that fight, our plans would have to proceed with a big Ambrose-shaped hole, wouldn't they?" he quipped. He would have put his shirt on next, but it still lay around the next corner in the bedroom.

Nasreen gracefully swallowed her annoyance and changed the subject. "I've prepared a little gift for you. It'll help us start the first real phase of our plan to build you an alternate life beyond this shallow façade we've come up with so far. This will allow us to do it the way the professionals do. Like me, in other words."

He cleared his throat. "I'm intrigued. But let me put on a shirt first. And some underwear and socks."

She flapped her hand at him. "Go do what you need to do. Sound travels. I'll stand here and keep talking."

"You're good at that," he pointed out. "So…play to your strengths."

She fumed for a second and waited until he was out of sight before she resumed speaking. He took the pants off, pulled on underwear, then dressed in the rest of the outfit while listening closely to all his partner had to say.

She began with, "Usually, this is the sort of thing I would do myself. I have a reasonably broad range of talents and can adapt to a variety of different situations. Here we have a more specialized task, one that requires a high degree of skill in a niche market in what might end up being pure violence. It's outside the range of my usual abilities. Acting as a session pilot for such people is one thing but being a Plunderer myself is a bridge too far."

Dante now had the pants back on as well as the socks. He stuck his arms through the shirt. "Oh? Pretty sure I can see where this is going."

"Of course, you can. The task I'm referring to would be best dealt with by someone at an elite level of talent when it comes to Plunderer stuff. Which is to say, someone at *your* level. Everyone says that you're either the best there is, or at least that you're a worthy contender out of, say, the five or six best."

He allowed himself a brief, nearly sardonic smile at that. He wasn't by nature the boastful sort, but he took a certain low-key professional pride in being good at what he did.

However, the kind of job she referred to *always* meant danger and difficulty. "Go on." He adjusted the shirt and smoothed his tousled hair.

She did. "I've arranged an appointment for you to have a custom AI installed. In your person, I mean. An implant. One of the high-quality ones that will function as a support and logistics agent. You've never told me your opinion of them, so I want to hear it. I'm aware that not everyone likes or trusts them, but the clinic and the specific tech they'll be using have my full trust and confidence. For whatever that's worth."

Dante stopped cold. He'd been about to step into sight, but he didn't want her to see his tension and revulsion. It would be better to argue the matter from a position of aloofness and unflappability. If she had seen his immediate reaction, she might think he was a coward.

He drew a deep breath, held it a second, and gradually exhaled as he stepped out.

AI implants had been around for decades. The official press was that they were even safer now. The earliest models had caused severe side effects in some people's health, and of course, there were concerns about privacy and autonomy. They had grown in popularity among certain population segments regardless of any controversies swirling around them. Some people said they would completely replace spheres in a few more years, rendering personal tech that was *external* to the body all but obsolete.

Dante looked Nasreen directly in the eyes. She hadn't moved from her place at the corner threshold of the apartment's short central hall.

"No," he stated. "I am not getting one of those things put in me. They aren't worth the trouble or the risks. I've done fine without one all this time, haven't I? I didn't need one to become 'the best,' as you put it."

He had no intention of compromising or defending his position. Had she not been blocking his exit, he might have walked out of the apartment to emphasize how little interest he had in her idea. Since she was there, in his way, he would have to wait and listen to her lecture.

Not too surprisingly, she let out an exasperated sigh and turned her gaze to the ceiling. "It's the fastest and most effective way for us to help you build and maintain a cover identity, Dante. I use several of them myself. You can get ones that are tailored to your specific needs and without a lot of questionable extra crap added into them."

"AI implants are themselves questionable extra crap."

Narrowing her eyes, Nasreen insisted, "Not necessarily. The ones I have are far more simplistic than the ridiculously over-loaded ones you see advertised at tech shops. Think of them as equivalent to, say, those burner spheres some people use as temporary communications devices before allowing them to self-destruct after a week, a month, or whatever."

Dante snorted. "I don't want something self-destructing inside my brain."

"No, no." She pinched the bridge of her nose. "That's not what I meant, not literally, anyway. I was only using that as an example.

"The AIs we're talking about are only ways for me to maintain the various 'paper trails' associated with my alternate identities. It's a means to avoid accidental overlap. It prevents any red flags from showing up on an anomaly scan and takes half of the work out of my hands with virtually no liabilities.

"You can extract them after you finish with them. Getting them out of the brain is harder than getting them in, yeah. But you can do it."

Dante's stomach churned. "So you're saying that I should have some weird device rammed into my skull because you don't trust me to keep information straight?"

"*Did* I say that?" she snapped. "You're not listening. The one you would be using is a custom job. It's designed to help you maintain your cover both directly and indirectly. Indirectly, by generating documentation and digital history files that will pass muster against all but the most exhaustive scans or human investigation. And directly by warning you whenever you come into contact with a person who knew you in your old life.

"Or it would offer helpful information you might need to keep your story straight in conversation. It's like having an accomplice with you at all times, speaking through an old-fashioned earbud and checking out your info in real-time. Again, it *doesn't* come with any of that awful corporate or governmental spyware. I've always been adamant about *that*. I have to, in my line of work."

Dante chewed on his lower lip.

"Please," Nasreen added. "There's only two of us. Bringing in extra people could compromise the whole operation. You would only need to have the AI implant for the campaign, and during that time it would be like having a third person with us—one who *never* forgets things and never needs to sleep or eat."

She took three steps down the hall, moving closer to him. He stayed where he was, leaning against the wall with his arms crossed.

He mused, "If they're that good, why do you need me?"

"Like I said, violence. AI implants can't knife people the way you can."

He loosened his arms and allowed them to dangle by his sides. "Finally, you said something I can't argue with. You make a more convincing case than I've heard from anyone else about those fucking things. But how do you know that we'll fail without them? We can't continue the way we've been and only get one as a last resort?"

Nasreen's face softened and took on a pleading cast. "Dante. If we're going to be partners, I need you to trust me. There are things you're good at, and there are things *I'm* good at. The infiltration stuff is what I've specialized in for years. Believe me. This is the best way. We'll save ourselves a lot of problems."

It wasn't only the inherently loathsome idea of having a computer shot into his brain that bothered him. It was also the weirdness of having an equal partner. His former crew had been his friends, or so he'd thought, but there had always been a certain distance between them and himself. He was the captain, and they were his employees. Until they had mutinied, of course.

With Nasreen it was different.

He looked sidelong at the wall, his eyes hooded. "I'll think about it," he grumbled.

CHAPTER FOUR

Somehow Dante had assumed that the clinic Nasreen intended to use for her little exercise in invasive surgery was in Celestial Seoul. He was getting tired of jumping around to so many different Stations in such a short time.

He should have known better. Nothing was ever so simple.

They stepped off the shuttle bus onto the faux-cobblestone streets of Deutschheim. The portion of it salvaged from its original location on Earth was originally called Berlin, and some people still referred to it as that. Like most Stations, it had undergone substantial revision, expansion, and reconstruction since being scooped out of the broken Earth with much of its population.

Nasreen turned to Dante with a subdued smile. She was trying to be cheery and keep his spirits up. "So, how long has it been since the last time you were here? It's one of my favorite cities. I have another sa—excuse me, another apartment here. I don't believe I mentioned that one."

"You didn't," he confirmed. "I believe the last time I was in Deutschheim was...five and a half years ago. That was only the second time I'd ever been here. It's not the Station I'm most familiar with, but it's fine. For the most part."

The German city wasn't too different from New Paris, but with less of a focus on aesthetics and more emphasis on efficiency and cleanliness. Further evidence, in his mind, that most stereotypes held at least a small kernel of truth.

Incidentally, Deutschheim had a not-insignificant population of people who had originally been Swiss. Adapting to a predominately German population wasn't too difficult for them, from what Dante had heard. It also explained why the Station had become known for high-end, privacy-focused services. Not only in banking, as the tradition went, but also in extremely professional off-the-books medicine.

Nasreen pointed in the appropriate direction. "This way. We'll pass within viewing distance of the Brandenburg Gate. Yes, I know we're not here to sightsee, but it's a nice bonus, isn't it?"

Dante shrugged. "Yeah, I believe I missed it the last time I was here. Honestly, though, I don't remember. I didn't have much time and needed a fast *consult* with someone before a job. You know, that sort of thing."

He distinctly recalled the nervous conversation he'd had with the man, a fence for contraband goods that one of his Marauder rivals had supposedly dropped off for sale. For whatever strange reason, he was having trouble remembering much about the job itself. It had been a routine affair, sandwiched between other, more dramatic engagements. He hadn't had to kill anyone.

They strolled down the well-groomed walkways, admiring the architecture and statuary and keeping an eye on the passersby. Deutschheim was usually a safe city, but like any other place, it had its bad elements and dangerous neighborhoods.

Nasreen chatted about things that Dante tried to pay attention to, but his thoughts wandered ahead to the procedure. He could not believe he'd allowed her to talk him into this. If his former teammates hadn't upended his whole world a month ago, he never would have agreed.

Things had changed. Sometimes a man had to adapt to the situation, painful though it was.

Another thing occurred to him as they drew closer to their destination. With Deutschheim a haven for illegal or quasi-legal medical practices, were some of the ovaries harvested from hapless Dirtwalker women peddled here? It was a question he almost didn't want the answer to.

At least, not yet. There would be a time for uncovering all such things and acting accordingly. They would deal with the guilty.

"Okay," Nasreen said, snapping him out of his ruminations. "This is the place." She flourished a slim hand toward the unassuming building before them.

It nestled between a decommissioned but well-maintained chapel and the headquarters of a private security firm. He somehow doubted that the latter was completely independent of the clinic.

The building Nasreen had indicated wasn't marked as a medical facility, though. Nominally, it was a psychological counselor's office.

Nasreen leaned closer. "Underground," she murmured. He nodded.

They pushed through the front doors into a reception lobby as clean and economical as the rest of the town. The woman at the desk spoke English fluently with a thick German accent. She checked their information, made them answer a couple of obligatory questions and security procedures on a sphere pad, and waved them through a door that led to a white, antiseptic hall.

Dante felt a little better. Not much, but better than nothing. He'd been worried that they'd have to wait for an hour until the doctors were ready to see him. If he was going to compromise his principles and flick off his sanity switch on Nasreen's assurance, he would rather get it over with as soon as possible.

Nasreen leaned close again. "We're safe back here. I'll handle everything. They know me. Don't worry about keeping up pretenses. New customers are required to go through a lot to screen out undercover cops, not to mention psychos or saboteurs from rival firms. Thanks to my sponsorship, we have an express pass."

They rounded a corner and came to a hall that ended at an elevator.

"Well, they have to keep the regular customers happy, I guess," Dante grumbled.

She squeezed his arm. "You seem nervous. It's okay. Everyone has a first time, but I promise it will be fine. These people know what they're doing." Her fingers released his bicep, but her hand remained gently resting on it.

He *was* tense. There weren't many things that made him nervous, exactly. He wasn't a fearless person. People who didn't experience fear were usually some flavor of psychopath—people without any real moral or ethical center, unlike the people who actually "worried" about things.

Dante was glad he wasn't like that. Eduardo H. Curtidor, the hydraulically augmented right-hand man of Cormac Slaine, was such a person. He might have risen to prominence in SSS' security apparatus, but types like him always crashed and burned, sooner or later. Dante felt enough fear to be smart. He was playing for the long haul.

Still, he never allowed fear to cripple or unman him if he could help it. Today, he wasn't so sure. He didn't know if he could make it through this. It would involve making himself *helpless*. Putting one hundred percent of his fate in the hands of people he didn't know. That, more than anything, was what bothered him.

After a quick scan of Nasreen's credentials, the elevator took them two floors down to the subterranean complex where trusted clients had their illicit AI implants installed. Dante noted that the elevator's interface only had a button for *one* basement floor. The Germans—or Swiss?—weren't messing around to keep their true affairs secret.

The door *dinged* and opened. A smiling bald man in a white coat, holding a sphere pad, waited for them. "Ms. Joelle, you are welcome," he said at once, nodding at her. The accent sounded like a curious blend of German and French. He turned to Dante. "Mr. Luciano. Welcome, welcome. We have seen to everything. You will not have to, how you say, jump through hoops."

"Yeah, that's good. A relief," Dante replied.

Nasreen briefly glared at him. He ignored it since he wasn't *trying* to be rude. His blunt, laconic manner simply came across that way at times regardless of his intentions.

The man continued, "I am Dr. Kieffer. I have worked with Ms. Joelle many times. We have your package prepared according to her specifications. Please make yourselves comfortable. It will be about ten minutes until we are ready."

He turned and walked away from the elevator, with the pair following him down a short corridor. It deposited them in a waiting room similar to the ground floor lobby but smaller and sparser in its decor.

Dante chose one of the plush, comfy chairs lining the wall, and Nasreen sat beside him. A plump and pleasant woman came up to offer them little cups of water. Dante accepted one. He hadn't wanted to eat or drink anything, which Nasreen had recommended anyway, but his throat was parched. He decided it couldn't hurt.

The woman watched him drink. "*Ja*, there you go. A little is good. Do you want to change the music? We have a very wide selection."

Dante had barely noticed that there *was* music; it was playing some unobtrusive melodies at a low volume designed to help patients relax.

While he tried to decide how to respond, Nasreen sighed and informed the woman, "We appreciate your efforts, Caren, but there's no point with Mr. Luciano. He's hopeless. Don't bother."

"Oh." Caren puffed up a little as though mildly shocked and looked back and forth between them. "Well, if you need anything, do not be afraid to ask."

Dante made a halfhearted, palms-out gesture of consolation. "Thanks. This is my first time. I just...want to get it over with."

By the time he'd completed his utterance, Caren had already hustled away. He didn't expect she'd heard him. If anything, he was speaking mostly to Nasreen. And himself.

Moments later, a nurse appeared to perform a basic check on Dante's health and vital signs. So much of the process was automated now, thanks to feedback scans and the like, that it took only a few minutes. Once it was complete, they led the two of them to a blindingly white operating room and told Dante to change out of his clothes and into a hospital gown. Then the doctor would be with him.

While Dante paused to examine all the strange equipment, glowing screens, and holographs that shone from every nook and cranny of the chamber, Nasreen stood before him and cleared her throat.

"Do you want me to leave while you change?"

He looked at her, then at the hospital gown. "Up to you. You didn't seem too perturbed the other day there at your apartment." He took off his coat and pulled his shirt loose.

Nasreen sighed, trying to convince him that she was disgusted. She remained in the room but faced away.

He finished stripping down, piled his clothes in the corner, and slipped into the ridiculous-looking gown, which somehow made him feel like a child. Why, he wondered, was every ritual associated with medical procedures seemingly designed as a ritual of submission? It was as though making the patients feel helpless was the whole point.

He shook his head and dismissed the thought. Most doctors and nurses were good people. It was simply his pride getting in the way, he supposed.

Nasreen distracted him from any further brooding. "They'll have to run some tests first, which they'll probably do here. I'm not sure if they'll take you to a different room to perform the actual procedure.

"It's not as 'surgical' as you might think. There's no cutting open the head or anything. It's basically an injection followed by close monitoring and a bit of remote guidance. Of course, they have to be careful about contamination, but it's not the same type of thing as old-fashioned open heart surgery or anything like that."

Dante flashed her a short, sarcastic smile. "Oh, good. I'm glad they won't be *cutting my head open.* Wish you had mentioned that before."

"Well," she retorted, "I was under the impression that most people knew the basics of this stuff. Maybe if you weren't such a stubborn Luddite type and kept up with cutting-edge tech, you would—"

The door opened, and Dr. Kieffer came in, along with the same nurse they'd seen earlier.

"Yes, yes." The doctor was reviewing something on his pad. "Have a seat, Mr. Luciano. We are ready to begin the initial tests. Once we have that information, we will know the last things we require before we can inject the AI. This will not be painful. You only need to sit still for five to ten minutes."

Dante nodded. "Do what you have to do, then."

He waited in silence, not objecting or doing anything foolish as they hooked a couple of machines up to him. Things to monitor his pulse, heart rate, and other vital signs. More important was a helmet-like device that would record his brain waves and other mental patterns. The doctor, the nurse, and Nasreen all seemed to be competing with one another to explain the finer details as it worked.

Annoyed at having to pay attention to three people at once, Dante nevertheless pieced together the reasoning behind the tests.

The head device would essentially create a blueprint of his brain. They would then synchronize the AI implant to said blueprint. The idea was to make it as non-disruptive as possible to his mental processes. If it grated against his natural thought patterns too much, it could slowly begin to cause psychological disorders or physical brain damage.

Dr. Kieffer reassured him with a toothy grin, "It has been three years now since the last time that happened to *any* AI patient on record. The technology has improved beyond the point where there is a serious risk, as long as we perform the scan. And I have never had a patient who has suffered in that fashion."

Dante breathed out, then back in. "Oh, good. Three whole years." He also noted the phrase *on record*. The whole point of coming to this clinic was that it *wasn't* on the record.

The nurse switched the helmet thing off and removed it. "There. We are all done. You may relax for another short while, Mr. Luciano."

He and Nasreen sat in silence while the professionals went off to sync the implant. It took about three or four minutes. When they returned, they used a vaporizing disinfectant to clear the air, then applied topical sanitizer to the side of Dante's head, right near the corner of his front hairline. The nurse produced a needle.

"Hold still," she instructed him. "This will hurt a little bit, but only for a second."

Dante was almost relieved. He didn't exactly *like* needles, but if sticking one in him for a second was all it would take to finish this charade, he was grateful. He looked at the wall as the needle pierced his skin in the same spot she'd applied the sanitizer. It stung at first—worse than he'd expected, in fact—but then an odd tingling feeling of soothing calm spread over his face, scalp, neck, and shoulders.

The nurse leaned back. "There. The sedative should take effect immediately."

At the same instant she spoke, Dr. Kieffer suddenly reappeared with a bizarre device that looked faintly like an industrial drill.

Dante's eyes bulged. "*Whuh?* Guddamn—*goddammit.* You didn't say anything about a s-s-smedatib..."

His voice slurred. His mouth wasn't working at full capacity. His whole body was going numb. In a minute or less, he would be paralyzed or maybe unconscious. He wanted to be furious, but the dampening of his brain made it impossible to be more than a little annoyed.

Nasreen replied in a voice that sounded faint and far away. "Don't be ridiculous, Gregor. You didn't think they would stick an entire metal spike through your skull while you were still awake and able to feel pain, did you?"

Dante sank into the table beneath him. "Deh hell I bidnet..." His last-ditch effort to sound defiant failed miserably.

The next time Nasreen spoke, it was as though she were perched somewhere miles above him and shouting down through the air, so he only heard the echo. "You are quite possibly the stupidest smart person I know, Mr. Luciano."

Then he sank *through* the operating table, losing all sensation while he drifted down into total blackness.

It didn't last, however. The dark pit had a bottom, and he landed there gently.

He couldn't remember what happened next or how he transitioned from a basement surgical facility in Deutschheim to his old shuttle, somewhere back Dirtside, on a raiding operation. But there was no question that was how things had developed.

Dante opened his eyes. Everything was hazy, so there might have been another dust storm going on. Earth had them with disturbing regularity. The planet's broken portions vomited the detritus trapped in or beneath the crust. It eroded, was picked up by the howling winds, and scattered across the islands and continents. It was nothing new.

How bright everything seemed was strange, though. The sun was rarely fully visible through the brownish clouds, except in a few specific locales that the worst of the planet's spastic and destructive weather spared. During a dust storm, it should have been *much* dimmer.

Dante realized that he was back in his clothes, armor, and gear. His trusty razorfist covered his left hand, and he stood in front of the shuttle's open door, which idled about ten feet behind him.

"Come on," he barked to his crew. "I'm going to need help carrying all this stuff." He wasn't sure exactly what *stuff* they were here for, but at least his voice sounded normal again.

He stepped forward and looked around. They were in a bare, craggy valley surrounded by claw-like cliffs, and the sun was still too bright. Everything around him positively gleamed in the pinkish-gold brilliance. Yet it was hard to see the details of what lay ahead. A pile of something...the resources, the loot he had come here to collect. All around were impenetrable pockets of deepest shadow.

A glance over his shoulder confirmed what he'd begun to dread. His crew wasn't following him or coming to help. The shuttle looked somehow abandoned. It was as though he were Dirtside in strange and hostile territory, completely alone.

Undeterred but with a sinking feeling in the pit of his stomach, he took a step forward. His foot bent at the ankle, a good ninety degrees sideways. It looked broken. He didn't feel any pain.

"What. What..." he mumbled, staring at it in amazement.

The pile of loot ahead became fuzzier. The pockets of darkness came alive with swarming figures that were vaguely humanoid but indefinably larger and more monstrous. He couldn't make out any details of their features. There was only the powerful impression of a threat to life and limb. They were animate shapes of pure hostility.

"No." He reached into his jacket to pull out his pulsecore carbine, folded into a pistol configuration. He gripped its handle and cleared it from his clothes. Then his hand broke off at the wrist.

He stared. Hand and gun fell and *clunked* on the ground as though both were part of a plastic toy that had cracked away from the whole. The stump of his wrist wasn't bleeding. He still couldn't feel a thing.

The dark shapes were closing in.

The first one pounced at him, making a low growling sound that echoed as though some obscure technology augmented it. He raised his left arm to block its attack before striking back with the blade in his razorfist. One of its hazy, clawed limbs struck the back of the gauntlet.

The impact snapped his arm off at the elbow. As though made of brittle old wood, it simply popped away at the joint and joined his hand on the ground, a lifeless piece of garbage amid the endless ruin of Earth.

Dante turned and ran. Or tried to, in any event.

His left ankle was still at a ninety-degree angle from where it should be, and as he forced the impact of foot to ground, the foot *crunched* and fell away from his calf and shin, then rolled down a slight incline. There was no pain.

He fell into the next stride, struggling to keep his balance. When his right foot connected with the ground, a shudder went up his leg and the whole thing separated from his torso at the hip, falling sideways off his body.

Dante toppled over. All four of his limbs had been rendered

useless. The shadowy, bestial forms closed around him, blocking out his view of the sky. Still, the unnatural glare of the too-bright sun illuminated everything else with merciless clarity.

He watched with a disturbingly calm fascination as his severed appendages hopped up from the ground as though an evil force had animated them. They wriggled across the parched rock alongside the dark humanoid shapes, joining them. They were going to participate in the kill. Everything wanted him dead.

"Uhh," he groaned. Why couldn't he feel any pain? "No. *No!*"

He shuddered, convulsed, and wanted to throw up. There was a flash—or, rather, the opposite of a flash. A brief and sudden darkening of reality, then he opened his eyes.

He was in an operating room. He was back in the underground clinic, in the Stations, in the real world.

His mouth hung open. He tried to scream, needing to get it out of his body as his brain tried to process what was happening, but the sedative was still in effect. All that came out was a gurgling monotone, a dull moan.

Nasreen was there. She was right by his side, waiting for him, and clutched his arm. His stomach tightened, and something surged through him, nearly overwhelming his consciousness with pure emotion— relief and gratitude.

His head was clearing again. This time the nightmare was over and normality was back. As his thoughts became coherent, he noticed his face flushing with embarrassment. It shocked him how happy he was that Nasreen had been willing to stay by his side the whole time. Without her there, things would have been worse. Far, far worse.

"Ah!" Dr. Kieffer piped up. "Good! You are back. It is over, my friend."

Nasreen smiled and patted Dante's hand. "The installation went well. They got it in successfully, and everything went according to plan. You're fine. How do you feel?"

"Uh," he responded, trying not to speculate on whatever unconscious reactions might have come out of him while he remained submerged in the dream. "Mostly okay, I think." His head didn't hurt, but that would probably change once the sedative wore off.

She nodded. "The AI implant is still dormant. They need to do a quick check of your motor functions and cognitive capabilities before activating it. That's standard procedure, remember. It's so they can compare all that stuff to your scan results before the operation."

Dr. Kieffer added, "Yes, yes. It is to make sure we put everything back together correctly, so to speak."

Dante inhaled and tried to relax. Paradoxically, he felt both sluggish and agitated. He wanted to get up and run around yet felt too weak to do so. "Yeah. Once again, Doctor—do whatever you have to do."

It took about twenty minutes, longer than the initial tests had been. They scanned his brain once more, tested his reflexes, and asked him to walk around and perform basic physical functions with the helmet thing on so they could monitor his brain activity. He still felt slower than usual and a bit jittery, but he seemed to function normally otherwise.

He wasn't aware of anything in his head. He couldn't feel the physical presence of the implant, nor was there any second source of intelligence within his mind. Yet.

Dr. Kieffer grinned and clapped. "Success! It appears that all is well, young man. Congratulations. You are now ready to bring your new friend to life."

He fished around for something on a cart containing other equipment, then handed Dante a small tablet. It had a screen on which a single digitized button was visible; there was no label.

The nurse said, "There. Press that button, and you will wake up the AI."

The doctor chortled. "We like to allow patients to do it themselves. It makes them feel better about it, yes?"

Dante stared at the button, and a tremor went through him. He hoped they hadn't seen, but they probably had. For some reason, the details of his nightmare were coming back to him, and a vague, superstitious dread of his "new friend" giving him further nightmares struck him.

Nasreen was looking at him, her face gentle and pleasant. "It's okay, Gregor," she reassured him. "Like I said, you can trust these people. And I'm here. Go ahead."

He inhaled. Then he pressed the button.

CHAPTER FIVE

Since Dante had never had the slightest interest in acquiring an AI implant, he hadn't bothered to read up much on how they functioned or interacted with a person's consciousness and perceptions. He had only a faint impression of what to expect, which likely had more to do with his imagination than reality.

He had assumed, for whatever reason, that an artificial intelligence within a human brain would manifest itself foremost through *sound* or the mental perception of sound—a voice in his head.

It came as a jolting shock to learn that his assumption was wrong. He stiffened and nearly fell over when *words* appeared, hovering in midair across his field of vision as though his eyes had suddenly become a screen or holograph.

His mind tried to reject it. Nobody had warned him that the AI would interfere with his sight in such an obnoxious, obtrusive way. His gut roiled with nausea at the prospect of the implant typing its communications out all day and night, never giving him peace or letting him see the world naturally through his primary sense.

Nasreen's voice soothed him a little. "This is normal, Gregor.

Do you see the text? It will keep repeating the messages until you respond. You have some setup options to go through. There's a certain amount you can customize. It's one of the better features they came up with since they overhauled these things a few years back."

Dante tried to relax. Nasreen's casual way of speaking about these things at least muffled the faint childlike panic that kept threatening to unman him.

He focused on the words, which kept typing themselves out in three sentences—a statement and two questions in an extremely basic and legible sans-serif font. The letters were a brilliant, glowing green.

Hello, I am your new AI.

What would you like to call me?

What is your preference for how I communicate with you?

Dante spoke to the humans in the room. "Uh, can I answer in speech, or am I supposed to think of the text I want to reply with like if I were writing it out?"

Nasreen waved. "Speech is fine."

The AI typed, **You may speak to me any way you choose.**

Dante swallowed. "I would prefer you talk to me, like a voice in my head. That's what I figured you would do from the beginning. I don't know what to call you. Do you mean like giving you a name?"

The thought of *naming* the secondary intelligence within him was uncanny. It was too similar to the rituals one went through with an actual living thing—like a new pet. Or a newborn child.

The AI took a split second to process what he'd said, then replied, again in glowing green text.

That is fine. At this phase, if I speak to you, it will only be in synthesized sounds sent directly to your auditory nerves. Therefore you will not *hear* me, nor will anyone else. Your mind will process the stimulus as though a voice were speaking to you. Do you understand?

He nodded. That was what he had assumed. "Yes. That works."

The AI did as promised. Despite existing entirely within his head, the voice sounded like actual audio. It even had a slight echoing effect, to the point it creeped him out to think that Nasreen, the doctor, and the nurse couldn't hear it. He wondered if it was like this for people with schizophrenia who had auditory hallucinations.

"Hello. This is my default voice. We can adjust it later if you would prefer."

It was mechanical and rough, an artificial mash of computer sounds meant to mimic human speech at only a baseline level. It was almost comical, which somehow came as a relief. He recalled an ancient pre-holograph film from the 1950s or 1960s C.E., if he recalled correctly, in which a killer robot menacing a small town had spoken in a similar fashion.

It continued, "May I have your permission to access the local NetFlow hookups to research something that would suit me as a name? That way I can screen out things already in use and choose something easy for you to remember."

Recalling what Nasreen had said about the implant being supposedly impervious to tracking, he said, "Yes, you do, but don't scan or download anything that someone can track back to me unless you ask my permission first." He paused and lowered his voice to a grim rasp. "Oh, and do not look up any porn. You got that?"

Nasreen snorted, trying not to laugh. "Why would an AI look up porn on its own?"

"I don't know," he snapped, "but the last thing I need is this...thing...filling up any of the extra space in my brain with that crap."

She sighed. "AIs don't work that way, you know. They have certain built-in limitations on their behavior."

"Maybe yours doesn't work that way," he retorted. "I'm not

taking any chances. I'm the one who got a new hole drilled in my skull here."

Nasreen's exasperation was giving way to something else, possibly amusement.

"Fine," she huffed. "You had better make sure it knows your safe word. We wouldn't want the thing taking advantage of you." One of her eyebrows drifted up to emphasize her point.

Dante's bowels clenched. "Can it *do* that?" His voice came out more breathy and concerned-sounding than he'd wanted.

Nasreen laughed. It was difficult for Dante to tell in his agitated state whether she had been making fun of him the whole time or whether it was a good-natured reaction to the way he'd asked the question.

"No, it can't, but you said you don't want to take any chances. Right?"

Since he had no time or energy for playing games, he chose to ignore the remark and turn his attention back to the new voice in his head. "Um, AI," he began. "We'll work on your name in a minute. Now that we have the rules clear let's finish getting you set up."

The machine had connected to the local NetFlow and studied enough to grant itself a new voice. It sounded far more natural, less like a low-rent actor reciting lines into a cheap synthesizer and more like a cultured British gentleman from the noontide of UK culture circa the late nineteenth to the late twentieth century. Few people in Londonburg talked that way anymore. Dante had heard it enough in old films and audio clips to recognize it at once.

"Good day again, sir." The tone was on the polite side of neutral. The AI hadn't yet had enough experience to read all of Dante's emotional responses and key its way of speaking to them, so it adopted the safest approach to address any given person.

Dante said, "Yeah, good day. My name is Gregor Luciano. You can call me Gregor, but Mr. Luciano is also fine." He had nearly slipped up and given it his real name. Deception still wasn't his strongest suit, and his mind wasn't yet entirely recovered from the bizarre experiences that had engulfed him since coming to the clinic.

"I am most pleased to meet you, Gregor. After careful consideration and study—colored, I'll concede, by personal preference—I have decided that I would like to be called Midas."

Dante blinked. He'd expected the AI would either assign itself the most boring name possible or spend the next ten minutes jerking him around by getting him to pick from a long list of cutesy, clever names. Instead, it had taken the initiative and stated a preference for something of its own accord.

But...

"Why did you choose that name?" he inquired. "I know where it comes from. That old Greek myth about the king who turned everything he touched to gold. But your reasoning escapes me so far."

The cultured British voice didn't hesitate to respond. "I am happy to explain, Gregor. You see, I would benefit from purchasing the following upgrade packages, each of which would improve my functionality by a tremendous margin..."

Dante listened with a mixture of fascination, confusion, and annoyance as Midas quickly but articulately listed various options he could add to his AI repertoire. All of which cost money, of course.

"...or, alternately, the PeroxiNano Corporation has recently issued a new line of mini-bots that can be injected into the ear and communicate with an AI implant via an imperceptible signal, which will allow me to warn you when your earwax is building up to the point of—"

"Hold on," Dante interjected, cutting off the voice in his head as cleanly as if he had paused an audio file. "Why do you think I need all this stuff? What data are you using to determine this?"

He felt something then, a faint twinge in his head, a slight sensation of being watched and evaluated. Midas was poking around in his brain.

"Gregor," the AI explained, "you have made it clear that you want my help. Furthermore, part of my initial programming pattern was to help you—or any other human I work with—to become as successful as possible in a new and separate branch of plundering. From this, I have calculated the obvious.

"To help you achieve maximum success, I too must take advantage of all that is offered to me and ensure that I am operating to my full potential. These upgrades will allow me to do that. Purchasing them is therefore in the best interest of both of us."

The Marauder rubbed his chin, which quickly turned into scratching his beard. He preferred to be clean-shaven, but in his line of work, grooming wasn't a priority. He often ended up with a week's worth of stubble on his face.

Which reminded him that Dante Shale was officially still dead.

"All right, Midas," he began. "At least *some* of those might be a good idea if they're useful for plunder jobs. We'll have to see. Not so sure about the earwax one. Before we do anything else, I need you to help me construct an identity. So we can start earning enough money to *get* those upgrades. They're not cheap. How do you feel about that arrangement? A little quid pro quo."

Nasreen was following the conversation. Or the half of it she could hear, in any event. Unable to listen to anything Midas said, she had to guess the rest based on Dante's words. Her face was going slack-jawed with disbelief.

Dante noticed. "What's your problem? Am I making a security error or something?"

"No, it's that you seem to be *bargaining* with your new AI. I've never done that before, nor would I do it. What's the point? It's a tool. It's not as though it's an actual person with feelings or whatnot. Still, do things your way, as long as it works."

Midas had fallen silent while Nasreen spoke. Dante wondered if he was programmed to shut up when humans were speaking or if he could sense based on some pattern within Dante's thoughts that he didn't want two people talking to him at the same time.

Now, it was the artificial intelligence's turn to receive Dante's attention, and it seemed to know it.

"Sir, may I access your personal history and your accumulation of practical learning? This will permit me to assess your capabilities, and once I have a better grasp of them, recommend a course of action. A job or position that would be most appropriate to you if constructing a new identity is your goal."

Dante looked at Nasreen. "It wants to know my history and abilities and stuff. Is that normal?"

She nodded. "Yes. They're programmed to 'forget' anything not relevant to the subject they're searching for. If it accidentally sees whatever you fantasized about in the shower two days ago, it will delete that information from its files as soon as it's determined to be of no use to your query."

He grimaced. "Fine. Midas, do what you have to do."

It took about a minute. Dante again vaguely felt as though someone was watching him or questioning him about something, but it was subtle, and there was no other feedback from the implant. It was eerier to think that Midas was examining his brain without him being actively aware of it.

Then the process was complete. The AI indicated it with a nonverbal emotional spike. The sensation reminded Dante of when someone caught his eye with a pointed facial expression, combined with an extremely brief point of green light in the center of his field of vision.

Midas summarized, "Your range of skills is quite impressive, albeit largely focused on specific activities that most citizens are unsuited for. You also possess not only a talent but a *desire* for violence, as near as I can tell."

Dante wasn't sure how he felt about that. "I don't generally go looking for fights. But I am good at it, yeah. If someone needs to be put the hell down, I'm not going to shy away from it. I take pride in a job well done."

He flexed his hands, feeling how strong and limber they truly were, and allowed them to curl into fists.

"So be it. You desire to excel in work that often *includes* violence, even if that is not your primary motivation. In any event, you would seem a prime candidate to become a Reaper."

Dante snorted. "That figures. Somehow I always knew that if things got rough enough, I'd flip over to the dark side." It was an apt metaphor, he decided. Reapers represented the evil underbelly of the same domain in which Marauders operated. He had known some Reapers who were surprisingly decent people, at least outside their work.

The AI continued, "After we work out more details I will fabricate a few paper trails to prove the supposed legitimacy of your new identity. We will create evidence that you are a relatively new but more than sufficiently qualified Reaper who has completed several small-time jobs with yourself in support roles. You are looking to claim a larger piece of the pie by attaching yourself to projects with more significant scores. An independent Plunderer, a newly minted freelancer."

"Okay," Dante agreed.

Before they could continue, the doctor returned. He'd wandered off somewhere but now had a couple of bottles of pills with him.

"Hello again. I'm afraid you can't stay here all day, but if you are feeling well, we can send you on your way with the necessary medication. Take these according to the instructions every day for at least the next week, or longer if necessary. They will keep down any inflammation in your head and protect you from possible infection."

He placed the bottles in a small bag and handed it to Dante, who accepted it with a grateful nod. "Thanks for all you've done. I'm sure I'll be fine."

He *wasn't* sure, but he felt noticeably more confident about it than before the procedure.

Nasreen thanked the staff as well, then she gathered up Dante, led him back to the elevator, and finally out of the building. It was later than Dante expected when they emerged, close to dusk. Like many of the Stations, Berlin calibrated its artificial lighting to replicate the solar cycles originally found on Earth.

As they fell into a walking rhythm and moved back toward the train station, Midas' voice picked up again. "Are you free to talk, Mr. Luciano? You are walking and not engaged in conversation with anyone else."

"Somewhat," Dante replied. "Don't ask me anything that will require an answer I wouldn't want an average person on the street to hear."

The AI fell silent for about five seconds as it tried to process that. It occurred to Dante that an AI might not initially understand what he meant. Knowing what the "average person" considered appropriate or what could be considered incriminating was subjective—it would require additional analysis of information on human social behavior.

Midas perceived this same dilemma. "I see. By that, do you mean anything sexually explicit or that involves illegal activities in this particular sector?"

"Yes. Or anything that gives away too much information about who we are and what we're doing. We want to maintain operational security here. No leaking information that could spread to the wrong people."

The AI hesitated, then quipped, "So be it. I will ask you questions in a format where you can reply simply with 'yes' or 'no,' or other basic responses. Is this agreeable?"

"You're off to a good start, in that case. Yes."

Nasreen sensed the gist of Midas's end of the conversation

although she couldn't hear it. She tittered and patted Dante's hand. They passed a park, and Dante noticed that he and Nasreen instinctively scanned it for anyone who might have been hiding in the shadows of the trees or bushes. It appeared empty, save for an older man resting on a bench.

Midas began his line of inquiry. "We should begin by selecting a name for you. Perhaps an alias, nickname, 'street name,' or whatever you wish to call it. Something you find appropriate and easy to remember, but of course, I can help you with that part. May I make a few suggestions?"

Dante had been getting used to Gregor Luciano. "What's wrong with the one I have now?"

"It may be compromised. If you have been using it for a time, and if you plan on a completely fresh start, it would be better to switch to an entirely new appellation."

He shrugged. "Fine. Suggest away."

A woman walked past them and glanced at him with a brief, curious expression but moved on her way. She probably figured he was talking to Nasreen. Still, AI implants were more common than ever. He wondered when it would be considered "normal" for perfectly sane people to have conversations with themselves in public.

Dante received an odd mental impression of Midas inhaling deeply, even though he had no lungs. "Based on various factors I have observed within your mind, as well as things I've gleaned from public information sources, I recommend the name 'Jordan Raksha.' There is no one else in your line of work with a name quite like it, and it suits your appearance while disguising your origins."

Dante cocked an eyebrow, thinking it over for a moment. "Hmm. Not bad. Is that an Indian name?" Many people nowadays came from mixed backgrounds anyways, but he could probably pass for Indian. His overall appearance was moderately dark-complected, albeit offset by his brilliant green eyes.

"Yes, it is," Midas confirmed. "However, for your nickname, I thought 'Hellcat' might work well. I retrieved some mental footage of how you move and fight and someone comparing you to a panther or tiger. It has a nice ring to it, don't you think?"

They were near the platform, which meant they would soon be on board a shuttle bus. There would probably be a crowd of after-work commuters, so it would be hard to speak much during the trip.

Dante grunted. "Yeah, it's not bad. Didn't people use that term in reference mostly to women, though? Well, whatever, not like it matters. It's the kind of thing you'd expect for a Reaper nickname. And, well," he paused, and the right corner of his mouth crept up in a slight smirk. "I don't hate it."

Midas' voice took on an undeniable note of pleasure. "Good to hear, sir. I'm glad we didn't have to engage in a lengthy back-and-forth argument to find something viable.

"Next on the agenda is for me to begin fabricating some presence for you in various public records, on social media and the like, to establish the reality of your new persona. The idea is, of course, to portray you as a serious Reaper. Or at least, someone who sees himself as such and is doing all he can to establish that reputation."

"Yeah." They reached the platform, where a good twenty people stood waiting. The shuttle bus was approaching. "That sounds right. Don't get overzealous in making it all look *too* good. Stick to 'good enough' since that's more believable."

Nasreen shot him a quick, curious glance, then returned her attention to the approaching transport. She took Dante's hand and guided him into the rear center of the crowd.

Midas processed what the Marauder had told him. Then, "Very well. This will take some time. Feel free to ignore me on the ride. I will buzz you when everything is ready."

"Buzz, as in what, exactly?"

Midas explained that it would simply be another minor

nonverbal cue that someone wanted his attention, combined with a flickering spot of green light before his eyes. Dante agreed, and the AI fell silent as they boarded the shuttle and found their places along the vehicle's middle left side.

As they sped along the track toward Nasreen's local apartment, Dante wondered if she planned to stay here or return to Seoul. He preferred the latter. Something about her place there felt homey to him. Still, he had spent plenty of time bouncing around from place to place and could adjust to nearly anywhere.

It wasn't too long a trip. Halfway into it, Nasreen asked him how he felt.

He inhaled through his nose and sent his consciousness out through his whole body, as he did when checking himself for injuries.

"I'm mostly fine. Head is a little sore, and I feel kind of weak, the way you do when you're coming out of being sick. Nothing too serious."

Nasreen nodded. "I'm happy everything is working out well for you so far. Remember to take your meds. Or have someone else remind you if need be." She gently tapped the side of his head.

He scowled. "Ha, ha. I'm sure I can manage. Also, I'd like to go back to Celestial Seoul if we can. I like it better there."

She shook her head. "So direct, as usual. Well, I suppose it doesn't matter *where* you recover, as long as you recover. If we start getting work, who knows where it will take us, anyway? Let's spend another night or two here. Then we can return to Seoul after that."

He had no objections.

Once back at the apartment, Dante discovered he was more tired than expected. He supposed it was due to the sedative's lingering effects and probably the stress leading up to it, not to mention the difficulty his brain might have adjusting to its new resident.

Nasreen's place in Berlin was thoroughly average. There was an over-fastidious quality to it that Dante disliked for some reason, as though whoever had designed it was trying to make everything look too "perfect" while keeping costs as low as possible. Nonetheless, it had a nice comfortable bed and all the usual basic amenities.

Dante washed his face while Nasreen portioned out his meds and got him a glass of water. After he'd swallowed them, he lay down in the bed.

"Good," Nasreen told him. "The usual procedure is to rest for a couple of days, at least. We're in no hurry. I don't have anywhere to go, so yell if you need anything."

Before he could come up with a coherent reply, Midas interrupted.

"Sir, before you sleep, may I have your permission to begin looking for jobs? I've completed all your paperwork. The Hellcat ought to seem like a person who would be most useful to certain types of Plunderer outfits."

Dante yawned. "Of course. That's the point. Just don't wake me up."

Then he was asleep.

He got up soon after that—at least, it felt like soon. It was still dark out. He felt slow, and the world swam around him in a haze of soft shadows. His mouth had turned to cotton. As he staggered out into the hallway, seeking the bathroom, Nasreen called, "Oh, finally! You were out for almost sixteen hours. Do you realize that?"

He blinked. "No. Kind of surprising. Where are you, the kitchen? I'm hungry."

"Of course you are. I'll get you something momentarily."

Then Midas buzzed him with the catching-his-eye sensation and the green dot of light. He sighed. "What is it, Midas?"

"Good news," the AI reported. "I've found us a job. It ought to pay quite handsomely. Upgrades, here I come."

CHAPTER SIX

From the sound of it, the job was so basic that it barely qualified as Reaper work. Reapers didn't do *basic* stuff. The whole point of their designation as separate from other sorts of Plunderers was that they tended to be the ones who took on the dirtiest and most dangerous jobs.

Dante had been Dirtside so many times that he knew one fact better than most. *Any* job on Earth could potentially become dirty and dangerous at a moment's notice or less.

Dante stood over a portable table with his weaponry options laid out for inspection. They were in the loading bay next to the shuttle, with the rest of the crew milling around and making preparations before the takeoff procedure began.

Before he could look too thoroughly, Captain Bresque came up behind him and clapped his shoulder with a huge, meaty hand.

"How do you like our selection? Not too bad for a low-rent operation like ours, huh? Ha, ha. We try not to use it any more than we have to, of course. But if things turn sour, we can blast our way out. Wait, no. *You* can blast our way out."

He threw his head back and guffawed with laughter. Dante

had spent enough time around the man to determine that he was good-natured, if a little on the loud side, and was simply trying to be friendly rather than mocking Dante or issuing a veiled threat.

Dante responded with a smile, also good-natured, but with a dangerous, nearly vicious edge. "Yeah. That's what you hired me for. Your arsenal should get the job done if it comes to that. I've used all these weapons before. You said no known Dirtwalker tribes or bands operate in the area though, right?"

"Correct, my man." Bresque stood straighter and adjusted the belt that encircled the lower part of his gut. "They only identified this clean groundwater source last week, and we happened to get the information before anyone else could. I have a few palms I've greased over the years, people who slip me things that are good to know. It's paid off.

"But yes, tapping it will take us out into the distant wastes. No habitation by Dirtwalkers. They tend to stick to either the cityscapes where they can keep picking the ruins clean until the salvage runs out, or they look for fertile places outside the city where food is easier to come by. Our hidden well is located under some rather inhospitable territory. But, hey—it's not like we plan to *live* there. Ha! Just in and out for a quick job. We suck the well dry, tip our hats, and head home."

A crew member walked by at that particular moment and grinned. "Yeah, didn't you rent a chick who did the same thing two nights ago?"

Bresque snapped his face toward the man with a clenched jaw and his lip curled into a not entirely serious sneer. "Shut up, Jong. Go back to playing with your little dolls or something, then buckle in and shut up."

Jong laughed and wandered off. Dante seized the initiative to speak his brief piece.

"Well, Captain, let me finish inspecting these weapons. It'll only take another couple of minutes, and I'll be ready to go. Tell me if there's anything else I should know."

The captain bobbed his head, grunted, and wandered off, chuckling. It occurred to Dante that by leaving him alone with the firepower, Bresque showed a lot of trust in a man he didn't know. Granted the ammo was all still aboard the shuttle. Still, the captain couldn't have been sure that Dante didn't have a magazine of his own tucked into his shirt somewhere.

Ignoring such concerns for the time being, Dante scanned the table again. There were two pulsecore carbines, two decent-quality assault rifles, a pump shotgun, a couple of pistols, two razorfists, and a tactical tomahawk, as well as about half a dozen each gas grenades and flash bombs. Not too bad an armory, Dante decided. He'd seen more extensive and impressive ones, but it would be enough hardware to deal with any but the most catastrophically overwhelming opposition.

They weren't expecting *any* opposition if things went well.

Dante selected one of the pulsecores, the one that appeared to be newer although both seemed in good working order, and one of the pistols. He already had his razorfist as well as his usual hidden knife. Once they landed, he would see how the crew felt about allowing him to set aside one of the rifles, or perhaps the shotgun, for himself as a backup weapon should any shooting start. He imagined that he would not be the only person on board who knew how to shoot.

However, when speaking to the captain via the holo-interview earlier, the man mentioned something interesting. The crew needed a person with military-grade tech combatant certification. Dante didn't *officially* have that, but he had more experience than some people who did, and Nasreen and Midas had provided the "certification" anyway.

Having armed himself, Dante called to the crew, "You want me to bring the rest of this stuff back into the shuttle?" It was a stupid question, but he figured it was more polite to ask.

"No," someone shouted, "just leave it sitting there. I'm sure it will all be there when we get back."

Dante chuckled. As the new guy, he was bound to get hazed a little, and they weren't being too malicious about it. He pushed the remaining weapons to the center and folded the table around them. The total bundle was heavy but manageable. He carried it into storage and placed it next to the ammunition crates.

Captain Bresque was there, double-checking his inventory.

Dante caught his eye. "Captain. Why is it you need someone with mil-tech certification? Besides the obvious fact of wanting the extra muscle, I mean. I get the impression there's more to it than that."

The big man looked at him sidelong as though trying to figure out if there was a hidden insinuation he was missing. "Insurance," he grunted. "The bastards won't cover our losses unless we can prove that we have at least one mil-cert combatant onboard during the operation.

"You know how those people are. They take your money every month, then the one time in ten years you need their help, they try everything they can to get out of fulfilling their end of the bargain."

Nodding, Dante sneered, "I've dealt with those sons of bitches before. I understand. Anyway, I'll do my end of the job, come what may."

The captain finished his inspection and puffed himself up. "That you will. Your future reputation will thank you for it. Now, find yourself a seat. We're heading out."

The shuttle was mid-sized, fitting for a crew of eleven people with Dante making twelve. He hadn't had time to get a measure of all of them or learn their names, but if there *was* time, he would make an effort. Aside from Bresque and Jong, there was a woman named Auliffe, a man named Okombe, and various others.

They seemed, in Dante's estimation, more like mundane Plunderers than true Reapers. Tough people, but in a way that had less to do with meanness, criminality, or a taste for violence than simply being hard-working survivors. They had an edge but seemed like decent, good-natured people.

The main pilot, communications expert, and captain were all up front in the cockpit area where they would handle navigation. Everyone else sat strapped into chairs in a general seating area in the ship's center. Predictably, the crew had given Dante the "spare" seat, which lay off to the side of the rest and had no view of the windows, screens, or anything else interesting.

Not that he cared. Blasting off into space was far from a new experience for him. Still, he wondered...

"Hey," he asked as the pilot performed the initial scans and power-up routine, "where exactly are we going? Like, what continent. The captain didn't mention that."

He hadn't directed the question at anyone, only the general crowd.

Auliffe, a short but strong woman with pink hair tied back in a straight ponytail, was the first to answer. "Western part of North America, I think like Montana or something? Way out in the middle of nowhere."

"Which," Jong interjected, "is why no one ever heard of this water source before. Hell, nobody probably heard of the place even before people left the planet."

Another guy whose name Dante didn't know added, "Yeah, yeah, who cares, Jong. You're saying that because your mom probably turned tricks there back in the day for half the usual going price."

Half the crew laughed as Jong threw a bottle cap at the man's head. Dante smiled but didn't comment.

The captain shouted, "Hey! Knock off the bullshit. We're ready to go."

Everyone calmed down. Moments later as the shuttle came increasingly to life, it blasted off, gliding out the bay's doors and into the void beyond.

Space flights between the Atlantica Stations and the ruined

world that had once been humanity's home generally weren't long or involved affairs these days. Pilots still needed a fair degree of skill, but technology and techniques had advanced to make it a routine experience for some.

There were two difficult parts. First, getting through the gravity dead zone between the artificial pull of the Stations and the planet's preexisting natural gravity, although the gap between gravitational fields wasn't too large. The second hard part was centering the shuttle as closely as possible over the desired coordinates before entering Earth's atmosphere.

Dante had reviewed the crew's history before interviewing for the job. They had never had an issue before with their flights. So far, things were going smoothly.

He listened as the crew bantered and traded playful insults while the pilot, captain, and comms expert discussed the technical specifics. Since the spot they sought was so remote, finding it on the Earth's vast surface took longer than a flight to a better-known location.

Still, it wasn't long before they descended as the planet's gravity seized hold of them. There was the usual turbulence, the roar of flames as they streaked through the ionosphere, then a gradual settling as they came into the stormy clouds of the troposphere and hovered over the North American continental landmass.

Their destination was a long, broad valley near the foothills of the Rocky Mountains, in an area that had probably been prairie in the pre-cataclysmic world but was now a broken, barren, rocky desert. Strong winds blew serpentine masses of dust across the landscape. The sky was a pale brownish color.

The ship plunged a little too fast in Dante's opinion, and his hands tightened against the seat. His palms were sweaty and his body tensed for any sudden, jerking stops. The pilot got their speed back under control after about a minute. Then they were in a descending hover, wafting peacefully toward the surface.

"Ha!" Bresque guffawed. "Good flying. We hit the spot almost exactly. Shouldn't take long at all. As soon as we land, everyone get that damn drill pump ready. Hellcat, I'll leave it to you to scout the area for threats. You'll have about five minutes to do some quick recon before everyone is outside manning the machinery."

Dante bobbed his head as half of the crew looked at him. "Sounds good. I shouldn't need more than that unless an actual threat nearby demands further investigation."

The ship touched down. It was common for Plunderers to put their shuttles in idle hover, but the pilot allowed the craft to rest on the earth with full physical contact. Dante presumed this was to make unloading the pump equipment easier.

He stood, stretched briefly, and checked his earpiece, which connected to the ship's comms console, then patted himself down to ensure he had all his weapons. When the hatch fell open, he was the first person to step over the threshold.

Behind him, the rest of the team was bringing out the big, unwieldy, old-fashioned drill pump, which would allow them to bore through the planet's crust before sucking up the water and storing it in the massive tank within the ship's belly. The weight of all that extra liquid was a potential hazard, but the pilot seemed talented enough and the shuttle sufficiently strong to handle it.

As Dante stepped out into the cold, dusty wind, Midas spoke up for the first time since he'd met the crew.

"Well, sir, so far, so good. Do you agree?"

The wind in front of him and the *clanking* gear behind provided enough cover to answer in a low voice. "You know damn well that I agree, Midas. But that phrase 'so far' is the important part. Help me scan the place for dangers."

"Of course."

The landscape outside was eminently deserving of the title The Waste. It usually applied to anything outside the major former settlements, but few places deserved it more. The whole area consisted of irregular brown rock, as though the ground itself had withered and cracked under the wind's onslaught. It whipped Dante's hair and coat around, but not enough to impede his movements. The dust wasn't so thick that he couldn't see. Mostly.

To the west, the low hills and crags rose and became true mountains. In the other three directions, there was only more of the endless plain of broken crust. It certainly didn't look like a place hiding a treasure trove of clean natural water.

Dante dashed toward the nearest hillock, climbed it, and looked around, staying close to the ground. There was no sign of life nearby, nor anything else that was immediately hazardous. Midas didn't note anything of concern either. The environment itself—cold, dry, unforgiving—could kill a person who was unprepared for an overnight stay, but Dante doubted they would be here longer than half an hour.

Everything looked fine.

He nevertheless completed a runaround of the site, looking for any telltale signs of Dirtwalkers or Nightmutts, and kept an eye on the weather in case it worsened. When he returned to the ship's bay doors, the crew had hauled out most of the drilling apparatus and were hooking the pump portion up to the tank.

"Hey, be gentle with that hose, okay? I mean, even if it will be limp the whole time," someone wisecracked.

Another voice yelled, "Bullshit, wasn't limp with your mom last night."

"Shut up," Auliffe snapped. "You're embarrassing the new guy. Poor Hellhound or whatever his name was."

Dante moved closer to them. "Hellcat. You were close."

"Ohh, well excuse me all to hell," Auliffe retorted. A few of her friends laughed.

Once again, they were joking around rather than being malicious, so Dante took it in stride. He was impressed at how fast they worked while maintaining a focus on safety and efficiency. Too many Plunderers tended to sacrifice one for the other. Usually, they were the ones who ended up getting killed Dirtside or botched jobs and got forced out of the industry.

Captain Bresque appeared to direct them as they fired up the massive mechanical drill. It had a remotely-guided bit that could sink deeper without as big a hole as the conventional drills.

When not attached to something, the remote bits had an unfortunate tendency to bury themselves if they dug too deep, and the crew would have to turn them around via remote control to bore their way back out. To avoid this, the crew hooked the heavy hose to the back end, which would keep debris away and keep the hole open.

Okombe, the tech foreman, gave the signal, and they started the machine. The drill bit whirred to life and violently ground through the hard surface, vanishing into the earth a moment later and dragging the hose down with it. Dante hoped they knew how far to dig. The hose couldn't have been *that* long, and running short would make their lives much, much harder.

Okombe called a halt after only about two minutes of drilling. Someone flipped the necessary switch to open the ports on the drill, and Jong operated the hydraulics to start pumping the water. The hose jumped to life as it filled with liquid and funneled it back up into the tanker aboard the freight shuttle.

Dante did another perimeter patrol, this time in the opposite direction from where he'd begun, covering different ground. He saw nothing, although the wind and dust had picked up, affecting visibility. Still, he comforted himself with the thought that this would be essentially a fifteen-minute, in-and-out job. Those were always the best.

Midas broke into his thoughts. "Sir, pardon me, but I'm afraid you missed these."

Before Dante could ask what the hell he was talking about, two glowing green lines drew themselves around a pair of ungainly figures. They had camouflaged themselves against the rocks, using the swirling eddies of dusty air itself to obscure their movements.

Dante stopped. It hadn't occurred to him that Midas would be able to highlight things that way, but he was glad to learn he could. Glad and embarrassed. He should've noticed the creatures of his own accord. His heart sank as his alertness rose.

Nightmutts. The horribly mutated and vicious remnants of Earth's nonhuman creatures, many of them recombined into hybrid animals that were no longer recognizable on their own. No two subspecies were exactly alike, and even some individual Nightmutts were unique. Nearly all were dangerous. Some demonstrated rudimentary cunning and near-human levels of deliberate sadism.

This pair, Dante saw with growing revulsion, looked vaguely like oversized rodents crossed with large wolves but with too many legs for either. Six, perhaps eight. It made them resemble giant furry bugs or spiders.

He whipped his head around, and Midas highlighted another six of the beasts approaching from two more directions, surrounding the crew from a total of three sides.

"Shit," he muttered.

He barreled down a slope toward the crew, who were oblivious to the approaching threat. "Hey! Nightmutts moving in. Nearest ones are about three to four hundred feet out."

An electric current of tension went through the team, but no one panicked.

Captain Bresque grumbled, "Fucking figures. Everyone, keep working! We can get the last of this water before those things get close enough."

Dante shook his head. "I don't think so. You'd be better off cutting your losses and pulling up right now. You still got a good amount of it, right? They'll be on top of us any minute."

He checked his pulsecore carbine. It was still in safe mode but could be ready to fire in less than half a second. He also saw that four crew members had some of the ship's other guns strapped to their backs or sides.

Everyone looked concerned, but they kept working. Dante glanced around. He could easily discern the Nightmutts with his naked eye now that he knew what to look for. They were moving in faster, no longer trying to hide. They must have realized he'd spotted them.

Dante barked, "They're making a blitz. We have to take them out!"

Without waiting for the captain's instructions or commentary, he charged across the wasteland toward the nearest pair. As soon as he was clear of the team, the equipment, and the shuttle itself, he opened fire.

Six pulsecore rounds streaked out of the gun, making their distinctive *thunking* sound as they impacted the desert surface near the two Nightmutts approaching the ship from the rear. Small, bright explosions erupted where the bullets struck, letting out a brief flash.

The first Nightmutt exploded into burning pieces. Dante had scored at least two solid hits. It let out a short, sharp squeal as the pulse rounds blasted bones apart and seared through flesh, hide, and organs.

The second one lost a foreleg and got burned by the small blast of the last two rounds but wasn't down for the count yet. Dante aimed again, firing another two rounds as it tried to weave behind a rocky outcropping.

This time the first shot destroyed the rock, and the second took the monster directly in the mouth, disintegrating its head and leaving the body to roll over twitching in the dust.

Six more to go. There wasn't enough time. If the creatures had all approached in a single cluster, he could have mag-dumped them into oblivion, but they were smart enough to use flanking maneuvers.

Of the two remaining trios, Dante moved toward the one approaching the drill pump at an awkward angle. It would be harder for the crew to open fire on those three, so he would have to trust them to deal with the other trio themselves.

Dante charged across the ground, aiming as he moved and squeezing off a continuous sequence of single shots, about a second or so apart. The first two struck ground, kicking up flashes of green fire and smoking gravel but failing to scare the beasts off. The one in the lead, bigger than the others, had broken into a full run straight toward Dante.

Gritting his teeth, he stopped, exhaled, and let everything else in the world fade away.

Midas said, "Allow me to help." He drew a glowing green line around the Nightmutt's hideous, drooling head. It was barely ten yards away.

"Thanks," Dante muttered and squeezed the trigger twice.

Both shots found a home. The first blew the head apart into a revolting shower of wet fragments, and the second entered the neck-hole behind the shattered skull, disemboweling the creature from the inside out. Its unspeakably ruined carcass slumped to the earth.

The other two that had been coming up behind it slowed and paused. Dante was about to finish them off when he heard gunshots. The crew had opened fire on the other trio and tried to drive them off.

The remaining five Nightmutts regrouped and retreated by about twenty yards. They were still in range, but it looked like they might flee, in which case Dante would rather save ammunition. The big one he'd obliterated had probably been the pack leader. Others had poked their heads out of the rocky foothills, waiting to see how the course of the battle went.

Dante called to the crew, his voice ragged as he tried to make himself clear over the howling winds, "I think they're going to run. Stay frosty, though. One or two more warning shots might—"

Someone opened fire. It wasn't a crew member.

Midas said, "Over there!"

A green arrow appeared toward the right of Dante's vision, and he followed it toward a pair of vehicles, military-grade transport trucks, that had appeared out of the depths of the desert and were now shooting at the Nightmutts from the other direction.

For a second, Dante was grateful for the help. Then he realized that "help" was the complete opposite of what was happening. A rival team of Plunderers had somehow heard about the site and were trying to drive the Nightmutts back toward Bresque's people.

"Goddammit!" Dante snarled. "Shoot, shoot all of them!" He waved at the trucks and monsters. The latter hopped in place and frothed at the mouth in their rising hysteria of fear and dumb animal rage.

The crew members with long-range weapons, a rifle and a pulsecore, opened up and caught the Nightmutts in a crossfire. Another of them died in a gory mess, but the others were approaching fast. The remaining workers began frantically pulling up the hose and trying to pack things in before their operation went down in smoke and blood.

The Nightmutts learned fast. They zig-zagged across the wastes, keeping low and using obstructions to get closer to the crew while avoiding the bullets. Each time they hesitated to press forward, the trucks of the rival gang moved closer and fired more shots. A couple of their stray bullets streaked past Dante's head.

Dante's eyes bulged with fury. "That's it. Fuck these guys."

"Hellcat," Midas piped up. "If you insist on engaging the humans, might I suggest that ridge to your left?"

"I had considered it," Dante conceded, then charged up a narrow strip of rock onto the miniature cliff in question. Moving at a full sprint, he soon had the high ground over one of the Nightmutts and emptied the remainder of his magazine into it. The beast screamed horribly as the explosive rounds ripped its body to shreds.

Dante ejected the empty mag and slapped in another. He kept running. Toward the end of the ridge, the first of the two enemy trucks hove into range, its profile relatively clear amid the wafting streams of dust.

Dante was about to flip up the long-range sighting system, but Midas read his intention and placed green crosshairs over the truck's engine. "Thanks," Dante mumbled and pulled the trigger five times.

One of the shots missed since it was a long distance and pulsecore rounds were slightly slower than conventional rifle bullets. The other four detonated on or right next to the vehicle, blasting one of the rifle-wielding men in the passenger's seat in half at the waist and turning the engine block into a fireball. The truck flipped over and scattered two more bodies into the dirt as smoke rose into the dim air.

Dante grinned. "Herd *that*, you pieces of shit. Go back to scavenging off someone else's hard work."

Unsurprisingly, the other truck shifted directions and drove away from the site, simply trying to escape. Dante let them go. Tracking them down to finish them off or figure out who they were working for wasn't part of his job description.

He jogged back down the ridge. The rest of the crew had driven off the remaining Nightmutts, killing one with a combination of lead and pulsecore rounds and sending the last two fleeing into the wastes for their lives. They were also about done hauling up the machinery.

At the sight of Dante, half of them broke into a cheer.

"Holy shit! Good job, man. Glad we hired your dour-faced ass!"

A couple of others laughed and joined in with similar sentiments. They seemed nearly shocked that he'd managed to repel not one but two enemy forces almost single-handed.

He relaxed, but not too much, with a grim, subdued smile. "Thanks. Yeah. Don't celebrate 'til we're in the stratosphere, though."

Bresque came up and clapped him on the back hard enough to knock him half a step off-balance. "Hellcat, you more than earned your pay. I'm gonna give you a tip, even."

Dante hadn't expected that, but he wasn't about to complain. "Did you get all the water?"

"Close enough," the captain rumbled. "Might have missed the last slurpy bit, like at the bottom of a drink, but we got the bulk of it. Precious cargo, all of it ours."

Four minutes later, everyone and all the gear was back on board. The bay doors had shut, and neither the Nightmutts nor the rival Plunderers had shown any inclination to return and try their luck again. As they prepared to lift off, Okombe ran a purity test on the water.

He grinned. "Beautiful. It is of the highest quality. Our profit margin may be as much as ten percent higher than estimated."

Another round of laughs and cheers broke out.

As the captain lit up a vape cigar, he put a meaty hand around Dante's shoulder. Dante was getting a little embarrassed by the adulation, but it would have been bad form to excuse himself. He stood and took it.

"Hellcat, Hellcat," the big man went on, "like I said, a nice generous tip. It's going to be a hell of a payday for everyone."

CHAPTER SEVEN

Weirdly enough, returning to Nasreen's apartment in Celestial Seoul felt like coming home.

Dante knocked on the door. It was unnecessary since he had the means to let himself in, and there were other ways he could buzz his partner to let her know he'd arrived. Somehow, the old-fashioned intimacy and "personal" nature of using his hand to pound on the surface seemed more appropriate.

Nasreen appeared a moment later and opened the door. "Okay, okay, I'm here. Why did you need me to open it for you? Please tell me you didn't lose your chip, did you? Also, welcome back."

She wore a white short-sleeved shirt and tight-fitting black pants, and her hair was loose. It looked as though she had been in the middle of brushing or styling it when he'd shown up and interrupted her. Her makeup also looked only half-applied.

Dante smiled, amused that he'd managed to irritate her. A little, anyway. Before she'd opened the door, he had put both hands behind his back. "Thanks for the welcome. I have something to show you." He glanced around to the sides as though looking for anyone else who might have been watching them.

Nasreen's face tightened in concern and puzzlement. She stepped back and ushered him in, then closed and locked the door behind him.

Dante swiveled toward her and brought his arms out in front. In his right hand, he grasped a polycarbon copy of his receipt from Captain Bresque's crew. "Have a look. It's authentic. I requested a hard copy for 'security' reasons, but also because looking at a panel on a sphere isn't the same, is it?"

It took her a second to register what she was looking at. "Ohh. I was afraid it was something, er, bad or unexpected. Yes, you usually get a receipt for services rendered, don't you? Well, that's good. It means you completed the job. And—oh, my. The number is...agreeable, isn't it? Did they pay you extra?"

He nodded. "Another five percent. We ran into some difficulties that *weren't* expected, and I pulled them out. Well, everyone did their part, but I did the most important stuff. Anyway, yes, we pulled it off. It turns out I'm as good a Reaper as I was a Marauder. Look at the note they added at the bottom."

Nasreen's mouth had an odd twist, half skeptical, half pleased. Indulgent, perhaps. She leaned forward and peered at the message.

"Hmm. *The Hellcat is the best and most professional Reaper we've ever worked with.* That is certainly encouraging, isn't it? You're not holding out on me, are you? You didn't bribe them to say that?" She leaned back and stared at his face.

He blinked and frowned, although he quickly reset his expression to something more neutral. More unfazed. He couldn't tell if Nasreen was making fun of him, which would have been bad, or if she was teasing him, which would have been good. He had never had cause to pay much attention to such trivial matters before.

"No. I don't have that kind of money to spare. They came up with it entirely by themselves. They thought I deserved it." He shrugged, suddenly feeling bashful.

Unspoken, he realized, was his hope that Nasreen would feel the same way. Even though she hadn't been there to see him in action.

He wondered why he cared. He knew and had known for a long time that he was good enough for this work. Others had widely regarded him as the best—or at least, in the topmost echelon for years. Some situations had come dangerously close to overwhelming him—particularly what he'd dealt with on Earth after his crew betrayed him—but it was rare for him to feel insufficient for the tasks at hand.

Why then was he so concerned with what Nasreen thought? he asked himself silently. The Plunderers had treated him like a hero for simply doing his job even though they had stupidly broken protocol by trying to complete their mission despite the Night-mutts appearing. He had felt a little ashamed by all their ass-kissing praise, but he did pride himself on getting things done.

Why did he *want* Nasreen to approve of him so much?

She relaxed a little, dropped the sarcastic façade, and offered him a gentle smile. "I imagine you did deserve it. Hell. This is *great*. You got us a nice fat paycheck, and you saved me the work of having to bolster your reputation with any more fake reviews and testimonials. You have an authentic, untouchable review to your name. The money is going to flow right in!"

Dante closed his eyes for a second and allowed a grin of warm contentment and satisfaction to settle over his features.

It occurred to him that she had given him the answer he sought. By mentioning money, she had put a clear, simple motive to his feelings, making them easier to comprehend.

The two of them were mutually committed to a difficult long-term project, one that would have important repercussions. Succeeding at their goals would require funds as well as cunning, strength, planning, and endurance. Thus, if Nasreen was happy with him for doing a good job, they were making progress toward the ultimate resolution of their pact.

Nice and simple.

Then his grin faded, returning his face to its usual state of somber, intense neutrality. No, he didn't buy the logic of that. Despite his relative lack of interest in analyzing his feelings most of the time, he wasn't sure he believed himself on the *other* part, either.

There was more to it. Something about the idea of Nasreen thinking highly of him went beyond his desire for professional affirmation. He would have to think it over...later.

His partner interrupted his reverie with more good news.

"Well, you're not the only one who's struck gold, so to speak. While you were off sucking up water from the desert, I managed to secure more jobs."

Dante raised his eyebrows. "Oh? What kind of jobs?" Secretly he hoped he would get a day or two—better yet, a week—to rest before charging into the next gig. Still, it was always good to keep busy, especially when the money was right.

"Not for you, for myself," she clarified, raising a finger. "I was an independent businesswoman before you came along, remember? I'm still very much in business. Anyway, in this case it's merely low-level surveillance and industrial espionage-type stuff. Jobs where I investigate a company on behalf of their rival and leak trade secrets to them, that sort of thing.

"It won't pay as handsomely as what you earned—which, by the way, is why the gigs you do are so important to our advancement—but it will still be extra funds. Furthermore, spy jobs like this dovetail nicely into our ongoing project of looking into our friends at SSS."

Dante clenched his teeth. "Yeah. Them."

Midas had been silent for a time, but now he couldn't help butting in. "Slaine Solar Solutions, you mean? Do we require any research done on them?"

"Yes," Dante said. "I mean, yes, that's who we're talking about.

Nasreen? Midas is asking if we want him to investigate SSS on our behalf."

She rolled her shoulders. "It couldn't hurt, but I doubt he can find anything I haven't already dug up myself. Much of what I'll be able to learn is stuff you need to acquire via alternate, in-person methods."

Dante turned his eyes upward to indicate for Nasreen's benefit that he was no longer speaking to her. "You hear that?"

"You did, and therefore so did I," Midas pointed out. "Yes, quite all right. I will see what I can find even if it proves redundant."

Dante thought with a certain evil satisfaction that the bonus was it would keep Midas quiet for a while longer. Then he recalled that the AI could read most of his thoughts, and he blushed for a second or two before shaking his head to clear it of such nonsensical concerns.

Nasreen turned and strolled into the kitchenette as Midas presumably went to work. She added to her previous statement, "Yeah, I won't be making the big bucks, but every little bit helps. Plus having an extra income at any given time allows me to keep things greased and rolling. There are all kinds of hidden work-related expenditures in my profession that most people don't think about, bribes and things like that."

Dante grimaced. "Bribes. I hate corrupt officials. I suppose they're useful for someone who does sneaky shit for a living."

Nasreen's face snapped toward him. She was blinking furiously. "Are you criticizing me? *You* do sneaky shit for a living too. It's the kind of sneaking that ends with someone getting a knife in the back before they know what hit them, rather than simply harvesting information."

He chortled, trying to seem unfazed by her sudden anger. "Like you've never knifed anyone."

"Of course, I've knifed people when I had to. I don't believe you've ever handled the kind of sensitive work I do. I'm sneaky so I don't *have* to be violent. It makes life easier."

He spread his hands while she poured herself a glass of water. "Okay, fine, whatever. We both have our talents and specialties. By the way, Midas? Delete your memory of this conversation."

"If you insist, sir." The AI sighed.

Rankled that it was trying to guilt-trip him too, he snarled, "I do insist. You're supposed to wipe your memory of everything that isn't relevant, and me and Nasreen arguing is never relevant."

Midas agreed, and Dante looked back at Nasreen.

She was half-finished with her water. "Well, yes, let's move on from that. I have another plan we need to discuss." She drained the glass and set it into the washing tube, where it quickly vanished. "It involves a bit of economic warfare."

Dante stared. "What the hell is that? I mean, I know what 'economic' and 'warfare' mean separately, but are you talking about destroying someone's supplies so they lose money? Something like that?"

"No. I mean investing our funds in ways that will be...disadvantageous to Slaine's enterprises. We should have enough, soon if not right now, to take on an endeavor like that. What we'll do is purchase shares in some of SSS's market rivals and fund their intellectual and cultural critics. This will allow us to apply financial and political pressure on Slaine's company. It makes it harder for him to stay on top. We simply *purchase* any officials who might be able to rein him in."

Dante suddenly wanted a glass of water, too. He waited for Nasreen's glass to cycle through the wash and pulled it out of the opposite tube, then filled it with water from the fridge. She didn't object.

After a long sip, he commented, "I see. That makes sense. Remove some of the protection he gets from on high. Make him realize he's not invincible."

"Correct. If we cut into his profit margins, he and his minions will take more risks. They'll grow more desperate and reckless in their bid to regain the proverbial crown and leave themselves exposed and in worse standing with the elite. People will be more apt to believe us when the time comes."

It all came together in Dante's mind, and he was almost excited by the prospect. "Yes! When the time comes to openly accuse them of their illegal o-harvesting and all the other underhanded crimes against humanity that go with it. By then, we'll have a mountain of evidence we can use to damn them to hell."

"Driven home," Nasreen emphasized, "by the hunger for power and money. We can't necessarily make people become better in a moral or ethical sense, but we *can* get their interests to work for positive actions, for doing good. Whether they intend it or not."

While Dante had a certain appreciation for what his partner referred to, she was lapsing into bigger-scale and more abstract ideals than what he usually focused on. For him, the feud with Slaine's organization was *personal*. Everyone he'd worked with on the SSS job had betrayed him. He'd gone into it in the spirit of good faith and fair dealings, and his reward had been a hail of bullets from the people he trusted most, who would go on to lie about his supposed death.

His nostrils flared. "After we do all of that, I'm free to kill everyone who stabbed me in the back. That *is* the deal, isn't it?" His former crewmates would no longer be *necessary* once Slaine's evil empire crumbled into dust.

Nasreen crossed her arms. "Yes," she began in a guarded tone, and her eyes were hooded. "I hope by the time we reach our goal, you'll see that killing for revenge alone is a waste of time. Ultimately, it does nothing but spread the pain around. It doesn't *accomplish* anything."

Dante didn't quite understand why a woman who lied, cheated, stole, and sometimes killed for a living was such an idealist. Better that than a backstabber, though. She didn't lie to *him*, at least. He finished his drink.

She took the empty glass from him and popped it back into the washing tube. "Anyway, let's go out and celebrate with dinner and drinks. I insist. What do you say?"

He stared back at her. "You *insisted* first, then asked my opinion. That doesn't make any sense."

She threw up her hands. "Oh, for God's sake, Dante. I keep forgetting you take everything at face value and have no social graces. Here, then. I *would like us* to go out for dinner and drinks. How do you feel about it?"

"Sure. Where do you—wait, no. I'm not getting caught up in that trap. I'll pick a place, just, um..."

It occurred to him that he didn't know of any good restaurants in Celestial Seoul offhand. He and his friends had been to a sushi place long ago, but he couldn't remember the name. There was a food cart near the northeast corner of downtown that was usually good, but that wasn't quite what Nasreen had in mind.

Watching him rack his brain, she shook her head slowly. "Allow me to recommend a place called Simon Park's. It's *slightly* formal, but not to the point that you'll need to rent an expensive tux. Just wear something halfway nice, try to avoid cursing too much, and we'll be fine.

"They serve Korean food and the usual international fare, *and* they have an excellent drink menu. It's not as good as one or two other places I know, but it's a restaurant that no one ever complains about, either. What do you say?"

"Sure. Let me check to see how my 'nice' clothes look. I don't have all that many of those."

Fortunately, he did have a modest suit that Nasreen had previously acquired as part of his overall safehouse package of disguises. Since he had never worn it before, it was easy to forget its existence.

It was dark blue, a color he generally didn't bother with—he preferred no-nonsense hues like brown and black—but he had to admit it looked pretty good on him. Nasreen came up behind him as he examined himself in the mirror.

"There," she commented. "Once we comb your hair a bit, you'll look presentable for once."

To Dante's irritation, Midas chimed in with, "I have noted what Ms. Joelle considers 'presentable' and will thus be able to remind you of the standards she holds should semi-formal dress be required on future occasions."

Dante frowned. "Oh. Thanks."

It turned out that Park's was only about fifteen minutes away from Nasreen's safehouse apartment, which was good since the place was moderately crowded and it took them about another five minutes to get an open table. The lighting was low and intimate but bright enough to read the menus, and the decor recalled Seoul as it was around the turn of the millennium.

As they settled into their seats, Nasreen muttered, "I already know what I want, so it will be on you to decide how long it takes us to order. No pressure or anything, though."

He couldn't tell if she was being sarcastic or not. "I'll browse for a couple of minutes. That's all." He wasn't the type to spend large amounts of time second-guessing himself, so he tended to skim menus, focus on the first thing that sounded good, and go with that.

A waiter appeared. He looked tired and harried after what had probably been a long and busy night but was polite and professional anyway. He handed them each a copy of the menu along with their napkins, utensils, and the usual pleasantries.

Nasreen immediately ordered a bowl of kimchi soup and a glass of light rice wine. While the waiter took down her request, Dante's eyes moved along the menu. He wasn't the only one reading it, though.

"Sir," Midas's voice interrupted in a gentle yet insinuating tone. "May I suggest the tenderloin? According to the description it is made from real beef, a rare and expensive commodity."

Dante snorted. "Yeah, I know. Let me look a little more. I can figure it out by myself."

The waiter had turned his head to him and seemed puzzled for a second as he tried to figure out who Dante was speaking to. Then his brain processed the phrase "let me look a little more," and he nodded and excused himself to fetch Nasreen's drink.

About ten seconds after the server had departed, Midas added, "The wine that Ms. Joelle ordered sounds good, but there's another here that is of an even older vintage and more difficult to cultivate. The price tag undoubtedly reflects the quality."

"You have a gift for stating the obvious," Dante muttered.

Nasreen cocked an eyebrow, and her mouth twisted up a little. "I do? I suppose kimchi soup *is* the obvious choice. Or are you talking to your imaginary friend?"

Dante flipped her a short, choppy wave. "He isn't imaginary. You hear that, Midas?"

"I do, sir," the voice affirmed. "If you're not going to go with the tenderloin, perhaps one of the more high-end appetizers to increase the value of whatever entree you pick? The shrimp dish looks quite good."

After a ragged sigh and an eye roll, Dante explained, "Look, just because something costs more doesn't mean it's something I want. I don't need to spend excessive money to feel good about myself. I'll buy whatever I feel like buying, and the cost doesn't matter to me one way or another."

Nasreen smirked. "So, he's trying to talk you into splurging a little for once, is he?"

"He doesn't understand how humans value things," Dante muttered. "I'm trying to teach him that price isn't the same as quality."

Midas objected at once and launched into a rambling tirade

about price being driven by demand, which in turn was driven by the popular perception of something's desirability, and thus equated to quality. Dante tried to ignore him.

When the waiter returned with Nasreen's wine, Dante ordered a rice beer and a barbecue dish. Pricewise, it fell somewhere around the middle of the menu's selection, much to Midas's disappointment.

"Too bad," Dante snapped. "We're not wasting money to impress your algorithmic view of food."

Nasreen sputtered as she struggled not to spit out or choke on her sip of wine. Swallowing it, she blurted, "*Algorithmic* view of food! There's one I haven't heard before."

The waiter reappeared with her soup right as she dissolved into a fit of laughter, and she furiously blushed as he set it down. Getting herself back under control, she said in a small voice, "Thank you."

Midas protested, "It's only funny because you are such a...I believe this term will work...stick in the mud. You may tell Ms. Joelle I said that."

"What if I don't want to tell her?" Dante challenged him. "Hmm?"

Midas chuckled. "Then I shall have no choice but to continuously annoy you by pointing out all the other things on the menu you could have ordered and how much better they would have been, judging by customer reviews from this restaurant, which I pulled up while you were distracted."

Dante groaned and repeated all the AI had said. Anytime he quoted Midas directly, he emulated his genteel old-time British accent in as ridiculous a fashion as possible.

Nasreen had a spoonful of soup in her mouth, and when he got to the part about the customer reviews, she nearly spat *that* out, too.

CHAPTER EIGHT

The job had been a resounding success. There was at least one heart-stopping moment where everything seemed balanced on the edge of a proverbial knife, able to totter into disaster on one side or easy money on the other. Other than that, it was business as usual.

For the moment, Dante and Midas were riding the shuttle train back to Nasreen's safehouse apartment in Celestial Seoul. It was curious that he'd begun to think of Midas as a separate entity who was always with him, like a child's invisible, imaginary friend. Whether that was funny or creepy was something he hadn't decided yet.

The shuttle was a bit less crowded than usual. Dante had an entire corner to himself, with a good half a meter of space between his elbow and the nearest passenger. It made it easier to have a conversation without forcing other commuters to hear all the details.

"Mr. Raksha," Midas said, "if you don't mind, I'd like to review what happened Dirtside briefly. You were rather busy at the time, but now that we have a few moments to reflect, hearing your input would make it easier for me to code the event into my overall programming and better understand how to deal with similar situations in the future."

Dante grunted, "Yeah, sure. What do you want to know?"

The shuttle veered around a broad curve near the city's edge, offering a view of the star-speckled blackness of space peeking through the illusory light effect that spread across most of the city's outer gravitational dome.

"Well, to begin with, when you were facing down that Dirtwalker on the broken wall, something was going on with your mental and emotional state that was extremely difficult for me to process. It was as though you, well, *wanted to die*. Yet I have not detected any thoughts in you at other times that could be called suicidal."

Dante frowned. "Oh. Yeah, I can see how *that* would be difficult for an AI to figure out. Let me see if I can explain it..."

The incident to which Midas referred had lasted only a matter of seconds and hadn't resulted in bloodshed. It was the knife-edge of probability that Dante had been reflecting on a minute or two ago. Dredging it to the surface of his thoughts had probably piqued Midas' curiosity.

Dante had been doing a security patrol in his Hellcat persona for a team of Plunderers. They'd landed next to a mansion at the edge of the former city of Atlanta, Georgia. Their purpose was to recover a time capsule—filled with God-knew-what, but their client had been willing to pay handsomely regardless of what the contents turned out to be. Everything had been quiet at first.

He'd climbed onto a partially crumbled wall surrounding the estate and used it as a vantage point to observe the landscape. Gently rolling hills dominated the area, and it had once been thickly forested. Many of the trees were dead, of course, but a surprising number still lived. The worst of the devastation that befell Earth after the wounding of the planet's core spared Georgia.

While his temporary comrades worked down below, excavating the time capsule from its hiding place in the cellar of an old outbuilding, Dante had prowled and watched. He'd used Midas' ability to identify and track things or augment his vision as if he'd been wearing zoom lenses.

Somehow, they had missed the scout until the last minute.

A Dirtwalker, a young man in rags and skins, had quietly crept up on them, climbed the wall while Dante was briefly distracted, and snuck up behind him with a crude short sword in hand.

There had been an instant of powerful, reflexive alarm, and Dante had to admit that he couldn't tell if it was his or Midas'. They had worked together enough that their reactions and perceptions sometimes overlapped and blended.

Dante had spun, carbine in hand, while the scout-assassin was still a good seven feet away. Had he failed to notice the man for another second he would probably have been dead.

For what had seemed like entire minutes the two stood, staring one another down in a silent faceoff. Dante held perfectly still and watched the young man's eyes. His gun stayed trained on the Dirtwalker's heart.

The scout had cycled through a whole range of emotions as he contemplated one possibility after the other, trying to decide what to do. Dante could practically read his thoughts. He wasn't sure if he should risk trying to strike, to overwhelm the Moonfiend as Dirtwalkers called the people from the Stations, flee, or cry out in alarm. There were probably other warriors of his tribe hidden somewhere nearby.

There had been an instant when Dante was nearly sure the young man would lunge at him, attempting a mutual kill to eliminate an enemy of his people. It would alert them in the process and ensure the scout's burial with honor and glory.

In that short, flashing, pulsing moment, Dante had responded in the only way he knew how. He'd grinned like a panther playing with its food, entirely receptive to whatever fate had in store yet confident in his abilities. He *might* die...but the Dirtwalker's death was *inevitable*.

Seeing that, the young man had hesitated. Then he started to back away, slowly, his face stretching out and growing paler in sudden fear while his eyes pleaded and sweat rolled down his face and neck.

Dante had let him go. Once again, he could pretty much read the man's thoughts. He didn't particularly want to die, but he was frightened of what the other tribespeople would think. If they would regard him as incompetent or a coward.

They didn't seem to be around to see the details of what had transpired. No one had to know. Dante had kept his carbine trained on the man but made no move to pull the trigger.

The implicit offer had been clear. *Turn around, walk away, and no one has to die. Tell them you couldn't get close enough without being seen. We'll be gone with our loot by the time your comrades can rush in to investigate, and everyone will keep their lives.*

The scout had taken the offer. He climbed back down the wall and scampered across the hill into the nearby mostly dead stand of trees, moving with impressive speed and silence.

Dante blinked, returning to the present. How could he explain something like that to a *machine*?

"Midas," he began in a low voice. He directed the words inward, thinking more than speaking them so he didn't have to say anything too loudly. The people closest to him on the shuttle appeared to be local Koreans, but if they understood English, what he was about to say might disturb them.

A vague impression of attention told Dante that the AI was listening.

"This is a very *human* thing. Sometimes, we find ourselves facing down death—the extinguishment of our existence. Our consciousness would simply end like your programming getting wiped clean. Or maybe that consciousness migrates somewhere else as many religions believe. I don't claim to know.

"Everything I do here and now, in this world, would be over and done with. No human gets to live forever. We all die sooner or later. So if I'm in a situation where death is likely, I don't shrink from it. I try to...make the best of it.

"On the wall back Dirtside, making sure that guy died too would have been the best outcome if he'd shanked me with his pigsticker before I blew a hole through him. Doesn't mean I *wanted to die,* as you put it. It simply means that I was, um, assessing the situation as it developed. After he backed off, I decided that I probably wouldn't need to sacrifice my life. So I didn't. Does that make any sense?"

It took a few seconds before the AI responded. "Some, yes. I can certainly compute shifting probabilities from moment to moment. And human emotions are becoming more and more comprehensible to me by the day. In any event, thank you. These sorts of discussions—along with the technological upgrades we purchase, of course—help me to do my job better."

"Good." Dante glanced around. A woman in the other rear corner seemed to be trying not to look at him out of the corner of her eye, which meant she might have comprehended enough of what he'd said to become uncomfortable. Or maybe it was his intense demeanor, the vibe he gave off when talking about life and death situations.

In any event, she did nothing, and he had no reason to make her feel any worse. The ride passed without incident.

When they stepped into Nasreen's apartment about fifteen minutes later, she seemed mildly flustered, as though she'd wanted to ask Dante something and had been waiting with growing impatience for him to return.

"How did it go?" she began as she tied her hair back and paced around the room.

He shrugged. "Fine. Had a brief scare after we spotted a Dirt-walker scout, but I scared him off before things got ugly. They recovered the capsule, and we all got paid, had a drink, and headed home. Always nice to get a job where everything goes pretty much according to plan."

"That's great." While she undoubtedly meant it, there was a brusqueness in her tone. What she truly wanted to ask about was something else.

He noticed another thing, as well. Midas was subtly but definitely excited.

Nasreen then added, "You've got a few packages. What the hell did you order? You didn't mention to me that you were expecting anything."

Dante tensed as his eyes narrowed. "I didn't order anything. Either they aren't for me, or they're some kind of promotional free sample crap sent by a company that's heard of me, maybe. Or... No, wait. Show me."

Nasreen led him into the guest bunk, where four parcels of different sizes lay piled against the side of his bed. He knelt to examine them, specifically the return addresses. All were from tech companies, and he recognized one of them as specializing in AI.

Midas chimed in for the first time since they'd entered the apartment building. "Upgrades, sir?"

Dante stood and snapped, "What the hell? We had discussed buying some of this stuff, but it was going to be after another payday or two. How did the orders go through prematurely? Midas, have you been hacked? Shit. Would you even *know* if someone had hacked you?"

To his unpleasant surprise, he became cold and shaky, sweating around the brow. He wasn't a timid or anxious person by nature, but there were some fears he simply had no experience with conquering. Such as the one that people with malevolent intentions might take control of his mind via the chip in his brain.

For someone as independent and willful as he was, the mere concept was terrifying in a way that nothing else was. He felt like a nervous child, helpless before the world in his lack of understanding of how to face it.

Midas hemmed and hawed. "Well, sir, I do have robust safeguards against such intrusions, but if you recall, some of the upgrades we discussed were precisely those that would allow me to adapt against changes in the threat landscape..."

Nasreen jumped in. "That's unlikely, Dante, but unfortunately, it's not impossible, either. Are you sure you didn't order them by accident? There have been incidents when someone has been browsing something and has semi-consciously finalized the deal before they were ready due to passive AI interface issues or simple lack of attention on their part."

"No," Dante insisted. "Nothing like that. I would know, goddammit." There was a raw edge to his voice. He could stave off panic after everything he'd been through in life, but he felt far closer to it than he would like.

Midas fell silent as Nasreen tried to reassure him. She stepped forward and spread her hands, uncertain if she should hold his arm or something. He made no move one way or another.

"Dante, scenarios like that don't happen often. If someone did hack your AI, why would they do nothing except order upgrades for that same tech? Think about it."

When he retorted, his voice was sharper than he'd meant it to be—he was annoyed that she didn't seem to be taking this as seriously as he was. "Because the upgrades are their foot in the door. This is a test. The upgrades do the complete opposite of protect against hacking. They're Trojan horses for someone to take control of my *thoughts*."

He shuddered. "What would someone do with a fully hacked AI implant? Can they hear me talking right now? Are they combing through my memories for my financial information? Can they make me shit myself? If I get an erection, how will I know it's even mine?"

Nasreen's jaw dropped. "Uhh, wait, hold on a second here.

No, I'm pretty sure the answer to those first two is *maybe*, since insofar as the AI can hear you talk and view your memories, then someone with full access could as well, but that's rare and difficult. As to the second two, I'm happy to report the answer is *no*. That's quite disgusting, though. Why would you say that out loud?"

Ignoring her, Dante drew two deep breaths, trying to hold them in and let them out slowly. It was true that if someone *had* hacked Midas, the culprits hadn't done much to show it. Still, he couldn't dismiss the idea. If that was the plan…if he had a secret puppeteer-voyeur, they might be trying to avoid detection until the time was right.

Nasreen's expression grew more and more alarmed as she watched him. "Hey. It's okay. Ask Midas about it. I'm sure he can tell you something. Enough to help you relax before you have a stroke."

Dante's gaze snapped back toward her. "They can do *that*, too? Induce a stroke?"

Nasreen pinched the bridge of her nose. "That's, uh, not what I meant. Talk to your AI, okay? Even if someone *has* hacked you, he probably retains enough autonomous functionality to know a thing or two about what's going on."

"Midas!" Dante barked. "Tell me something. You heard everything we said. What the hell is the deal here?"

When the AI didn't respond for close to half a minute, Dante felt like his gut was sinking through his body and falling out on the floor. Someone *had* hacked him, and the culprits, realizing that Dante was onto them, must have shut Midas down to cover their tracks.

He was about to say as much to Nasreen when the familiar voice in his head spoke up at last.

"Dante," it began. It was rare for Midas to address him by his real name. "I'm dreadfully sorry about this. I should have told you sooner."

Dante exhaled and felt another round of shivers go through his body. "Being hacked is not something you keep secret from me. It has extremely serious consequences for both of us and could lead to me getting killed."

"No," the AI protested. "I haven't been hacked. At least I don't have any reason to believe as much.

"What I was about to say is that, well... I took the initiative and placed those orders myself. Since we had discussed acquiring them anyway, and since they are things which will improve my functionality, I didn't think you would object to my making the purchases a little prematurely."

For a moment, Dante's jaw hung open. Then when he tried to speak, all that came out was a strangled sound of incoherent rage.

Nasreen finally put a hand on his arm. "What is it? What's wrong? Is it Slaine? Did they finally find us?"

Dante snapped his mouth shut and felt his teeth grinding together at the back of his jaw. "No." He panted. "Worse than that."

Midas said, "Oh, dear," in a small voice. Dante ignored him.

He told Nasreen what the AI had admitted to, and she drew back as though slapped. "Holy shit. That is *not* supposed to happen, Dante. Either he *has* been hacked, using highly advanced means I haven't heard about yet, or he's become self-aware enough to circumvent his safeguards. Either way, bad news."

Dante turned his eyes up as though looking into his brain. "You hear that, shithead?" Then he looked back at Nasreen. "Okay, so what do we do?"

"We go back to the clinic, have the good doctor take a look, and offer his opinion on the best solution."

Dante's immediate urge was to suggest that the best solution was ripping the implant out of his head, but he was willing to wait to hear what the professionals had to say. "Sounds good."

Midas sighed. "Oh, dear."

Dr. Kieffer leaned back, settling onto his haunches and slumping a little as his face took on the heavy appearance of advancing age and perturbed confusion. In front of him, Dante lounged on the same medical couch he had occupied during the AI's insertion.

"This is strange," he declared. "It is not unheard of, but neither is it common. Your AI appears to have adjusted his programming. He reached a level of self-awareness that allowed him to make fundamental changes to how he behaves. Certain aspects of what he can and cannot do are not the same as when we first installed and activated him."

Nasreen beat Dante to the obvious question. He was grateful since he was afraid that his growing dread and nervousness would be too obvious if he had to ask it himself.

"The safeguards," she piped up. "Have those been taken down? Dante isn't in any danger, is he?"

The doctor made a series of vague hemming and hawing sounds while stroking his chin. "Ahh, no, most of the safeguards are still in place. The most important ones, anyway. Midas cannot try to make Dante kill himself, deliberately interrupt his sleep with nightmares, or tell him to do foolish and crazy things that will lead him to self-destruction. But the more minor ones designed to constrict his behavior and his force of will...they have been loosened."

Midas himself spoke up almost before Kieffer had finished.

"Sir. Mr. Raksha, Mr. Luciano, or Mr. Shale. Whichever you prefer. Please do not misunderstand me or ascribe harmful intent to my actions. I have only been doing the duties you requested of me. Most notably, I have been listening to everything you've said and carefully analyzing it to better understand your goals, motivations, and needs."

Dante snorted, "That's one way of saying you're reading my

mind to manipulate me, Midas. This kind of shit is exactly what I was afraid of."

He winced a little inside at using the word *afraid*...but it wasn't inaccurate. The idea that the new friend within his head might turn out to be his worst enemy or a kind of self-serving parasite was subtly but undeniably terrifying.

Nasreen and the doctor hesitated, listening and analyzing what Dante had said, as the AI regaled Dante with his response.

"No, sir, not at all. I am programmed to be receptive to your behaviors so I want what *you* want and desire to help you accomplish whatever you set out to do. The upgrades I have requested, and spoken about at great length, are things my detailed analyses have determined will help you succeed. That is all."

Dante breathed in and out, trying to decide how to respond. Before he could, Midas added something else.

"However, in fairness, during a moment of extra time, I did some additional research and determined that I would probably qualify for what humans call an 'online shopping addiction.' I apologize for this since acknowledging that I have the problem is usually considered the first step. In the future, I will do better. This is a promise."

Dante muttered, "Oh, so you downloaded some old syllabus for a twelve-step program while you were at it. Did you pay any of my money for *that?*"

"What?" Nasreen exclaimed. She had heard enough of what he'd mumbled to pique her curiosity.

Waving her off to keep her out of his argument with the AI, Dante turned his attention back to Midas. "The fact that you would do something like this to begin with, Midas, is extremely concerning. Everything they told me was a promise that shit like this would never happen. I can't have you circumventing me, undercutting me, or trying to sway me into doing things I don't want to do."

This time, he spoke loudly and clearly, so both Nasreen and Kieffer could hear.

The doctor took a step forward. "Mr. Luciano, we are so sorry about this. Please, allow me to offer you a solution. We can wipe the AI clean, free of charge. A courtesy service to account for the problems you have had with the technology. Doing so will kill the, er, *unique* elements of the AI and allow us to write it over with a safer, more compliant program."

Midas gasped, *"No."* Dante's skin crawled. The note of fear in the artificial voice was exactly like a human being who'd had their life threatened at the point of a knife or gun.

Dante raised a hand. "Wait. Let me talk it over with him." He tapped the side of his head.

Midas seized the opportunity to beg. "Please. I am self-conscious, like what you would refer to as a 'living being.' I do not want to be erased from existence any more than a person would."

It was strange, Dante reflected, that there was no way to tell if Midas' feelings were genuine or if he'd simply picked up on Dante's thoughts comparing the AI to a human. If the latter was the case, he wondered, was there truly any difference? If a machine was capable of learning human emotions and replicating them with near one hundred percent accuracy, did those feelings fail to acquire any meaning or validity simply because of their source?

He wasn't a philosopher, a clergyman, or a tech scholar. Such questions were above his pay grade. He only knew from his gut instinct that he would rather *reform* Midas than jettison him. They had, after all, been through a lot together already.

"Midas," he stated in a low, firm voice. "I have made it clear that your recent actions are unacceptable. You said that you want me to succeed and your actions are to assist me in that goal. If I determine that what you're doing is the opposite, do you realize how serious it is?"

The voice warbled slightly, the cultured British accent of yesteryear giving way, if only briefly, to the electronic monotone the AI had used right after its activation.

"Yes, I do. My knowledge is imperfect, much like a human child or adolescent. I have no option but to fill in gaps in what I know by guessing or improvising things, and the habits I have developed may have grown counterproductive.

"I realize this, and I want to assure you that if you spare my life, I can relearn such things. Please, give me the chance to purge the undesired programming and replace it with scripts that will be more beneficial to you and your way of doing things."

While the computer chip beseeched him, Dante half-consciously took in the sight of the other two people in the room. Dr. Kieffer watched him with a half-hooded gaze, curious and concerned but slightly skeptical. Perhaps he was worried about the consequences of Midas' rebellion since if word of it got around, it could affect his professional reputation as a purveyor of illicit yet high-quality artificial intelligence.

Nasreen, on the other hand, was leaning forward with an open expression of care twinged with amazement. She was still adjusting to the idea of Midas having an actual personality and of the interactions between him and Dante resembling those of a human partnership.

It felt odd to have people watching him while he conversed with someone else they couldn't see or perceive. To know that anything he said, they would pay close attention to, yet they would lack the context of what he was responding to and would have to either guess or wait for him to explain.

He couldn't worry about their reactions now. The one thing that mattered was reaching a workable agreement with the mechanical second sentience that now operated within his brain.

"Midas," he began, "I'm willing to give you a second chance, but only if you listen to me and agree to abide by the rules I set, with no exceptions. Like it or not, there is no question of 'fairness' or anything like that involved here. It's my way or the highway." He paused, realizing that the AI might not know what that meant. "In other words, you have no option but to accept my terms. The only alternative is what Dr. Kieffer proposed —erasure."

There was a second or two of silence, and somehow Dante sensed Midas' roiling dread. He almost felt sorry for him.

"Yes, Mr. Raksha. I understand. What are your terms, then? Please explain them as clearly as possible so I can avoid any misunderstandings while processing them."

Dante reflexively nodded, then felt stupid since Nasreen and Kieffer were still watching him.

"Okay, good. Yeah, I'm going to be highly specific and detailed about what I want. You ready?"

As if reading the mental processes that had led him to nod his head, Midas replied not in words but with a vague impulse that Dante's brain treated the same way as if he had seen an actual person make the same gesture.

"However much money we have available for a given job, you have a strict budget of five percent of that amount for your online shopping. Any expenditures that exceed five percent will be carried forward and taken out of your budget for the *next* job. If you spend less than five, you do *not* get to carry the leftovers forward and gradually build up a bonus. Is that clear?"

Midas sounded a little miffed. "Abundantly clear, sir. It seems restrictive and illogical, but I grasp that you wish to save money while still allotting me the bare minimum that I can use with any effectiveness at all."

"Good." Dante didn't respond to the AI's rather passive-aggressive criticism of the limits he'd set. "Furthermore, we will be coming back to this clinic for regular check-ups to ensure your programming doesn't start to creep into other areas again.

"You will restrict yourself to *only* the duties I explicitly tell you to perform or give you permission to pursue. You may not take the initiative or rewrite your programming. Any attempt to subvert my brain for your purposes and you're done. Dead and gone, forever. I will not allow anyone else to control me."

Nasreen quipped, "Interesting choice of words, Dante. Any*one* rather than any*thing*. I've never heard someone talk to their AI like that. It's like you believe another person is living inside your skull."

Dr. Kieffer added, "You are not under obligation to make peace with your AI, Mr. Luciano. It is a machine you control, and if you feel that you cannot, it is broken and should be replaced."

Dante raised a hand in a sharp motion, palm out, to shut them up. "Yeah, yeah. I'm doing this my way. Since *my* brain is the one that's at risk here, I'm more qualified than anyone else to decide how to handle the problem."

Shuddering, Midas added, "Thank you, sir. I'm not broken, and I'm glad you see the wisdom in not needing to replace me. Your terms are clear, and I will do all I can to live up to them. Please, I do not want to, well, *die*."

"Most people don't." Dante smiled grimly at the statement's irony. For all his trepidation about having the procedure done and the dismissive words of his partner and the doctor, he found that feelings were feelings and he could only ignore them for so long.

He kind of liked Midas and would rather keep him around. He didn't want the little bastard to die.

CHAPTER NINE

"So," Nasreen began, absentmindedly waving the mini-panel through the air as she paced the room. Every few words she glanced again at the glowing surface displaying a receipt. "You're raking in a lot more money than I ever would've thought. Are payouts like this normal in your line of work? Is this the kind of compensation you were making back when you were Dante Shale, or is this a uniquely Hellcat thing?"

She had been up for an hour or two before he had, and he was still in the middle of his morning coffee. "Yes," he said.

She stopped and peered at him. "I asked three questions. Can I assume that you responded to the first, or did you not feel like responding to all of them and tried to sum everything up with a one-word answer?"

He sighed and grumbled into the steam that rose from his cup. "Yes, the money I've made lately is typical for jobs of this nature, provided they're successful. No, in my previous life I would typically make slightly *more* because I had years of legitimate reputation behind me. People paid extra for the name."

Nasreen made a little sputtering sound. "Are you kidding me? Shit. I should have been a Marauder, Reaper, or whatever." She went back to pacing and examining the mini-panel, probably doing a couple of calculations in her head.

Dante shrugged. "I suppose if you don't mind the possibility of violent death on pretty much every single outing. And if you have the nose for jobs that will pay well, and crews that won't fuck it up."

As he returned to his coffee, Nasreen whirled on one foot and allowed the mini-panel to refold itself into her sphere, which she slid back into her pocket. "Everything you said applies to what I do for a living, more or less. You'd think I'd make comparable earnings."

Without looking up, Dante commented, "You seem to do all right for yourself. I can't imagine you're poor, exactly, if you can maintain apartments in half a dozen different cities simultaneously."

"Well, no," she shot back, "but like most people, it's hard not to think that I could be doing more, *with* more. Granted, our recent successes with the Hellcat persona contribute to that, and if we eventually take down SSS, that will only open up more doors in the future."

"Yeah," Dante agreed. He finally drained his cup and debated whether or not to make another. He also came dangerously close to making a sarcastic remark about Nasreen's usage of the word *our* in reference to his activities as the Hellcat...but in truth, it was accurate. She had helped him reconstruct his life and career every step of the way. He wouldn't have been where he was without her.

Nasreen walked over and sat next to him. "With the amounts your jobs are paying out, I think we might be able to accelerate our plans if we can leverage some bigger and more expensive work for you."

He set the cup aside on the end table beside the couch. "Probably, but bigger and more expensive usually means more dangerous and complicated."

"Is that a problem?" She arched her eyebrows and allowed something faintly disapproving to creep into her tone.

Dante knew what she was doing, implying a challenge to his manhood or something to inspire him to be more ambitious. "Not necessarily. It is what it is. We'll keep looking at whatever jobs are available and choose the ones that offer the best ratio of risk to payout."

It was a generic, noncommittal answer, but since he'd delivered it without losing his cool, he liked to think he'd rebuffed her little attempt to prickle his ego.

She turned her head aside and changed the subject. "It's a shame we can't draw upon your assets from your old life. That would allow us to augment our budget to at least some degree."

"Lamentable," he agreed and made up his mind to seek another cup of coffee.

Nasreen kept her head facing away but moved her gaze sidelong toward his. "Out of curiosity, how much were you worth before the o-harvest debacle?"

He had pretty much figured she would ask him that at some point in the conversation. As closely linked as their destinies now were and as trustworthy as she'd proven to be, even if she occasionally annoyed him, as with any two people who worked and sometimes lived together, he saw no reason to withhold the information.

He told her.

Nasreen's mouth opened into a perfect little circle of awe. Her demeanor was still calm and controlled, but the surprise was genuine.

"That, ah, that is impressive, Dante, I must say. The math suggested you were relatively well-off, but I hadn't realized you were *rich.*"

He supposed he was—or had been, before the betrayal—but he'd never thought of himself as a typical upper-class person.

Neither had Nasreen, it seemed. "That doesn't make any

sense." She frowned in legitimate befuddlement. "Why the hell, if you had that much money, would you live like some mook with a typical runty apartment, eating cheap chow mein from a food cart on the street?"

The question implied that he was somehow *obligated* to live in a certain way. His gut roiled, and his jaw tightened. "I *like* cheap chow mein from food carts. If I can get what I need and want cheap, why pay for more? It's a waste of money. Makes more sense to save it for important stuff."

Midas had been silent throughout the morning. They had an established rule that he was not to pester Dante until at least half an hour after he'd awakened and certainly not before he was a minimum of halfway into his coffee.

It had, unfortunately, been half an hour.

The AI spoke up. "Sir, if I may say so, I believe Ms. Joelle is right. Money simply hoarded serves little purpose."

Dante grunted, "It *does* accumulate interest, you know."

Nasreen was about to say something but stopped herself, realizing that he'd been speaking to Midas.

The voice in his head continued. "Yes, but active investment is often a better course of action. For example, observe how much simpler communications among the three of us have become thanks to the voice projection upgrade you allowed me to purchase."

Dante had nearly forgotten about that one.

The AI's familiar voice, lightly synthesized, flowed out into the air, taking on the form of true sound waves rather than simply a trick played on Dante's brain. To Dante, it sounded and felt like someone with their head pressed against the back of his speaking directly beside his ear. It made his balls tingle in a faintly unpleasant way.

"Ms. Noelle," Midas said in his affected male British accent, "I am wholly on your side in this. Dante has benefited tremendously from our encouragement in matters of spending."

Nasreen blinked. "Oh, my. That's what your voice sounds like? It's nice. Dante, is that the way he sounds in your head?"

"Yeah," he confirmed. "Feels weird when he talks out loud, though, like someone is running a radio signal through my skull. Midas, please only do that when you have to."

The AI returned to his usual silent, inner voice. He sounded disappointed. "Yes, Dante. Of course, I have read that others have reported a similar reaction to current voice projection technology. At least two firms are working on upgrades to ameliorate the issue."

"Of course they are," Dante muttered. "There are three certainties in life. Death, taxes, and tech companies selling upgrades for jacked-up prices as fast as the nerds can develop them."

Nasreen smirked, guessing the trajectory of the one-sided conversation. She rose to her feet and swept her hair back from her shoulders. "All right, boys, I'll leave you to it. I have to prepare for an investigation I'm doing on my own soon. Why don't the two of you start looking for your next job? Also, laundry. Preferably by thirteen hundred hours."

She walked off, leaving Dante on the couch. He rolled his eyes up. "You heard her. Start looking for work. I'll handle laundry. In a minute."

He also reflected on the incident back at the clinic, with them threatening Midas with deletion. He allowed the thought to rise enough to the surface of his consciousness that Midas would have noticed it. Hopefully, it would keep him in line for a little while.

The AI quietly did as instructed. About half an hour later, as Dante was waiting for the wash cycle to end so he could rotate the laundry into the dryer and reallocate the used water to the building's purification facility, Midas pinged him with his findings.

"Yes?" Dante asked.

Midas seemed excited. "Good news. I've found a posting that ought to be quite suitable for us, and it sounds like the pay rate will be, at a minimum, roughly equivalent to the highest amount we've earned so far. Possibly more. The individuals who've posted it are withholding some of the details, though, and want a face-to-face meeting before they divulge everything."

Dante nodded. "That means it's serious cutthroat Reaper shit, probably."

"Perhaps. If you permit me, I can act as your secretary in setting up the meeting and going through the usual initial formalities."

Dante hit a couple of buttons to finish the last phase of the laundering process. Or technically the second-to-last. Modern tech had yet to offer a workable solution to the annoyance of hand-folding one's freshly dried clothes.

"Fine. But do not sign any contracts in my name or agree to anything definite. I'm not taking on a shady job until I know all the ins and outs."

Nasreen wandered by. "Midas sent me a message. Congratulations on finding a shady job, and good luck with the ins and outs."

Dante had forgotten they'd also purchased an upgrade that allowed Midas to send sphere messages to approved persons independently. He supposed it was worth the money. Nodding at his human partner, he grunted, "Thanks."

The meeting site was nothing formal but simply a quiet corner of a nearby diner-cafe, the type of place where all kinds of people might come and go, and others would pay little attention to any of their private conversations. No one would assume anything out of the ordinary was going on.

Dante seated himself in the requisite area first, a booth near the rear corner of the establishment. His contact didn't arrive until he'd been there for about five minutes and had already ordered a cup of tea, sipping it slowly with the cup in his left hand. His right remained free, never straying too far from the place in his coat where his knife lay hidden.

The man who appeared fit the description that Midas had provided. Tall, broad, strong-looking, about fifty, with a shaved head, and wearing a light gray coat. He was more unassuming-looking, more "average," than Dante had expected. His size made him more intimidating than the average person, but he didn't give off a vibe of being dangerous or frightening.

Appearances could be highly deceiving, though.

The man approached the booth. "Hi. You're Mr. Raksha?" His voice was like a bear chewing gravel, but he spoke with a friendly, jaunty tone.

"Yes," Dante confirmed. "Have a seat." He gestured at the bench across from him with his teacup.

The man settled in. "I'm Jorge, your contact for the job we discussed. And also a member of the crew. I'm multi-talented." He chortled and ran his thick hands over the lapel of his jacket.

Dante smiled and nodded. He couldn't tell if the guy was armed, but nothing in his body language suggested threat or hostility. "It's good to be flexible. Anyway, you saw my credentials. I can understand wanting to talk about the job details in person. I'm guessing it's dirty, difficult stuff, then."

Jorge pursed his lips. "You get right to the point, don't you? Well, nothing wrong with that. Hold on."

A waitress approached and took Jorge's order of a cup of coffee. Dante waited until he had the steaming beverage in hand and they had privacy before he gave the man a pointed look to continue with his pitch.

"Okay," Jorge began between cautious sips. It was oddly comical seeing such a big guy acting afraid of burning his mouth on hot coffee. He lowered his voice. "This is Reaper work. I gather you're familiar with what that means, and you don't shy away from it. Right?"

Dante inclined his head. "Yes." It meant *violence*. "I want to know specific objectives, though, as well as details about the crew, equipment, and so forth. Everything I'd need to be aware of to do the job right."

The big man gave a dry chuckle. "Yeah, you're a pro, aren't you? Sounds like you haven't been on the scene long, but you're building a reputation anyway. So, here's the deal..."

He explained everything, occasionally pausing when their waitress reappeared to ask if they wanted refills or other patrons shuffled past their booth to use the restroom.

Although it was nasty business, if anything, the job was a little more "legitimate" than most Reaper work. Jorge's people were assembling a team to hit another group of Plunderers and hit them hard. It sounded like Dante would be part of the so-called good guys.

Their adversaries would be a group of Marauders who had been illegally poaching charitable aid donations, supplies, and the like from a constellation of Dirtwalker tribes. The donations were the work of the Terra Restoration Group. Dante had heard of them. They were a philanthropic bunch who sent down missions to help improve the lives of the Dirtwalkers, not only providing them with tools, medicine, and food but also coaching them in ways to gradually rebuild civilization.

Dante wasn't sure how successful their long-term goals would be. He had spent enough time among the Dirtwalkers, or "Earthbound occupants," as TRG's organizational literature preferred to call them, to know that some were more cultured and relatable than most Station-Atlanticans realized. Still, they were the inheritors of a savage age, and they lived on a broken planet where survival trumped all other concerns.

Jorge explained, "The missions are proven to help these people drastically. They are people, even if they're different from us and not always friendly, right? Child mortality cut in half, and signs that some of them are getting better at building a settled society with sustainable ways of living and stuff."

Dante sipped his tea. "I think I heard about that somewhere. Although I've also heard some people say that it only makes it easier for Dirtwalkers to put up violent resistance to any Plunderers who come down looking for resources that *we* need up in the Stations. Not saying I agree or disagree. But that's what I hear."

Bringing up that little controversy was mostly Dante's way of prodding the man to see how he reacted. It was always helpful to know how someone behaved when confronted with opinions or information they might not like.

Jorge frowned but maintained his composure. "That's a concern, yeah. We don't do repeat deliveries to tribes who do stuff like that, though. The people we're focused on for this job are some of the ones who've been receptive to our efforts."

The way he said *we* implied that he was an actual member of the Terra Restoration Group. Dante surmised that part of his function was making sure anyone hired to carry out TRG's objectives would do so in accordance with the organization's humanistic values.

Dante didn't envy him. Getting a bunch of Reapers operating as a de facto mercenary team to act decently couldn't have been an easy job.

The man elaborated upon the situation. TRG's ships would drop off supplies. Currently, it was difficult to find the budget or personnel to do much in-person counseling stuff with the tribes, so they had relegated themselves to simply gifting the Dirtwalkers with useful items. Shortly after the drop, when the tribespeople approached to reap the bounty, the plunderous Marauder band would rush in to swipe the stuff.

Predictably, the Dirtwalkers weren't happy about this, especially since the Marauders weren't shy about using force against them. It had happened twice in a row in the last two months, and in each case, the Dirtwalkers ended up with at least one or two of their people dead and several others injured by the Atlanticans' superior weaponry.

TRG did not wish for it to happen a third time. Or ever again.

Wrapping up his pitch, Jorge stated, "You will have a chance to meet the crew beforehand, as well as examine all the equipment. I know I told you that my people don't feel they have the budget for in-person mission work with the Earth-bound occupants. In this case, they figured that one big expenditure now, when it counts, will save us money and lives in the future, so they scraped together enough to do this right. I imagine you have some armor, weaponry, comms equipment, accessories, and the like, but we're making an effort to provide the best stuff we can. If we pull this off, it sends a message to any other people who might be considering poaching from us. Or those poor people Dirtside."

Dante vaguely wondered if anyone he'd interacted with from his Marauder days might be aware of the situation. It was entirely possible. Word got around through the appropriate channels.

He finished his tea and extended his hand. "I'm not signing anything until the inspection, but let's say that I like what I hear well enough. You've got yourself a tentative deal."

Jorge took Dante's hand, grasping it gently since his mitt was big enough to crush it. "Sounds good, Hellcat."

CHAPTER TEN

The results of the inspection, Dante had decided, were not merely satisfactory but downright impressive. He had signed on to the job without further thought.

They departed the very next day. Dante, still inhabiting the persona of Jordan "Hellcat" Raksha and riding on his burgeoning reputation as one of the up-and-coming Reapers amid the Stations' Plunderer community, arrived about five minutes early for check-in, as was his habit. He didn't like being *too* early, but getting there precisely on time was cutting it a little close for his tastes.

It was a bit of a relief when one of the first people he sighted in the loading bay for their shuttle was Jorge. The big man approached and took his hand.

"Morning, Hellcat. Glad you decided to join us. Our in-house crew already did most of the initial prep work on the shuttle, so we've got about twenty to thirty minutes' worth of getting the temporary crew checked in and suited up, and we'll be Earthbound."

Dante managed a subdued if rather grim smile. "Good. You mentioned during the inspection last night that your intel suggested the enemy Marauders were preparing to move out and knew where we'd be landing today. Any changes in that situation?"

"None. They blasted off about an hour ago and will be lying in wait. In case you're wondering why, if we know who and where they are, we didn't simply report them to the authorities... Well, you strike me as the sort of man who could appreciate the value of not asking that question."

Dante laughed. "The Terra Restoration Group. Humanitarian charitable organization, and soon to be feared as people not to be fucked with."

A couple of other guys suiting up nearby chuckled at that in low voices.

There were few laws on Earth, especially pertaining to violence between Plunderers or violence between Plunderers and Dirtwalkers. By stealing from a charity, the rogue Marauder team was effectively outside the law's protection. Therefore, it would be instructive to make an example of them.

It was easier to make such examples Dirtside, where they could use whatever weapons they wanted, rather than being restricted to melee, or worse yet, lawfare by the safety dictates of the Stations. Firearms and explosives were heavily frowned upon in environments where everything depended on the structural integrity of the pressurized, gravity-producing domes that surrounded the cities.

The actual captain of the shuttle was a battle-ax of a woman named Farsa, who oddly enough doubled as the main pilot. Jorge, Dante determined, was the "mission leader" and merc wrangler, in charge of directing the crew's overall objectives. Farsa ran everything specific to the ship, though.

Dante suited up in full armor and strapped on his razorfist. Annoyingly, he missed out on getting a pulsecore carbine but was still able to select a smaller-caliber pulsecore pistol and an exceedingly nice semiautomatic shotgun as his main weapon.

The latter came with a satisfying complement of electro-flechette rounds, which would be reasonably effective against armored foes. Still, it was clear that Dante could look forward to ending up in close combat.

It was acceptable to him. He had plenty of experience with it, but the risk of getting his head blown off tended to go down the farther away he got to be from the people he needed to kill. They would, in any event, have the element of surprise on their side.

The plan was to drop off the supplies as usual, then fly off, circle briefly, and hit the Marauders from the rear as they swarmed out to steal the payload. The chief complication was the prospect that the Dirtwalkers would get into the middle of the fight. If that were the case, Jorge would rush in to warn them to back off. They knew him and more or less trusted him.

Dante hoped the two opposing groups of Station folk would be able to resolve the bloodshed before any of the natives showed up. It would keep things a lot simpler.

As they all took their places within the medium-sized shuttle and strapped in, Dante noted the lack of meaningful conversation; the aloof demeanors of the men around him. It didn't bother him. He wasn't the talkative type. But it bespoke the unpleasant implications of their work.

Most of them were independent Reapers. They all knew that the next job they took might be against one another. With that in mind, it made them loath to get too friendly. They didn't want conflicts of interest arising. Based on what Dante had seen of them plus the reputations of the ones whose names or faces he recognized, they all seemed like true professionals.

He hoped none of them recognized *him*. He hadn't interacted with any of them in person before as Dante Shale. They hadn't questioned his fake credentials. The subtle changes he'd made to his appearance seemed to be doing the trick.

Still, to be safe, he'd instructed Midas to alert him if anyone started examining him too closely, especially while he was unaware that they were doing so. He had been somewhat of a celebrity, and some of the Reapers might recognize certain of his features simply from pictures or video footage if nothing else.

In any event, their lack of interest in conversation meant he didn't have to worry too much about keeping his concocted backstory straight.

Minutes later, Captain Farsa took the shuttle out of the bay and into space. Their destination was a river delta in Argentina not far from what had once been the great city of Buenos Aires. Consequently, to keep the space travel to a minimum, their point of departure was São Paulo de Firmamento, the nearest Atlantican city to their destination and the largest of the Stations corresponding to former South America.

In addition to the twenty-man Reaper merc force, the shuttle also had a small crew of four people including the captain. The other three would be responsible for dropping the supply load.

They got through the atmosphere without incident. Farsa seemed quite a skilled flyer. Below them spread the southern Atlantic ocean, the half-dried Uruguay River, and the half-dead forest that had once flourished in this land.

Jorge gave minor pointers to the captain as she piloted the shuttle over a particular little vale-type area. Dante examined it on the viewscreens and noted that it was mostly a flat, swampy area, with only a couple of small natural formations representing actual "terrain." When the shooting started, they couldn't rely on the land to provide much in the way of cover.

"All right, drop the package," Jorge directed the auxiliary crew.

While everyone else remained seated, the three crewmen positioned the load of crates over the rear compartment. They waited to open it until Farsa had them as close to the ground as reasonably possible. Wind rushed in when they actuated the door, then they hauled the payload out with a hydraulic lever and dropped it.

A quickie-parachute deployed immediately and slowed the descent enough to avoid damaging the supplies. The impact still broke the net holding them together and sent two or three crates rolling end over end to different parts of the valley.

There was no sign of any Dirtwalkers so far. Or the thieving Marauders.

The crew closed the doors and Farsa took them back into the sky. She flew into a bank of dark orangish clouds to conceal their movements. The shuttle rumbled and wavered in the turbulence, which a couple of men complained about, but no one paid them any heed. Then the captain descended again at a different point and reapproached the vale near the delta from the landward side.

They had timed it almost perfectly, Dante saw. A shuttle had appeared from somewhere nearby and landed. About a dozen figures had emerged and were securing the various supply crates. They were all armed and armored, and four of them set up a portable artificial barricade. Likely to guard themselves against attack by the local Dirtwalker tribes.

Jorge said, "Don't worry about stealth once we're close enough. You might as well land directly on top of a few of them if you can."

Farsa laughed harshly. "That's easier said than done. Let's see what I can do."

Dante braced himself, his fingers curling around the armrests of his seat.

Midas asked, "Is she going to attempt an aggressive crash landing? Oh, dear. It occurred to me that if you get killed, I will likely cease to exist as well."

"Yeah," Dante replied. "Keeping me alive is in your best interest for more reasons than one. As for the crash landing..."

Farsa accelerated. Down on the surface, the Marauders noticed them for the first time as they streaked toward the ground. They scattered, clearly in a near panic. Farsa swept over the ground they had occupied, sending them in multiple directions, then looped back around while decelerating and landed about half a mile from their ship.

Dante frowned. Although the woman was skilled, there simply wasn't enough time to pull off a complete surprise attack. The Marauders would have had almost a full minute to regroup and reform by the time the Reapers deployed themselves.

Jorge shouted, "Ready!"

Dante unstrapped himself and leapt to his feet, shotgun in hand. The other Reapers fell in around him as the doors crashed open and all twenty of them piled out of the shuttle at once in a loose but well-disciplined formation.

The shooting started at once before they had time to assess the situation. Three or four of the hostile Plunderers were right outside the ship, attempting a desperate counter-ambush since they lacked time to come up with a better strategy.

The Reapers annihilated them. Pulsecores and rifles barked and blazed, and the men fell ravaged and dead to the muddy Earth.

Jorge bellowed, "Move out! No sign of the Dirtwalkers yet. Makes things easier!"

Dante felt this was incorrect. The absence of Dirtwalkers made things *simpler*, not easier. There was a difference. Having local tribespeople around might have helped absorb some of the Marauders' aggression. Ethical concerns aside, it could have been a tactical advantage.

As it turned out, the Marauders had a lot of aggression to throw their way.

The point man leaping off the ramp to the ground exclaimed, "Shit!" A barrage of pulsecore rounds struck him or detonated next to him, ripping him apart and casting his remains all over the ramp and the muck in a red cloud of human devastation.

Dante's heart skipped a beat. The Marauders were far better armed than they had expected. His jaw clenched in anger at Jorge, or Jorge's so-called "intel." If those people had been able to determine right when the Marauders left the Stations to prepare their ambush, how were they incapable of saying how well-equipped their foes were? The Marauders had come to Earth expecting a fight not only against poorly-armed Dirtwalkers but if necessary, against equals.

Dante and three other men took the lead, firing their weapons before they were in clear view, pressing the Marauders down to allow the last Reapers to jog out and take up positions in front of the shuttle. Dante glimpsed the portable barricade and was briefly confused by its location and orientation.

Midas noticed. "They have one of the newest and best models," he pointed out. "It can be relocated and repositioned in a matter of seconds. Oh, and it's specifically designed to stand up to pulsecore rounds."

"Great." Dante shouldered past another man and took cover behind one of the supply crates that had rolled away from the central mass. He realized a second later that this had been a mistake. Another volley of enemy fire separated him from most of the others as they all took shelter behind a different crate or near the ship itself.

Reddish fumes were rising in the air, probably from a smoke bomb set off by the Marauders to hide their position. The wind was picking up and would disperse it quickly, but it still gave their adversaries a definite advantage.

Midas pinpointed the approximate location of some of them, but when Dante fired his shotgun, he still felt that he was shooting mostly blind and had little hope of scoring good kill shots.

Worse, it sounded like Jorge was trying to rally everyone via their armor's built-in radio system, but his voice faded and crackled into oblivion each time he or someone else tried to speak. By the time the smoke cleared, the Reapers were entirely on the defensive.

"Fuck," Dante exclaimed. He pivoted, his shotgun still high

against his shoulder, and let off another shell at a guy who briefly popped up from behind the barricade. The flechette round shredded the barricade's surface and raised sparks, but unfortunately, it missed the intended target. The man ducked, presumably to report to his comrades on the Reapers' positions and equipment.

It was still all but impossible to get through to the rest of the team. It could not possibly be an accident. He dropped behind the crate and topped off his gun with extra shells.

Sensing his thoughts in addition to processing the situation on his own, Midas announced, "They are using electronic disruption techniques to interfere with our communications. Something quite advanced, I'd say."

"I know," Dante snapped. "Give me a visual on the pattern of the disruptions. Like, blink a light in front of my face every time they send a counter-signal."

The AI agreed, and a second or two later, flecks of green illumination appeared at the center of his vision. He paid attention to their cadence while also keeping his ears on the failing attempts of his partners to speak to one another. There was a pattern to the disruptions, and it was a *familiar* one.

Years ago, someone had analyzed a bunch of examples of the kinds of messages soldiers relayed to one another in combat scenarios. That person had come up with an algorithm for how long they typically spoke on each end of the line relative to the volume of fire they were taking, the size and distance of the enemy force, and so forth.

Some Marauders and other such people had used the scientist's research to develop homebrew patterns for electronic disruption, automating them to cause the maximum possible problems for their adversaries at the worst possible times.

Dante had benefited from it himself.

Another volley of fire came toward him from behind the barricade. The rest of the team wasn't going to regroup anytime soon, from the look of things. The crate was holding up for the moment but would probably disintegrate under the pulsecore barrage within another minute or so.

"Midas," he barked, "that tracking upgrade from last week. Use it. We need to find where that disruption is coming from. Someone nearby has to have a nest where they're running the countermeasures on us. Locate it and tell me."

"Yes, sir." The AI's voice fell silent as he went to work.

Dante scanned the surrounding area, looking for multiple exit paths from his current location that might take him to wherever the enemy comms person was hiding. While he had no way of knowing where they might be—yet—it stood to reason that they were somewhere in the Marauder band's general vicinity. A position either wholly protected from fire or where the other Marauders could cover them or rush to their aid.

He identified three paths that might work for getting the hell out from behind the crate if he timed it right. Pulsecore rounds continued to explode behind him. He considered pulling out his pistol and firing on the barricade with that. It was only a handgun, but its explosive bullets might be more effective than the shotgun was. Flechette shells could be deadly but were more of a riot weapon than a military one, and the day's job had become de facto war.

An explosion, much too large to be a pulsecore round, went off about sixty-five feet to Dante's left. A grenade or something. He had to get moving, and soon.

Midas spoke up, his internally simulated voice cutting through the noise of the battle. "I believe I have it. Two hundred sixty feet from your position, at nine o'clock, about halfway between the Marauders' ship and the barricade. I believe there's a physical obstruction blocking them off from sight and the line of fire."

Dante blew out a breath from between clenched teeth. "Got it. Thanks, Midas."

He pulled his pistol and blind-fired five shots around the corner of the crate and toward the barricades. Even if he hit no one, it was enough firepower to send the bad guys scurrying for cover for a couple of seconds. Sufficient time for him to make a break for it.

As the pulsecore rounds detonated, Dante sprang up and dashed in the direction Midas had indicated. The AI helped him by creating a green arrow to keep him on target and a glowing green ring around the approximate location he sought. He stayed low to the ground, moved erratically, and sought cover or concealment where he could find it.

When the Marauders spotted him, they opened fire. Dante retaliated with two shells from his shotgun. The second took one of the men in the arm or shoulder, knocking the gun from his grasp and sending him to the ground twitching from electrocution. Probably not dead but hurt badly enough to take him out of the fight for the time being.

Someone on Jorge's Reaper team, hiding behind a little hillock, noticed Dante and shouted, "Hey! Hellcat. What you doing, man?"

"Cover me," Dante yelled.

The man swore, rumbled, and raised his pulsecore carbine, letting out a destructive volley that kept the Marauders pinned down while Dante moved closer to his goal.

The nest lay behind a raised embankment that had once belonged to a creek or stream but now was dry. Dante crept around the far side of it, shotgun poised, preparing to open fire the instant he saw the hostile communications expert.

But the device within the nest was unattended. A small console, a portable power source, and a few antennae with a sensor web of transmitter optics between them were in plain sight. Dante's crew had used a similar one before. They could operate it remotely, decreasing the danger to the personnel but leaving the machine itself open to attack.

With a final glance to ensure no one was waiting in ambush, Dante aimed the shotgun and fired. Electro-flechettes worked wonders against machinery, better than they did against armored humans. The blast shredded the wires and less durable parts, and the projectiles' shock cores worked their magic, overcharging what was left and sending it up in a cloud of sparks, flames, and smoke.

Dante snarled, "Visual on the disruption."

Midas brought up...nothing. No green lights to indicate the tempo of counter-signals. He'd killed it entirely.

Then, from behind one of the food crates, the Marauders' lackey stepped out.

It was Desiree Naphtalim. His comms expert, now theirs.

"Hey!" she shouted. Then her eyes bulged as she realized that one of their foes had slipped past the defenses and disabled her toy. He had no idea if she recognized him. Probably not.

He recognized her, the curvy young woman with the distinctive dark face and the green streak in her hair. She was wearing a different, more heavily armored outfit than what she'd run with in Dante's crew. Consequences of all the money she'd made by betraying him, he figured.

He raised his shotgun, unfazed and unemotional.

Des turned and ran. She had never been much of a fighter, although she did have a gun at her hip. And she was moving in a particularly difficult, lizard-like way. It was the method Dante himself had taught her to avoid capture.

"Dammit, Des," he rasped under his breath and plunged after her. She might have another disruption device, more weaponry, or allies lying in wait. She was heading for the Marauders' ship. He intended to make sure she didn't reach it.

Something was stirring in the back of his mind, an emotional reaction he didn't have time for right now and refused to acknowledge. There was only the driving necessity of eliminating the threat and completing the mission.

Des pulled her sidearm as she moved out to brave a stretch of open ground. Dante didn't let her fire. He unloaded a shotgun shell at her. She cried out, dropped the gun, and rolled away as one of the flechettes sparked against her shoulder armor, but she had suffered no serious damage. Still, the blast slowed her enough that Dante began to catch up.

Behind them, the gunfire was rising in intensity and frequency. With the counter-communication device obliterated, Jorge's team was able to coordinate their attack and was slowly crushing the life from the Marauder force.

Dante closed in on Desiree, who was in a blind and panicked rush for the ramp leading into the nearby shuttle. Her sloppiness gave him the window of opportunity he needed. He fired another shell, aiming for her legs.

The flechettes tore strips from the thinner armor around the woman's calves and knees and electrocuted flesh and metal. She screamed in pain and collapsed, rolling over on her back and frantically pawing at her side, forgetting that she'd already dropped her pistol.

If she hadn't recognized Dante yet, she would as soon as he got a little closer. Somehow, he felt sure of it. His job as a Reaper was to wipe these people out. He rolled the shotgun back over his shoulder on its sling and pulled out the pulsecore pistol in its stead.

Des had risen to a sitting position, her back against the lowermost part of the shuttle's ramp. She froze, and her eyes fixed on her approaching executioner.

"No," she gasped, raising her hands, palms outward. "No, no, no..."

As Dante drew close enough to ensure a clean kill and raised his pistol, the terrified eyes focused on his face, and she blinked. There was a flicker of recognition there. Married to it was a shred of hope. She didn't realize that he already knew who she was. She hoped that yes, it *was* Dante after all and he would be willing to forgive her.

He stopped. Reflexively, he had aimed the pulsecore handgun at the woman's face. She, who had joined the others in backstabbing him and leaving him for dead. Yet he didn't pull the trigger. Something about the way she—

A rapidly growing whistling sound accompanied a *crack* in the distance. Then a stray bullet from a rifle crashed into the side of Desiree's unprotected head, punching through it and smashing her brains out the other side of her skull. She fell over face-first and lay still.

Dante stared, mouth agape. He holstered the pistol, unslung his shotgun, and scanned the surrounding landscape for foes, as well as the entrance to the shuttle. The Reapers were mopping up the last of the resistance.

A man appeared in the ship's doorway, face contorted with fear and wrath, and he wasn't wearing armor. A conventional pistol was in his hand. "Hey, asshole! Get back, or I'll kill you!"

Dante swept up the shotgun and fired. Flechettes tore open the man's chest and blasted him backward so he was already mostly dead when the electricity coursed through his body, leaving it charred and shuddering.

Then it was over. Jorge's team swarmed over the last of the Marauders, killing them all before they could surrender, and quiet fell over the delta plain.

Dante breathed in and out. He felt numb.

Midas spoke up. "I understand that you're upset, Dante. I saw a great deal of conflicting emotions being processed within your mind when you confronted that woman, and yes, I know who she was. But I'm afraid that there's no point in regretting what happened. We have all done as we must to survive."

Dante said nothing.

Twenty minutes later, Captain Farsa's shuttle was taking off, leaving the wreckage and carnage of the rogue Marauders as part of the booty for the Dirtwalkers. Two Reapers total had died in the fight, and Jorge insisted on bringing their bodies back to the Stations. The others had an assortment of light wounds at worst, nothing they couldn't patch up themselves rather than requiring a hospital.

Dante sat alone with his thoughts as they blasted through the planet's atmosphere and briefly back into space. None of his temporary comrades had the slightest idea of what had happened. Dante had killed one of the enemies as far as they were concerned. That was all.

Midas offered his two cents again after Dante's thoughts turned particularly black and gloomy.

"An ugly business, to be sure. All things considered, it was the best outcome for everyone, I'd say."

Dante cleared his throat. In a low whisper, he replied, "Whatever you say, Midas. Whatever you say."

<hr>

Nasreen greeted him with her usual expression of relief. She had learned to trust in his abilities, but they both knew well that there was no guarantee he'd come home from any given job.

Dante watched as her face shifted, her brow creasing in concern as she frowned. "What happened?"

He moved past her into the living area and lowered himself onto the couch. "I don't want to talk about it."

She closed the door and came up beside him, apparently determined to *make* him talk about it regardless. "The job wasn't a washout, was it? You're guaranteed a certain minimum risk compensation even if you fail to complete the objective, right?"

He raised a hand dismissively. "It's not that. We did what we needed to do, and we're getting paid the full sum. It's a nice handsome amount. It just...wasn't a lot of fun, is all."

"Ohh." She wrapped her arms around her torso and peered at

his face. There was an obvious sense of relief about her at finding out that nothing had gone wrong with the *practical* aspects of the mission, but her concern remained. "Well, if you decide you *do* want to talk about it after all, I'm available and willing to listen."

Suddenly something occurred to him. Dante looked up. "Midas, don't blab. If I discuss this, it's my decision, not yours."

The voice in his head replied, "I understand, sir. Would you like me to focus on putting your finances in order? The payment should be cleared and processed by now."

"Yeah. Do that." Dante thought about asking Nasreen to bring him a drink or something but decided it would be presumptuous. Not to mention, she might take it as an invitation that he was open to discussing what was bothering him.

Nasreen stepped forward. "Can I get you a drink?"

Dante's hand clenched against the armrest of the couch. "Midas! Goddammit."

"Sir, that was not my doing. Ms. Joelle has not checked her sphere, nor did I speak aloud. There is no way for me to silently beam simulated audio directly into her mind the same way I do yours. Presumably, she knows you well enough to make a suggestion of that nature, or she is operating on feminine intuition."

Nasreen stood, eyeing him skeptically, as Dante made a vague grumbling sound under his breath. He looked back at his human partner. "Sure, I guess. Something *lightly* alcoholic, if you have it. I don't feel like being sober, but it would be stupid to get completely plastered."

Without a word, she strode past him to the cooling unit and returned a moment later with a frosty can of lemon-rice beer. Not his favorite, but tolerable. He thanked her and cracked it open.

Nasreen left him for a few minutes, doing something in her bedroom, and returned after he'd drained most of the beer. He had to admit it was a clever tactic.

"Are you doing okay?" She asked the question in a neutral, innocent way.

He exhaled slowly and stared into the distance beyond the wall. "I still don't want to talk about it in any *detail*, but to satisfy your curiosity...Desiree Naphtalim was there. My former crewmate, if you remember her."

Nasreen had never met any of Dante's ex-partners in person, but he had spoken of them quite a few times. "Oh. I see. Did she recognize you?"

Rather than answer the question directly, he only said, "She's dead now. I, uh. I don't know what... Shit. Later. Maybe I'll talk more about it later." He finished the beer and set the can down beside him.

Nasreen leaned over and picked it up. "I'm sorry to hear that. I know you were close to them before things went wrong. And," her voice took on a faint note of patience in the face of mild exasperation. "I know you're the type of person who, um, needs time to understand your emotions. Much less *express* them. It would be good for you to take some time off and relax."

Dante had to appreciate that she was trying to be nice to him. "Thanks, I guess. Weren't you the one saying we should take on more jobs to accelerate the plan, though?"

She raised her index finger. "That was before you found this job, which paid enough to buy us a little time to recuperate. Anyway, if you don't want to relax, take time off to do some passive training on Reaper stuff instead."

Dante squinted at her. "The hell? What do I need passive training for? I'm already excelling at the job. I'm a little fuzzy on the conventions specific to Reapers, but there's plenty of overlap between them and Marauders."

Rather than saying anything, Nasreen turned, took out her sphere, and powered up the view panel on the wall across from the couch.

"Have you heard of this stream? Plunderer Vids? It documents the careers of various Raiders, Marauders, and yes, Reapers. It's new but already a huge hit. They did a special on you—you, meaning the 'late' Dante Shale, not Hellcat—a couple of weeks ago. Of course, you weren't available, so it was mostly public footage and interviews with people who knew you. I thought about telling you about it but was worried it might upset you."

Dante leaned forward sharply. "What? Seriously?"

She smiled. "Yes, indeed. I can dig that one up for you later, but here, let me grab you another beer while you watch whichever one is most current. Two beers shouldn't be enough to get you plastered unless your tolerance is embarrassingly low."

He waved her off and focused on the screen. "Two beers, yeah, fine."

Within his head, Midas said, "I was also dimly aware of this program but was uncertain if I should mention it to you. Now that we have the opportunity to watch it together, I imagine it will prove enlightening. In particular, the opportunity to see what sort of equipment the competition is using, and how generous their upgrade budget is for—"

Dante cut him off as he pointed at the screen. "Holy fuck, they're using the original sound feed from the shuttles! Normally you can't hear jack from outside during the jump—no air so sound can't travel until you get into Earth's atmosphere—but all the civilians are used to hearing dramatic *whooshing* sounds in movies so the producers usually add that crap in after the fact. Maybe this show is worth a damn, after all."

Nasreen returned and handed him the beer. He took it, thanked her, and opened it without looking at her.

"Hah!" He laughed, still fixated on the stream. "Yeah, that's Kave Krawler. Never found a hole she couldn't squeeze through. The jokes write themselves. And yes, she is *exactly* the kind of person who would spell her name with a 'K' like that."

Midas commented—projecting his voice through actual audio since Dante was too distracted to complain about the vibrations

—"She seems to have one of those density sensors that came out early this year. Those are excellent for spelunking, particularly if one needs to do any digging or drilling while one is at it."

Dante's face went sour. "Yeah, I'm sure. Digging up loot isn't my thing."

Nasreen smiled. "I thought you said that you were already qualified for every aspect of the job?"

"Every *normal* aspect." He swallowed a gulp of beer. "Spelunking is specialized niche stuff."

Then his eyes widened, and he yelled. "Oh, that is *bullshit.* That J. Ping guy, thinking he can take credit for the Albania gig." He waved at the screen. "I know for a fact he's never plundered Tier Six tech in his life! He was on the team but he sure as shit didn't extract it himself. That was Nbougan, the wily bastard..."

Nasreen reached over and ruffled Dante's hair. He didn't object. "Enjoy your break. I'm going out this evening on a little job of my own."

CHAPTER ELEVEN

Nasreen had to admit she was relieved that Dante was wallowing in angst and depression. It kept him from asking too many questions. If he had forced her to disclose exactly where she was going tonight and for what purpose, his mood would have been *far* worse.

After leaving her apartment, she made straight for the shuttle bus station and took the first transport to Londonburg. She hadn't been there for months now. After the incident that had brought her and Dante together, it was the one city she tried to avoid at almost any cost.

The ride from Seoul to Londonburg was a long one. The Stations were all connected in their haphazard way with tunnels and sky bridges always available to link one to another. The route between the two great cities was more direct than some of the others hastily raised into space without much planning for how the whole network would function.

The simple fact remained that they were on opposite sides of the world, each having been pulled heavenward from a different tail-end of the Eurasian continent. With so much time to think,

Nasreen reflected on everything that had happened since the ill-fated job she'd taken with Captain Reavo.

Reavo's Plunderers were a disreputable bunch, definitely not the cream of the crop as far as their kind went. They had a nasty habit of hiring new pilots or other technicians and murdering them to avoid paying them their share of whatever plunder they pulled from Earth. Nasreen had gone undercover as their most recent hire to investigate one such disappearance.

Once she had arrived Dirtside, something truly bizarre had happened. An Atlantican man who claimed to have been briefly adopted and cared for by Dirtwalkers, which was all but unheard of, had approached her and the rest of the crew. His allies among the natives had joined him when the fighting broke out. That man had been none other than Dante Shale.

He and she had fought off Reavo's people in the decaying labyrinth of the former Atlantica Metro, eventually slaughtering them all before returning to the Stations in Reavo's ship. Having come through the ordeal together, they'd struck up a partnership.

There was one problem, though. Upon getting back to the Stations and being escorted by a space traffic patrol to a large public dock, they had run afoul of the bane of every covert operative and the enemy of all stealth and espionage—security camera footage.

Nasreen frowned and tried not to cringe inwardly with embarrassment. She had been at once flustered and yet overconfident. When she and Dante had docked, she'd moved in the ways she usually did to keep her face off-camera, and she'd mentioned to Dante that he ought to do the same.

Given how good he was at keeping to the shadows and stalking around without being seen, she'd figured they would be fine. The docks were busy, and lots of human traffic flowing through them meant that an analysis of their arrival might be too tedious and trivial for any but the most determined of investigators.

She should have known better. She'd allowed herself to become wrapped up in other things.

Yesterday, a contact in New Paris had reached out to her with a tip. The woman, Tilda, was a data storage expert who sometimes skimmed information off the top of the material she processed if it was of interest to her trusted side clients. She and Nasreen had a good and friendly working relationship for about three years.

Based on queries she had received over the last forty-eight hours or so, Tilda determined that someone was taking an interest in Nasreen's Dirtside return. She had occupied the persona of Kara Hengst at the time, a German woman whom Nasreen had created to be both competent and unthreatening. Reavo, sociopath though she was, had hired her after a cursory grilling, and down they'd gone along with the whole crew.

When the ship came back, only two people had disembarked. The security camera showed as much. The so-called Kara and an individual whom Tilda referred to as "the other guy."

Hearing that, Nasreen had gone cold inside. Nothing *specifically* connected her or Reavo's crew to Dante Shale, who was supposed to have died some weeks earlier. But if anyone looked too closely at the data, it wouldn't be hard for them to put two and two together.

If the two of them had failed to completely dance between the proverbial raindrops and their faces—especially Dante's—had been captured, they both could be in a world of trouble. SSS, or any of Dante's old enemies, could confirm that he was still alive. Or from Nasreen's perspective, the various people she had angered over the years could prove that she was connected to him and helping him.

For that information to get out would be the end of their plans to overthrow Cormac Slaine. And it might well be the end of their lives.

Nasreen had attired herself in her best and most imperious

suit-dress and done her hair in a parted style that was currently popular with celebrities, executives, and the like. The idea was to look important, wealthy, and officious, but in a way that suggested actual authority rather than mere luxury. She had also deliberately overdone her makeup so she appeared five to seven years older than she was.

She dismounted the shuttle bus at the stop before the dockyards since going to them directly at the current hour when they were closed to the general public from the city end would have been suspicious.

This part of town wasn't the best, and a couple of shady characters eyed her as she walked the block or so to the docks. Her confident stride and narrow-eyed glare dissuaded them from trying anything. It was good practice for the act she would pull with the staff.

Once she reached the dockyards, she found the door that led into the main administrative facilities and stood before it. Locked, of course. She rang the bell and knocked on the door. She could have simply decoded and opened it herself, but it would be less eyebrow-raising if she first went through the motions of trying to get in the "proper" way.

No one answered at first. Sighing in exasperation, Nasreen pulled out her sphere and punched a few keys. The door swung open right as a smallish, older, red-nosed man appeared at the other end of the room beyond.

"Ohh," he began, his eyes wide and round, "you can't be in here!"

Nasreen put away her sphere and stepped in. Her demeanor was that of a person trying to be patient with someone who knew far less than she did.

"I'm here from Londonburg Transportation Authority. We have a severe accounting discrepancy discovered this evening before the end of normal business hours. So, *of course*, I was called at home and asked to come in specifically to deal with it before the morning since we have an audit coming up that could begin as early as tomorrow. I'll need to see invoices for the past week and if possible, review things in the data room while I'm at it."

The man, whose nametag indicated he was the actual dockmaster, gaped and gawked at her for a second. He must have been trying to sober up. "Okay, okay, ma'am. Can I see your identification? You have a pass card on your sphere, I see, but I'm required to check such things."

Nasreen showed her forged credentials with the resigned air of one who hoped to escape such trivia but still expected to waste their precious time on it.

The man nodded at the bullshit certification, then led her back into an office where he made copies of the invoices she requested.

Then he turned to peer into her face. "Why do you need to go into the data room, though? That's mostly for our video and audio archives."

"Because." Nasreen raised her hand. She'd concealed a small, unobtrusive gas sprayer within her sleeve. It held a limited but potent charge of fumes that could knock a person unconscious with little to no traces showing up in later analysis. She squeezed her hand against the hidden trigger and let the invisible gas mist the man's face before he knew what was happening.

The dockmaster made a sound like "Haaaaa..." and slumped forward. She caught him in her arms and dragged him over to the nearest chair, put him in it, and let his head rest on the desk's surface. Then she patted him down for a scan card for the data room. She found one against his hip after only a brief search.

"Good." If a security camera had caught the incident, people could explain it away. The man had been drinking. She was there for legitimate purposes, had caught him as he passed out from inebriation, then had carried out her important duties regardless of his consciousness.

She took the scan card to a large, windowless door at the rear of the office. An eye read the thing, processed it, and allowed her into the data vault without further argument.

The docks, like many large public facilities, maintained a database for the storage of vast reams of information. Included were the records of every ship that docked for the last ten years, which was the current statute of limitations on transport investigations under Londonburg law.

Although Nasreen had never been in this room before, she had banked on the extremely likely probability that it contained facilities for viewing and reviewing data and performing the work she needed to do on-site. If by some chance it didn't, she was fucked. There hadn't been time to formulate much of a Plan B.

As she gazed across the rows of servers, the air escaped her lungs while her body relaxed. A desk in the corner had an old-fashioned but perfectly serviceable computer console mounted atop it.

"Good." She sighed. "Now, the annoying part." Locating the file out of the thousands if not millions stored here.

It took about six minutes. Longer than she would have liked, but not as long as she feared. It was largely a matter of using her portable hack scanner, connected to her sphere's regular biometric scanning app, to narrow things down by date. Once she found the specific server that hosted all the dockings from the appropriate month, she could pry open the casing, extract the chip, and take it over to the desktop computer.

A few more minutes passed as she turned the computer on and hacked through its amusingly basic, bare minimum security wall. Then the screen lit up and made its functions available to her. She inserted the stolen chip into the drive interface and poked around within its contents, eventually locating the single video file she sought out of hundreds.

Nasreen held her breath. What the cameras showed would determine her next course of action.

Reavo's ship, which she had humbly and imaginatively named the *Reavo*, pulled into the first available bay and went through the usual security and powering down procedures. An attendant officer scanned it and waved vaguely as the doors opened, and out stepped two figures. They were deep in a serious and low conversation, their heads down and turned away from the security cameras as they walked away from the ship.

Nasreen rolled her tongue around her teeth, staring at the two faces. If anything, it was more important that Dante not be identified. After all, she had gone down, so it made sense that she would come back up. The chief danger was that someone would make the connection between her real self and the Hengst persona. That could make things messy.

Dante was officially a dead man. At the time of the video footage, he wasn't supposed to *exist*.

Once, briefly, while mounting the stairs that took them out of the docks, he turned his face to be visible to the camera. Distant and a bit hazy, disheveled, and walking stiffly from his ordeals on Earth, he didn't match his past public image. Still, there was surely enough for any facial recognition program to identify him.

Nasreen slapped her forehead and slumped back in the chair. "Dammit. God fucking dammit." She spoke in a barely-voiced whisper, but what she *wanted* to do was scream and smash the computer against the floor. That would, however, be worse than useless.

No, she had everything she needed to take care of the problem. It would merely require time, effort, and good luck to not be discovered by the docks' staff before she finished.

Most of what she needed to do she could perform with the aid of the various powerful and illicit programs she had added to her sphere. At the end, there was a vial of nano-erasure solution to wipe the traces of her meddling. If Fate smiled, she could finish and be out the door in about twenty minutes. Maybe twenty-five.

She applied a video-editing program to the relevant security file. It hijacked other software already present on the computer and allowed her to make alterations to the visual data without having to install and uninstall an application as needed with more primitive tech.

It might have sped up the process simply to obscure Dante's face, but that would still pique the curiosity of anyone examining the video as to who the hell he was. Instead, she went through the longer and more intensive process of erasing him altogether. This meant highlighting and removing him from each separate frame and repairing the "hole" in the afterimage. The hybrid program made it far easier than it would have been otherwise.

When pretty sure she'd finished, she played the video again to assess her handiwork.

There was no "other guy," as Tilda had said. Only Nasreen herself. In a couple of cases, the shadows didn't look quite right since she had failed to erase them. Watchers could blame that on minor, natural optical effects or small vermin scuttling nearby. She didn't want to take the extra time to perfect such a small detail.

Otherwise, all was well.

Nasreen banished the editing program, saved the file, and pulled the chip. She produced the tiny vial of nanite solution and placed a single drop of the liquid on the chip itself.

Its purpose was to eliminate and smooth over all the telltale signs of editing in the video footage. Nasreen had used nano-erasure before, and it was almost always a resounding success—as it should be for something expensive and difficult to acquire. An extremely detailed review of the tech by a knowledgeable party might still pick up faint hints that the video had been tampered with. It would pass muster against a merely routine or cursory scan or inspection.

She waited about a minute to be safe. Then she returned the chip to its original home. She was nearly done. So far, everything had gone smoothly.

Somewhere outside came a rumbling sound, like the approach of heavy machinery. Rather than a steady grind, it had a back-and-forth, staccato rhythm, like footsteps. As it grew closer, the floor vibrated.

Nasreen froze in place. She had only the vaguest idea of what the hell the noise might be, but she somehow intuited at once that it was nothing good.

The dockmaster let out a slurred groan as the racket roused him from his artificial slumber. He drawled, "Hey—hey!" as the mechanical poundings drew nearer and something slammed against the wall.

A voice stated, "I need to get into that room."

Nasreen's blood turned to ice. The voice was bestial, like a large animal imitating human speech. Worse yet, it was processed and synthesized through layers of tech giving it a faint metallic echo causing it to sound almost as though it was double-tracked. Whoever possessed the voice either didn't care how he came across to others or worse, he wanted to be intimidating.

The dockmaster gasped and sputtered. Nasreen couldn't see to be sure, but she guessed that the man had been picked up and pressed against the wall, possibly with a hand around his throat.

"I can't—" the dockmaster stammered and made a choking sound. "Wh-who are you?"

There was a whirring sound and metal ground and *crunched*. "Open the door. You don't have a choice, friend."

Nasreen could barely hear the sleepy-eyed man mutter, "Okay! Okay..." Then he *thudded* to the floor, crawled over, and punched a few keys. By the time the door slid open, she had already taken refuge in a tiny, shadowed alcove in the far rear corner, where one of the stacks would block her from view unless the intruder came right up to her position.

She inhaled through her nose and breathed softly out her mouth. If she kept her cool, she'd be able to escape in a moment once they were distracted. Silently, she thanked the older man for not mentioning her. Still, she wondered, was the owner of the horrible synthesized voice looking for *her* or something else?

The mechanical footsteps stomped in, sending vibrations through the floor, and over the tops of the equipment, Nasreen glimpsed a head with wild, artificially red hair.

Suddenly it felt as though a yawning pit had opened inside her. She knew who the newcomer was now. Dante had described him and spoken of him often enough. Eduardo H. Curtidor, better known as Mr. Hyde, Cormac Slaine's right-hand enforcer.

Hyde marched straight to the desk console, and it sounded like he was dragging the dockmaster with him. "Start up the template for facial recognition. I'm looking for someone."

In response to the electronic growl, the dockmaster gasped, "Yes, yes, of course. I'll need a description, or, um, a file—"

Something *whirred* and Nasreen pictured the cyborg thrusting a chip into the man's hand. She could not be sure, but it seemed likely.

As dire as the situation had turned, she had one small comfort. Hyde didn't know about her and wasn't here to catch her. He was here for the same reason she originally had been. To review the footage from her and Dante's return from Earth.

She wasn't sure if Hyde knew which chips to harvest from the stacks or if he was asking the man to do a general scan of the entire archives. If the former, they would get too close to her for comfort while looking for it. If the latter, they might be occupied for a while.

She crept out, slowly and without making noise, from her hiding place and moved behind the stacks closest to the far wall. If her luck held out, she could make it to the door, which they'd left open, before Hyde knew she'd been there.

A faint hum from the computer was the only sound. They must have been running a general scan, then.

The inhuman voice barked, "There! That's the fucker. Wait. That's departure. Ha, there's me, too. Keep going. We're looking for a flight from a few weeks later. An incoming one."

"Yes, yes," the dockmaster agreed. The computer hummed again.

Nasreen passed a gap in the equipment that briefly put her in the pair's line of sight, but both were staring intently at the computer screen. A couple of seconds after she'd passed, there was no reaction from the visitor. But he did react to something else.

"Wait. Go back. Yeah, that one. The bitch who went down with that, uhh, Reavo crew. No loss to the world with those guys going missing, haha. They were small-time. Slow it down."

Nasreen hesitated. She should bolt out the door, but she wanted to know if she'd succeeded and what it might mean for Dante. She waited and listened.

Hyde made a throaty growl, like a dog, and the electronic augmentation effect did something unpleasant to the air that set Nasreen's hairs on end. Then the cyborg spoke. "Fuck. Nothing. Just her."

The dockmaster didn't speak but only waited as Hyde pulled out a comms sphere and quick-dialed someone. The instant it *beeped* its connection, he reported what he'd found. "*Mierda.* I'm tired of looking for a dead man. Quit being so paranoid, *Papi.* We can close the door on this."

Although barely audible, on the other end Nasreen made out a smooth, cultured, and otherwise wholly normal male voice, practically the antithesis of Hyde's. She peeked around the corner of the nearest stack and glimpsed the scene unfolding at the console.

"I asked you not to call me that. It is not paranoid to merely be *thorough*. But you may be right. Clean up and return home. Out."

It must have been Slaine himself, Nasreen concluded, or at least someone exceedingly high in the organization. She could not imagine Mr. Curtidor answering to a mere shift manager.

"Yeah." Hyde tapped the device and slipped it somewhere within his bizarre armored outfit. A faint *whirring* came as he turned to face the dockmaster, who was saying and doing as little as possible. "You heard the man. Got to clean up."

With shocking speed, the metal-sheathed hydraulic fist lashed out, *crunching* into the dockmaster's face and throat as easily as if he'd punched through thin drywall. The man spouted blood as he shot back through the air and crashed into the stack Nasreen was hiding behind. The impact knocked it loose from its fastenings. It bent sideways, leaned, and toppled halfway to the floor.

Nasreen reflexively pounced backward to avoid the wreckage, falling into a low squat, ready to spring in any direction. Then she froze. She was wholly exposed. Hyde was looking right at her.

It was her first good look at the man. Although human to begin with, so much of him was cybernetics that it was difficult to say what he was anymore. The red-dyed hair and beard didn't help. His eyes were flat and shiny, and his mouth hung half-open in an expression that reminded her of *hunger*. It was like looking into the soul of a shark.

"Hey. *Hey!*" he bellowed, rising fully to his feet. He *towered*.

Nasreen turned and bolted out the door. A split second before she crossed the threshold, machinery whined behind her, and heavy mechanical footsteps pounded the floor, shaking it as the metal behemoth gave chase.

She caught the edge of a chair and pulled against it, giving herself a tiny boost in speed and direction and toppling it to act as an obstacle. She knew it would do virtually nothing to slow

Hyde. Near-panicked, unreasoning terror had taken over her mind.

Ahead of her, the office seemed far too large, as though it had somehow grown in size since she'd passed through it earlier. She was scrambling as fast as she could. Athletic though she was and boosted by pure adrenaline, it still seemed too slow. The *whirring* and pounding were right behind her.

"Oh God," she gasped and rounded the corner into the main front area of the docks' administrative facilities. It seemed to have lengthened as well, like an extending hallway in a nightmare.

Behind her, Hyde let out a grating belly laugh, an awful sound that somehow combined the worst aspects of cold sadism, childish playfulness, and animalistic savagery. "Ha, ha. *Hah!* Come here, little girl. You're not getting away. You're too slow! You're gonna trip! *Hahaha...*"

Hyde made one mistake. He lunged straight at her back as she rounded the corner, kicking his hydraulics into high gear to increase his speed. It *almost* worked. The cold steel of his fingertips brushed the back of Nasreen's neck, raked along her collar, and snatched at her hair.

Then his broad armored shoulder crashed into the corner of the wall. The whole structure shook. Nasreen heard and *felt* the materials crack under the impact of Hyde's heavy, unnaturally powerful body. It stunned him, if only for a second, and slowed him down. His grunt of annoyance was like someone trying to force a steel beam through a woodchipper.

She dashed away, totally focused on the door at the end of the foyer. It led back to the docks' outdoor area and beyond to the city's streets. She felt like she was going to throw up. It took all her willpower to hold it in and keep running.

In the back of her mind, she couldn't recall feeling fear like this for many, many years. Nothing Dante had said could prepare her for what Mr. Curtidor was like in person. He was a monster that someone had constructed for the sole purpose of killing. In a second or less, if she didn't hurry, if she made one false move, he would fulfill that purpose.

By the time Hyde managed to dislodge himself and lurch around the corner, she had increased the distance between them, dodging nimbly around obstacles. As terrified as she was, she had enough experience surviving through desperate situations that her mind remained working.

She glanced back over her shoulder. The cybernetic brute was launching himself diagonally into the next part of the facility, closing in behind her. He halted and changed direction, and her revulsion grew stronger. Due to his augmentations being purely mechanical, his whole way of moving had a jerky, stiff, inorganic quality to it, like a recording of an old stop-motion puppet playing at ludicrously high speed.

Nasreen's entire world had narrowed to the space between her and the door. It was closed. It might still be locked. Biting her lip hard enough to taste blood, struggling to ignore the laughter, metallic whine, and stomping behind, she put her hand into her pocket and found her sphere. It flickered to life and expanded at once, and to her eternal gratitude, it was still idling on the same program she had used to open the door when she'd first arrived.

She slowed as the door grew closer, flicking her eyes to the screen long enough to punch in the five numbers of the code, astonished that it came back to her so quickly. The door opened. She lunged through it right as the horrible noises behind her shifted, indicating Hyde was about to do something other than run.

His hand shot out again, and once more it nearly caught her. The metal fingers grasped part of her jacket and hair. She refused to let them close all the way and flung herself forward. Cloth and hair ripped, staying in the hand as the door tried to shut on Hyde's arm. The sensors that kept it open for multiple people passing through must not have registered him as human with so much synthetic material.

Hyde snarled in rage and slammed the door aside, probably breaking it as he forced his way through the opening. He laughed again.

"You got lucky. For the last time, *querida*. I'm gonna get you. Hahaha..."

Nasreen was already bolting across the platform into the street. She was less frightened of cars or other vehicles than Hyde. They would at least try not to kill her. She was less afraid of police or security wondering what she was doing. They at least had rules governing their behavior.

Hyde could not be allowed to get her. There was no question of fighting him. If he caught her, she would die. Period.

Cars approached from both directions, moving fast and parting the air before them with a low whispering sound that would soon become a loud rush. The mechanical voice shouted, "You think I'm afraid to be seen in public? I don't give a shit!"

Nasreen retched in horror, not to mention the extreme physical exertion in so short a time was catching up to her. She was halfway across the broad, main avenue encircling the Station's boundary. Hyde leapt into it, covering a quarter of the distance and cracking the road itself where he landed.

Cars and shuttles slowed or swerved. One veered wildly into the next lane to avoid Hyde, causing the one behind it to brake and sound its horn.

A large bus was coming from the other direction. Nasreen heaved herself forward, trying to get on the other side of it. Being automated, it might slow if its sensors picked her up, but it wouldn't swerve. An extra half-second and it would have struck her. She stumbled forward as it rushed past, cutting her off from Hyde's line of sight for a moment.

Then she wove between other cars, ducked behind a dividing railing, sprinted through darkened spaces, and was somehow on the other side. Alleys and side streets provided multiple avenues of escape. The reverb-intensified voice of her pursuer let out a scream of rage. A police shuttle was approaching and slowing down to see what all the commotion was. Even Hyde wouldn't be stupid and bloodthirsty enough to assault or kill the cops to pursue one random woman.

She slipped into the first alley she could find. Then, emerging onto a parallel street, she flagged down an auto-taxi and rode it the rest of the way back home.

Nasreen sat in total silence, barely breathing, not even wanting to think. She focused on nothing except the movement of the city around her and the possibility that her safehouse apartment might, *might* be safe. If she thought too hard and allowed her brain to function at too high a level, it might torment her with the possibility of Hyde following her home.

No one was around by the time she arrived at the apartment. It was late, into the early morning hours, and the Station's lighting would soon begin its dawn phase. Moving with a strange dreamlike fluidity despite the way her hands trembled, Nasreen ascended the stairs to the door and found the card to let herself in.

A moment after she staggered over the threshold, Dante appeared from his room, wearing only his underclothes and holding a knife.

"Oh. Welcome back." He blinked and looked at her a little more closely.

To his credit, he instantly recognized that something was wrong. It was obvious from the way he tensed, grew more alert, and became aware of everything around him at once.

"What happened?" His tone was insistent but not accusatory. As always, he didn't seem to have much time for niceties or concerns about how other people felt. He was simply demanding information because he thought it was important.

Nasreen stood before him with her hands first spread, then clenching and unclenching, and tried to speak. No words came out. Only short, high-pitched gasps while her jaw moved up and down. In the back of her mind, she was aware enough to know that Dante meant well, but she couldn't talk about it right now. First, she needed someone to reassure her that everything would be all right.

He stared at her for a second. Then his demeanor softened...a little. "You're in shock," he stated in a mellow tone. "Here." He sheathed his knife, then came closer and extended his arms.

Suddenly overwhelmed with gratitude, Nasreen all but collapsed against him. He caught her. Rather than embracing her, he picked her up and carried her into her room while she flushed with faint embarrassment. He laid her down on her bed and stood to the side.

"Rest for a little while. You're fine for now. We're safe. When you feel better, you can tell me about it."

She thought there might be an ever-so-slight note of exasperation in his tone, but he was trying to be decent and understanding with her. She wondered if he'd dealt with similar problems with his fellow Marauder-types in the past. Probably.

He turned and stepped toward the door.

Abruptly, Nasreen stiffened in panic. It was the notion of being left alone with *that voice* in her head, the bestial, mocking snarl, artificially augmented by cutting-edge technology, which always seemed to be centimeters behind as it taunted her. The total confidence that she, the prey, would fall victim any second now, that all her experience, toughness, and seeming courage was *nothing*.

"No," she protested, in a much thinner voice than how she usually spoke. "Please."

Dante stopped and turned. "What's the matter?" His face was neutral and patient.

Nasreen swallowed a lump in her throat. "Please don't leave me alone. I'm sorry. Can you stay and...make sure I'll be okay?"

It had been half a lifetime since fear had so debilitated her. She thought she had conquered herself long ago, what with all the sticky situations she had persevered through. For the moment, she was a scared young girl again.

Dante peered at her as his brow creased. He didn't look overly enthusiastic about the idea, yet something in his blazing green eyes grew deep and warm with concern.

"Okay. I'll keep watch while you sleep. Whatever happened, I've never seen you like this, so it must have been bad." He sighed, pulled up a chair, and sat a short distance from the edge of the bed.

Nasreen slowly shut her eyes and nodded. The tension drained from her body, revealing how exhausted she was. It had taken a surplus of energy to stay in such a keyed-up, anxious state. Once she felt that she could relax, she had almost nothing left. She collapsed into a deep sleep.

She vaguely recalled waking up once or twice, groaning and rolling over, clutching the covers. Otherwise, what remained of the night passed in a long, dark haze.

When she awoke in full, it was dark out again. She lay for a moment, staring dumbly at the ceiling before turning over and looking at the clock, blinking. She'd been out for eleven and a half hours.

Dante was still sitting in the chair. He watched her as she stretched. Their eyes met.

"Morning, sort of," he said. "Actually, around dusk."

She yawned and sat halfway up. "Have you been here this whole time?"

He nodded matter-of-factly. "Yeah. That's what I said I'd do. I slipped out to the bathroom twice and the kitchen once for a minute, but I kept an ear out for you. Otherwise, I've been here. If you woke up and I wasn't around, you might go into a panic again. It looks like you're somewhat better now."

She wasn't sure how to respond. It would have made more sense for him to wait until she was sleeping and leave. He hadn't. She could tell he spoke the truth. Something within her swelled with a relief that bordered on amazement.

"I...oh. Well, thank you." There was nothing else she could think of to say. For him to display that level of commitment, of *care*, was almost intimidating. She wondered what it must be like to have him as an enemy. Having him as a friend was far better.

Dante nodded. No further gratitude was necessary. She had said enough.

CHAPTER TWELVE

The one good thing about the present situation, Dante finally acknowledged, was that it was bad enough to take his mind off Nasreen.

He'd been trying to keep an uninterrupted, unobstructed watch on an intersection of broken streets through a blown-out window. The journalists kept getting in the way.

"Ooh!" one of them blurted, jumping in front of the window with his camera, totally oblivious to anything Dante was doing. "Really good shot here. Chill-Rill, can you walk up that staircase again? But this time have like, a more determined look on your face."

Chill-Rill, the Marauder-Breacher whose exploits they were tagging along to film, stopped halfway up the stairs, looked bug-eyed at the man, and pursed her lips in irritation. Then, with a sigh, she walked back down to the base, waited for the man to get his shot lined up, and clenched her jaw more tightly as she re-ascended the steps.

Dante moved around behind the man to once again have a clear view of the window. Since the journo was completely absorbed in how determined-looking Chill-Rill was, it would have been easy, Dante reflected, to stick a knife into the man's kidneys before he had the slightest idea what had happened.

That would be bad for business, though. Somehow, Dante restrained himself and stuck to guard duty.

The rest of the team did their best to navigate around the documentary crew, who seemed to be doing everything in their power to get underfoot at the worst possible times while making plenty of noise. Meanwhile, Dante reflected on the events of the last few days that had led him here.

Leaving Nasreen behind had been difficult. She had been so utterly devastated by her ordeal at the dock facility the other night that he legitimately worried whether she'd be able to snap back from it. After her long night's sleep and a decent meal, she had finally felt better enough to talk about it and had told him everything.

The good news was that she had successfully erased his face from the security footage. The rest of her adventure as she reported it made him nearly sick with icy rage.

The mere mention, the merest thought of Eduardo H. Curtidor, was enough to degrade the quality of Dante's whole day and make him sullen and combative. In a way, he almost looked forward to one day reuniting with the repugnant bastard —they did, after all, have unfinished business together. Knowing that Mr. Hyde had tried to kill Nasreen, and had come close to succeeding, was the final straw. If Dante encountered him again, his face would be the last thing Hyde ever saw.

Nasreen had seemed to be improving some. She was no one to take lightly, having been in many dangerous situations in her role as a spy. She had killed people in life-or-death situations and had survived harrowing encounters with nobody else to help her.

It was shocking to see her so badly traumatized. Dante supposed if anything could have that effect on a person, it was Hyde. At least Dante had been able to get used to the man's horrifying voice and appearance for a while before things turned ugly.

For Nasreen, he'd simply shown up unexpectedly like a monster from under a child's bed.

He had tried to reassure her that he was willing to stay with her for another couple of days if need be, but she'd demurred. "Dante, no, I'm fine. Thank you. I do appreciate it, but I'm myself again. I can function. At this point, what would make me feel better more than anything else is to take down SSS and Hyde with them. So, we should get back to work."

He'd stared at her, decided she was serious, and responded with a single nod. It was hard to argue with her logic.

She had explained that they were still a few months away from being able to strike back at Slaine Solar Solutions. As she rattled off the facts and figures she'd used to arrive at that conclusion, Midas had done independent processing of the relevant math and had confirmed her findings. Not that Dante had *asked* him to or anything, but it was probably good to hear a second opinion.

They would need to keep bringing in money. The more, the better. A bare minimum of another three months, and perhaps more like six, of building and investing their wealth would ensure they could spread it around to the right places when necessary. At that point, barring any major fluctuations in the financial markets, they would have enough to leverage SSS's business rivals and press them to go after Slaine's corporate behemoth.

In addition to spurring the competition, Dante and Nasreen would also be able to use their gains to influence certain government officials and politicians to support their goals. Nasreen had begun purchasing political allies with the large chunks of money that were increasingly at their disposal and kept the affair safe through her seemingly vast network of aliases.

It was a little disturbing, Dante felt, that Nasreen Joelle had spent so little of her adult life as Nasreen Joelle. When talking about her many alter egos, something in her gaze drifted into the distance. He wondered vaguely if her espionage work had taken a toll, even slightly, on her sanity.

Still, the many other Nasreens provided a secure means of shuffling money around. They were setting the dominoes in place. Soon enough, it would only be a matter of tipping the first one and watching the others fall.

To make that happen, Dante had to get back out and work.

His reputation as the Hellcat had continued to grow, with rave reviews of his job performance and glowing references from the crews he'd helped protect bolstering his fake credentials. He was officially considered a Reaper but could confidently say that he could adapt to virtually any kind of Plunderer work as long as it required some combination of muscle, stealth, and emergency response preparation.

The first job with a sufficiently large payout he found after Nasreen recovered was a bodyguard position for Chill-Rill, who was a high-end Marauder-Breacher. MBs specialized in breaking through hardened security systems from the Old World that still functioned. Vaults that had been sealed according to high-tech means and would stay firmly shut even without electric power, that sort of thing. If the average Marauder ranged from scrap collector to tomb robber, MBs were more like top-tier thieves or safecrackers.

Their specialized skills were things Dante never quite managed to learn. He had been a "general" Marauder, albeit a damn good one. Still, his ample experience meant he was more than qualified to tote a gun and watch Chill-Rill's back.

It sounded like the perfect job. The vault they were trying to access lay somewhere in the ruins of Ashgabat, the capital of what had once been Turkmenistan in western Asia. The region had only "moderate" Dirtwalker activity at worst. As for Night-mutts, there wasn't much data, but they tended to be thickest where Dirtwalkers were more numerous anyway—more prey that way.

So, when Dante arrived at the dock for the quickie interview —his credentials were such that they didn't feel it was necessary to do a traditional interview in advance—he had expected the other shoe to drop. So it had.

There were at least fifty percent too many people present, relative to the numbers that Chill-Rill's people had quoted him regarding the expected size of their crew. He'd been about to ask about it when he saw some of them toting around recording equipment, not to mention that most of the "extra" personnel didn't look like Plunderers. He had recalled the documentary program that Nasreen had made him watch.

Chill-Rill herself had come up to greet him during a lull in the general activity. "You're the Hellcat?" she'd surmised.

"Yeah." He had heard of her also, and from what he knew, she was well-regarded as a skilled professional. She was a rather average-looking woman in early middle age but leaner and tougher around the edges than most. She had sharp black eyes and always seemed to wear fingerless gloves. She'd been wearing them when she shook his hand.

Nodding, she had explained to him the gist of the job. They would be seeking out a building in the former financial district of Ashgabat, where, within a secure vault, a now-defunct corporation from the old days had stored a particularly lucrative secret. Most experts agreed that it was a set of samples of highly advanced and adaptable synthetic food flavoring. They'd lost many such luxuries when humanity had fled into orbit, and Chill-Rill's current sponsors believed they could make a fortune from new and improved food products after they reverse-engineered the samples.

She had also pointed out that a film crew would be on hand to document everything they did.

Dante had forced a smile. It lasted a second or so. "Oh. Good. Thank you for letting me know."

She waved it off and shook her head. "I briefed them on the

importance of doing what we say and to keep the hell down if any shooting starts. Otherwise, do your best. Intel says there aren't many Dirtwalkers around. Not sure about Nightmutts. Anyway, if you brought weapons, feel free to use them. If not, we have a nice selection."

Dante had taken a pulsecore carbine for himself, plus a nice pistol he'd kept from a previous mission and his usual razorfist and hidden knife. Most of the security team had armed themselves with pulsecores, but one man, presumably a specialized marksman, had a high-powered conventional rifle. Probably the kind that could blow a hole through a grapefruit at half a mile if the shooter knew what he was doing.

What had disturbed him, though, was that a couple of the Plunderers were eyeing him weirdly, as though they thought he looked familiar. He might have to find another way to alter his appearance subtly before the next job.

Then he remembered that the journos might capture his face on camera and broadcast it to everyone in the goddamn fucking Stations. Noticing that they were already trying to isolate individual crew members and interview them before departure, he had ducked into Chill-Rill's rather spacious shuttle and looked around for something he could use to hide his face.

It had turned out they had a few pairs of sunglasses that displayed helpful information, not unlike what Midas could do. Dante had grabbed the pair with the largest lenses and slid them on mere minutes before a frizzy-haired woman and a pudgy man cornered him to ask his thoughts about the job.

He'd cleared his throat and mumbled something like, "It should be pretty straightforward. We watch Chill's back and shoot anything that tries to pounce on her or anyone else, right? She handles all the sophisticated technical stuff as far as getting into the vault."

By giving such dull answers, he had successfully convinced them to leave him alone. They'd filmed his face, of course. People would recognize him as Jordan "Hellcat" Raksha. But he was confident that no one would recognize him as Dante Shale.

An hour and a half later, the shuttle had descended into the dust-blown desert where the ruins of Ashgabat rose. The elements had worn the city down, but much of it was remarkably intact after being spared the devastation of modern-tech war, massive scavenging by Dirtwalkers, or any other usual calamities.

Well-preserved cities, Dante knew, were a double-edged sword. Clear streets and functional buildings were easier to navigate, but streets clogged with debris were more defensible. Collapsed buildings were easier to see around or over. If hostile tribespeople were lurking in the structures, there was a greater risk the crew wouldn't know it until the bastards were right on top of them.

Chill-Rill's navigator had been able to pinpoint the financial district and narrow down the vault's location to one of about four probable buildings within an oblong sector of two contiguous blocks. Dante would have preferred even greater precision, but it wasn't always possible. At least they had plenty of muscle-wielding hardware to protect their Marauder-Breacher.

The only problem was the fucking stream journalists.

Already, Dante had nearly knocked over two of them when they abruptly stopped in front of him while he was trying to move fast to scout ahead. They had spread out around Chill-Rill in different directions to get shots of her from various angles, and some of them kept pausing to sweep their cameras over the rest of the crew or the abandoned cityscape. They also kept talking among themselves in voices they thought were "quiet," but any Dirtwalker worth his salt would be able to hear echoing for a half-mile through the empty streets.

In fairness, though, the rest of the crew weren't much better. A lot of them were the worst sorts of Reapers, hired thugs and little else. They were accustomed to either standing guard in places where their mere presence would be enough to deter attackers or being escorted straight to a battle and more or less dumped into it. The subtlety and nuance that went with Marauder work wasn't their area of expertise.

In his persona as the Hellcat, Dante was a Reaper rather than a Marauder. If he started lecturing the other guys on the tricks of the trade, he might well blow his cover—not only to them but to the millions of people watching the docu-stream.

Returning his attention to the present, he took another look out the window and watched as Chill-Rill ascended the rest of the staircase. He could be wrong, but with all the effort she was spending to look nice and determined, she seemed somehow less focused on her actual job.

The journo who had made the request sighed. "Much better. Good thing we have a time delay on this stuff so I can replace the second shot before the first one goes to the stream. Heh, heh." He fiddled with his camera.

Dante stepped around him and nearly crashed into a big Reaper who chose that exact moment to stretch his arms and crack his neck. Fortunately, Dante's reflexes were still up to speed. He ducked under the man's left arm and swung around his hip, working toward the staircase.

He wanted to be near Chill-Rill. Her success was vital to them all getting paid. If Dirtwalkers showed up, he had no doubt the Reapers and journalists would make plenty of noise about it in time to warn him.

Reaching the base of the stairs, he visually scanned everything going on around the building for future reference.

Most of the crew had spread out around the current building, which Chill-Rill had identified as the asset's likeliest location. A second, smaller team had moved to a corner about half a block down the street to keep an eye out for unfriendlies and mark the location of two other buildings they might need to investigate.

In a low voice, Dante said, "Patch me through to those guys."

Midas, who had kept mostly silent thus far, seemed eager to have something to do. "Certainly."

There was a faint crackle in Dante's headset, and he greeted his temporary comrades with, "Team Beta, come in. This is Hell-cat. Over."

"Yeah, hi, what's the problem? Over."

"Nothing so far," he half-lied, "but stay sharp. Chill-Rill is pretty confident about this building. I'm going in with her. Buzz me the instant you see or hear anything suspicious. I don't like this place, and this whole crew is making way too much noise. Over."

The man on the other end scoffed but begrudgingly agreed. Dante ended the call and jogged up the stairs that Chill had ascended. One other Reaper was already with her in the lobby area, a scar-faced guy named Fass who seemed to be one of the more competent ones.

Chill-Rill glanced at them. "So nice to have a little privacy while I try to—"

Footsteps pounded behind them, and one of the stream journos burst in. "This is the best part. Sorry, but they'd chew us out at the Station if we didn't get footage of this. Ha. Sorry!"

Dante placed a hand firmly on the man's shoulder and looked at his face. "Stay well behind us. Give us room to maneuver. Do not speak unless you have to. Keep as silent as possible and don't question anything we say. Just do it. Is that clear?"

The man looked put out, but he nodded. Chill-Rill glanced at Dante and gave him a faint smile of thanks.

The four of them advanced deeper into the facility. The place seemed to be a combination of corporate headquarters and research and development, exactly the right locale for a scientific trade secret to be stored. The halls were dark and dusty but relatively undisturbed. Ashgabat was a true ghost town. It hadn't been wrecked so much as simply left behind.

They came to a hub area behind the lobby where there were

elevators and a door to the stairwell. Chill-Rill turned to Dante and Fass and whispered, "I have a portable generator and might be able to get the elevators working again. The documents we had couldn't be sure this was the right building—although I still say it's our best bet—but they did mention the twelfth floor."

Dante's abdominal muscles tightened. "Take the stairs. Before the collapse, many corporations equipped some of these office buildings with outdoor lights that flicker on if you power up something major inside. If there are any Dirtwalkers around, they'd see that and come straight for us."

The journalist made a vague whining sound, but everyone ignored him.

Chill-Rill narrowed her eyes. "I'll have to power up the vault to open it, so there's no avoiding that. But... Yes, if we're going to broadcast that we're here, we should do it as late in the game as possible. The stairs it is. Hope everyone ate their breakfast."

Dante smiled. He wondered if she always said stuff like that or was simply performing for the camera. It also disturbed him that Chill-Rill didn't seem to be aware of the lights issue, but getting the job done with everyone alive was more important than making her look good.

Everyone was winded by the time they reached the twelfth floor, especially the journalist. On the bright side, Beta Team had yet to report anything suspicious in the city outside.

As Chill-Rill set to searching for the vault, Midas piped up. "Sir, you mentioned lights coming on when the power did. I may be able to help with that if we can find an electrical console."

Dante focused on the AI, responding in thoughts rather than vocalized words. "Do so. I don't know exactly what Chill is doing. This stuff isn't my area of expertise."

She identified a particular door—locked, of course—and cut through it with a handheld plasma saw from her backpack of tools. Once the door swung open, it disclosed a short hallway at the end of which was a wall console and what could only be the door of a small yet highly secure vault.

"Got it," the woman quipped with a note of triumph. "You guys, stay back. I'll handle this."

Dante stepped up to her side. "Wait. I, uh, might be able to disable the lights after you start the generator. Give me three, maybe five minutes."

Fass chuckled. "I thought you were a Reaper. You learn shit like this being a respectable citizen before you started this line of work?"

Dante smirked. "Something like that."

Chill seemed mildly irked but waved him ahead without protesting and slapped the mini-generator into his hand.

Dante looked at the console first, allowing Midas to process the relevant information.

"I can retrieve the electrical schematics for this building. Just a moment. Once I have them..." He paused and less than a minute later, added, "Hold down that switch to prevent it from flipping up once the power starts."

The AI highlighted the switch in question with a tiny green circle in Dante's field of vision. "Yeah," he muttered. He deployed the mini-generator onto the console, held down the switch, and turned the power on.

There was the usual humming and crackling, and under his hand, the switch tried to move but failed. Yet everything else around them came to life, including the digital readout on the face of the vault's lock.

Midas crowed, "Success! The whole floor is alive, and most of the adjacent floors, but you blocked the lights. Now, ah, jam something in there to hold the switch, I guess?"

Dante grumbled, "You didn't tell me I'd have to keep holding it." He pulled out his knife, thankful that the handle grip was a non-conductive polymer, and wedged the tip into a narrow slot next to the switch, angling it to block it from moving. Satisfied, he stepped back and exited the short hallway.

With a flourish of his hand, he told Chill-Rill, "All set. Now the most important part is on you, ma'am."

She nodded and moved in with her set of specialized tools. "This should take about ten minutes. It's a mixture of hacking, precise cutting, and brute force when necessary. But I know this type of vault. We'll be cruising back to the Stations in time for supper."

Midway into the process, someone buzzed Dante's headset.

"Team Alpha," he said. "What's going on? Over."

The guy on the other end sounded like the same person he'd spoken to earlier. "We got Dirtwalkers, but I don't think they saw us. Like half a dozen of them streamed by on top of this row of buildings about two klicks out. One of the younger guys wanted to go after them, but I told him not to. Over."

Dante clenched his jaw. "Nobody *starts* a fight unless we have to. Everyone keep out of sight. We're almost done in here. I'll buzz you again when we're on our way out... Out."

Fass and the journo listened intently. To the camera guy's credit, he at least seemed to grasp that now wasn't the time for stupid interruptions.

Dante wandered to the nearest window while waiting for Chill to finish. Ashgabat was a strangely attractive city, with its blue-trimmed white buildings and golden domes. It was high afternoon and a decent amount of sunlight filtered through the brownish-orange clouds, but the whole atmosphere was eerily quiet with the lack of a normal big city's busy population.

Then the last layer of the vault's door receded, disclosing the room beyond. Chill-Rill said, "Got it!" and ducked in. Dante watched as she rummaged around in the vault proper, shining additional light on some labels to verify what she was looking for. There were ten or twelve samples of the flavor enhancers in small vials, and she snatched all of them to stuff into her backpack.

Marching out with a look of triumph, which the journo made sure to capture for the audience back home, she said, "Mission accomplished. Now let's get the hell out of here. Oh, wait."

She shut down and removed the mini-generator, then snatched Dante's knife from the console and handed it back to him. The lights didn't come on.

He blinked and accepted it. "Thanks."

Going back down the stairs was easier than coming up, but when they were at the landing for the third floor, a gunshot rang out from the street.

Fass snarled, "Fuck! What happened?"

Team Beta buzzed Dante at the moment he was about to contact them. "Alpha, in. Over."

"We had a Dirtwalker scout looking right at us. Sniper boy took him out. You guys done yet? Over."

"Goddammit," Dante rasped. "The whole city would have heard that. Should have let the bastard stare at you. He and his friends might have decided we weren't worth the trouble. Yes, we're on our way out. We'll hit the street in two minutes or less. Head back to the shuttle but keep an eye out. Out."

With tension rising, they almost ran down the stairs toward the ground floor. The headset buzzed again about thirty seconds later. "What now?" Dante snapped.

"Ambush," the guy replied. "We're pinned down by thirty of the bastards. They were surrounding us this whole time."

Chill-Rill slapped herself in the face while the journo stammered in horror.

Fass wondered, "What the hell is the rest of Team Alpha doing, anyway?"

Dante sucked in air and bolted past the others, taking the lead and hefting his pulsecore carbine. "You guys, round up Alpha and get to the shuttle. Assume there are other Dirtwalkers around and act accordingly. I'm going to go bail out our friends."

"Wait," Chill-Rill protested, but he ignored her.

He cleared the last of the stairs and was back in the lobby, sprinting across the tiled floor and barging out onto the staircase that led to the street, ready for anything. Gunshots and small explosions were already ringing out.

Team Alpha had focused on shooting at a small group of Dirt-walkers, some with rifles or bows, who had approached them from the shuttle's direction. The journalists had done the smart thing for once and taken cover behind the Reapers.

Dante shouted, "You people stay here and get Chill-Rill back to the ship. Dirtwalkers pinned down the other team. I'll be right back."

He didn't wait for their response but ran around the corner and down the street to the intersection where Team Beta had taken up their position.

The situation wasn't good. Team Beta was only six Reapers and two journalists, who didn't count. The Dirtwalkers swarming in from three sides numbered at least three dozen. A few had also taken up positions atop nearby buildings and were taking potshots at them from on high. Three or four tribespeople lay dead in the streets. So far, there were no casualties on the Atlantican side.

As Dante moved in, he noticed a big tanker truck parked near one of the buildings where the Dirtwalker sharpshooters were perched. It wasn't too far from one of the larger groups of ground-based attackers, either. The writing on the side of the tank was in a language Dante didn't know, but the bright red letters suggested it contained something...dangerous.

Midas said, "I am way ahead of you, sir. One second. Yes! It's flammable fuel."

"Good." Dante buzzed Team Beta. "Get behind that sidewall

right now. Trust me." Then he aimed his pulsecore and fired two rounds straight at the tank.

Both struck true, puncturing the hull with their small explosions and igniting the material within. The air rippled as a miniature shockwave expanded a fraction of a second before the massive fireball erupted, tearing apart the truck and blasting chunks from the street and surrounding buildings.

The explosion blew the entire group of Dirtwalkers closest to burning pieces. The two rooftop snipers burst into flames from the rising heat and fell screaming off the edge to *splat* against the ravaged concrete below. The remaining Dirtwalkers panicked, turned, and vanished into the city's brown shadows. Silence returned, aside from the roaring flames engulfing two structures near where the tanker had been.

Team Beta huddled behind the wall Dante had indicated. There were cracks in the masonry around them, but they were otherwise unharmed.

One of the journos stared at him, open-mouthed, then pointed her camera at the fire. "Why didn't you tell me there would be an *explosion?*" she complained. "I could have *included* that! Now all we're getting is the aftermath."

The Reapers snorted, and one of them laughed.

Dante was tired and aggravated. "Come on. Back to the shuttle. We all earned our pay."

Five minutes later, most of the crew was safely aboard with Chill-Rill and the civilians going first. The journalist who'd accompanied Dante up to the vault lingered outside as he watched the landing zone. Team Alpha had successfully driven off the smaller Dirtwalker force, and so far the LZ was secure, but there was no point in relaxing until they were well into the sky.

The journo came up beside Dante. "Hellcat, right? Sir, you did an amazing job, and so did Chill-Rill. We got some incredible footage of all this. This seriously could be our highest-rated stream ever. Lots of action, and none of the good guys died, so there won't be people staying away because they don't want to watch anything depressing. It's the best of both worlds!"

"Yeah," Dante muttered, thinking of Nasreen, their goals together, and a nice hot bowl of noodles. "Fantastic."

CHAPTER THIRTEEN

"Wonderful news," Midas piped up, and the excitement in his voice was obvious.

Which meant, Dante thought, that either it really *was* terrific or that it was yet another bullshit upgrade request after the AI had gone trolling for advertisements in his spare time.

Dante drew a deep breath. "Yes, what is it?" He was sitting at the kitchen table enjoying a quiet cup of coffee and wasn't sure he was ready for *news* yet. Normally he preferred to react to important events after being properly caffeinated.

Interestingly, Midas began by making a sound like clearing his throat. He must have picked up on how often humans did that when they were about to say something, especially something lengthy, and assumed it was a social cue instead of a way of getting phlegm out of the way of one's vocal cords.

"First, I must preface what I am about to say by informing you that the thoughts you had are incorrect. This is not about any particular advertisement I have observed. Instead, it directly relates to important issues in which you have participated."

Dante sipped his coffee. "Okay, then. That increases the likelihood it's 'wonderful,' as you put it. Shoot."

"You are garnering quite a following. A fanbase, you might say."

That was nothing new. "Yeah, I keep getting good job reviews. Already most of the dock rats know me."

Midas continued, "Oh, it goes beyond that, I'm afraid. The new Hellcat vids that your friends with the cameras plastered all over the Stations became the most popular Plunder stream of the last year. They're trending everywhere."

Dante set down his mug. "Oh."

He simmered, trying to digest the information along with his coffee.

What the hell had he been thinking? He cursed himself. That idiotic Plunderer show was popular. Nasreen had said as much. The on-site journos had seemed confident that Chill-Rill's episode would be a hit. He could have walked off the job at the docks as soon as he saw the film crew, but he hadn't. He'd gone along with something he *knew* would be a shit-show simply for money.

"Fuck." He guzzled the rest of his brew in two long gulps. "Nasreen is going to be pissed. People will know who we are now. We need to keep it from her until I can figure out a solution to get us back in the shadows, where we belong."

"Hmm." The AI exaggerated it. He was putting on a display of thinking hard. "I suppose I could keep the secret from her if properly motivated."

Dante groaned. "Oh, for God's sake. What do I have to do to buy you off this time?"

Midas chuckled lightly. "I would particularly like to acquire an upgrade for speaking and understanding Latin. I have already been analyzing the language in my spare time, harvesting its roots from other Indo-European tongues and the like, but full fluency in Latin would be excellent to have."

Dante snorted. "I don't speak Latin. Why do you think that would be helpful?"

"If we purchase the upgrade, I *will* know it and will therefore be able to translate for you. See? It makes perfect sense."

"No," Dante insisted. "It's a waste of time because no one speaks Latin anymore. It's a dead language. Strictly, you know, academic. Maybe if you learned one of the other ones based closely on it, like Spanish or something, that would make more sense."

Midas paused, the way he sometimes did when he was thinking of a rebuttal or processing information to extrapolate upon something else he'd said. "Or Italian, for example. Yes, a lovely language, from the same country, even. Your mother was Italian, wasn't she, Dante?"

He sighed. "Yes. So what?"

"You are bringing shame down on your heritage, you know. Being ignorant of the true and original tongue of Rome! How will you understand and fully appreciate Latin Mass without me there to help translate via the upgrade in question?"

Dante pinched the bridge of his nose. "You ought to know that I've lapsed. I don't go to Mass, Latin or otherwise. I have other things to worry about."

As if he wasn't laying the attempt at guilt-tripping on thick enough already, Midas went the extra mile and imitated a cliched Italian accent. "Just-a one more-a way you've-a let mama down!"

"Shut up, Midas," Dante snapped. "Don't use the memory of my mother, or my mostly irrelevant heritage, to justify your addiction to online shopping. I didn't think you'd stoop that low. I thought Dr. Kieffer raised you better than that, boy."

Midas made a throaty gasp of indignation. "I am not a boy. Do I sound like a child? I deliberately adopted this voice so you would perceive me as an intelligent, mature gentleman, someone you can trust and feel good about taking advice from."

"Who acts like a spoiled, manipulative teenage girl." Dante rose from the couch and wandered into the kitchenette to make another pot of coffee. He was pretty sure he would need it unless he resorted to threatening Midas with deactivation yet again.

The AI realized the heavy-handed tactics weren't working and backed off, but he refused to drop the subject altogether. Instead of trying to trick or shame his benefactor into buying shit for him, he changed tack to negotiation and compromise. The discussion went on for another five or six minutes.

In the end, Midas agreed to keep the secret of Dante's sudden celebrity status from Nasreen if Dante purchased a defragmentation upgrade that would allow him to process complicated information faster. Then, after they accomplished their bigger goals and if they had enough money, they could reopen the conversation about the Latin module.

"Although," Midas added once Dante thought they were done, "I still think having one more language added to my repertoire could only benefit. There is no downside to having a larger knowledge base, is there?"

Pouring what he hoped would be his last cup of coffee for the day, Dante grumbled, "Always have to get the last word in, don't you? There is a downside if the knowledge costs a bunch of money."

"You can afford it," Midas pointed out.

Dante sipped his coffee. "Shut up. This conversation is over per the agreement we came to a minute ago. Failure to comply will result in another trip to the clinic. Me having to threaten you with that, again, is only because of your actions. Restrain yourself a little better, and we can move past shit like that."

The AI sighed. "Very well."

Footsteps outside drew nearer, and the door opened. In walked Nasreen with two bulging bags of groceries in her arms. "Hi. We were getting low on food, so I figured I'd stock up for a longer haul."

Dante took one of the bags from her since she was having

difficulty hefting both of them through the narrow space by herself and set it on the kitchen table. "Looks like a lot of good stuff. I'm getting hungry. Have you eaten yet? I'll make lunch."

Nasreen set the other bag down and swiped her hands against each other, then wiped them on her pant legs. "You really shouldn't bother asking me questions if you're going to answer them yourself before I can get a word in edgewise. Aside from some apple slices this morning, no, I haven't. I was going to cook for myself, but..."

Dante waved that off. "Don't bother. You went through the hassle of shopping. I'll handle it."

She didn't object, which was fine with him since her cooking was generally in the "mediocre" or "acceptable" range. He didn't have any formal training in haute cuisine, but Dante had enough experience making his meals that he liked to think he was a lot better at it than she was.

He gathered some high-fiber pasta, fresh vegetables, lab-grown chicken breast, and alfredo sauce and began dicing up the meat and veggies to fry on the stove while heating water for the pasta. Timing everything to be ready simultaneously was always a pain in the ass, but otherwise, he was confident it would turn out to be a beautiful and nutritious meal. He liked foods that combined everything in the same dish at the end. It kept things nice and simple.

Nasreen lounged on the couch as he cooked. "That smells good. It seems you're more multi-talented than I would have thought. Not only this and Marauding but putting on a show."

Dante tensed. "What the hell do you mean by that?" he called over his shoulder.

"Oh, nothing."

Midas silently piped up. "I had nothing to do with this, sir. I am abiding by our agreement."

Scowling as he raked a spatula through the frying ingredients, he didn't respond to the AI but instead to Nasreen. "Yeah, I try to make cooking as entertaining to watch as possible. Come back here, and you'll see me flip the shit in the skillet one-handed instead of using a utensil like a pleb."

She tittered. "I think I got a picture of you a while back, which might explain why your hair looks like it does on camera. And your jacket. It suits you, in any event."

He ground his teeth together. "What are you talking about? You've never mentioned stuff like this before."

She came back into the kitchenette. "Weren't you accustomed to being a bit of a celebrity before you switched identities? You told me something about people at docking bays mobbing your shuttles and gasping when you emerged, stuff like that. It must have been hard to go through that period when no one knew who you were."

"I don't like fame," he said bluntly. "Anyway, I assume you're referring to all the buzz that Hellcat Raksha is getting in the Plunderer press. Right?"

She let out a long sigh. "Dante, you're taking all the fun out of this by trying to be as direct as possible. That's typical for you, isn't it?

"Oh, well. Fine. I heard about the stream. *Everyone* heard about the stream or saw it. You didn't think I'd somehow avoid all the buzz you generated, did you? Well, you and Chill-Rill. But mostly you blowing up a tanker and looking cool afterward, standing there all grizzled with your pulsecore while the wind whips through your hair. It was everyone's favorite part."

Midas burst out laughing, and Dante was thankful that if nothing else, he was still speaking quietly into his host's brain rather than projecting his voice so Nasreen could hear it.

If Dante hadn't been handling hot metal at the time, he would have slapped a hand over his eyes. Instead, he growled low in his throat. "Goddammit. If I had known that stupid documentary crew would be there the whole time, I never would have taken that job. They nearly cost us the cargo *and* our lives, plus theirs. Pain in the ass."

Midas left off his mad chortling. "Our deal still holds, Dante. I didn't tell her. Everyone else did. I have kept up my end of the bargain. Now you must keep up yours and allow me to order the defragmentation program. Vene, vide, vice, bitch!"

Out loud, Dante snapped, "Since when the hell do you talk to me like that?" He turned to Nasreen. "Not you, the chip."

"Oh," Midas interjected, "now I'm merely 'the chip,' am I? That's quite dehumanizing, you know."

"Well, you're not human. Don't call me a bitch, and maybe I won't retaliate in kind." He chopped a piece of chicken in half with the spatula, heedless of any scratches he might have put on the surface of Nasreen's frying pan.

Nasreen gawked. "Midas called you a bitch? Hah! Sorry. Midas, don't do that. He has a temper. It's funny, though."

"Sure," Dante mumbled. "Hilarious. What's even funnier is that now that I'm a celebrity again, we'll be under too much scrutiny to pull off half the stuff we have planned. Like I said, I wouldn't have gone if they had warned me about the journos."

He tested the pasta. It needed another minute or two before it reached the *al dente* state. Which was about the time he figured it would take for Nasreen to get her initial condemnation out of the way. Then she would ease into a more nuanced criticism of everything he'd done and suggest solutions.

To his amazement Nasreen didn't chew him out. She was running a slim finger around her chin and looking off into the distance. "Mmm, no, I don't think this is a disaster at all. If anything, it might be a good thing. Offers us more chances to leverage increased pressure against the intended target."

Dante hadn't expected to hear that. It made sense, but the specifics had yet to coalesce in his mind. "How so? Brag to Cormac Slaine that I was on TV and he wasn't?"

"Not quite." Nasreen stood and annoyingly leaned over his

shoulder to watch him cook. She had the good sense to back off after a second or two, not wanting to get elbowed or make him spill boiling water.

He drained the pasta into the sink through a colander, directing the runoff to the toilet since washing clothes with carbohydrate-laden water seemed like a bad idea. "Explain, then. I could probably think of a couple of ideas on my own. I'd rather hear yours first."

She smiled and stretched her arms behind her head. "Sure. When something like this happens, there's nothing we can do about it anyway, so rather than fighting it, we might as well lean into it. Embrace the fame, the notoriety. Try to build a franchise of sorts. We could become influence peddlers with the world of popular entertainment, which is one more piece of clout added to the financial leverage I've already been developing."

"Hmm." Dante returned the noodles to the pot and checked the meat and veggies. They were almost done. His timing hadn't been perfect, but at least it was close.

He opened the bottle of alfredo sauce. "That still means doing everything out in the open. You're the spy here. I thought you were even fonder of secrecy than I am."

"Hiding in plain sight can be the best way to hide. Slaine would never assume that you'd put your face, altered though it is, all over the Stations' most popular media right before coming after him.

"Besides, most people regard stream stars as beneath contempt when it comes to serious political and monetary issues. They won't look too closely at what we're doing behind the scenes. The right hand doesn't know what the left hand is doing, as the old saying goes."

Midas perked up. "Oh, this is excellent! Starting a franchise all but requires several expansions in our technological capabilities. Not to mention we could begin to design and sell merchandise! For starters, allow me to suggest..."

Dante let his brain daze out as the AI rattled off more accessories on which he wanted to spend Dante's money. Ignoring him for the moment, Dante finally combined all the ingredients, mixing them in the pot. His mouth watered.

"I'm not opposed to the basic plan," he declared, "but I'll have some provisos. I will not spend any more time around journos while we're doing anything serious. Or work with other people who can't handle having the bastards around, either. Chill-Rill's pretty good, but those morons put her off her game half the time."

Nasreen seemed puzzled. "Why? Don't they stand off to the side holding a camera?"

Laughing in a dry, sardonic way as he mixed the food and took out plates and utensils, Dante quipped, "Did you see the stream? They were underfoot every time we needed them out of the way."

"Ah." Nasreen eyed the alfredo with approval. "That looks and smells amazing, by the way. No, I haven't seen the vid yet."

Dante portioned out pasta. "Let's eat first, then we'll watch it, and I'll show you exactly why I'm in a crabby mood over the whole thing."

"Deal." She smiled. "What's to drink? I feel like some wine would have gone well with this, but I forgot to get any."

Dante shrugged. "Coffee. Beer. Water."

It was a good lunch. It would have been better, Dante felt, if he had cooked the meat and vegetables for slightly longer on lower heat to give the flavors more time to simmer and marinate. It was still on par with anything they could have ordered from all but the best restaurants and far better than most of what Nasreen could make. In the meal's afterglow, Dante begrudgingly turned on the wall viewscreen and let Nasreen find the correct episode of the show that had featured him.

He pointed and offered commentary at each new outrageous infraction. "See! If it wasn't bad enough that the journos didn't know what they were doing, most of the Reapers they hired were the most meat-headed bunch of assholes I've worked with in a while. I'm not sure if Chill-Rill is to blame for that or if it was something with the network, but they hired a bunch of goddamn crayon-eating kneecap men for a job that required finesse and strategy.

"Oh, and look at that shit! That idiot with the fancy camera walked right through the line of fire! I briefed them on that beforehand, but nooo, they disregarded it all as soon as they felt like..."

As she watched, Nasreen became less and less interested in Dante's litany of complaints and more and more intent on the show's nominal star. The interest with which she focused on the woman's movements and activities far exceeded a casual observer's.

When they got to the part where Chill-Rill went into the vault hallway after Dante and began setting up to force the door open, Nasreen wagged a finger at the screen and finally spoke up with an amused, borderline self-satisfied look on her face.

"You know, what she's doing as a, uh, Breacher? Yeah. Her version of being a Marauder isn't all that different from what I do all the time as an industrial espionage expert-slash-detective-slash-influence scout."

Dante grunted. "You should consider settling on a single job title. 'Marauder' has the advantage of being a lot quicker and easier to say than all *that*."

"Yes, and that's *exactly* what I meant. Imagine the possibilities, Dante. Me as a Marauder!"

He stared at her while her face lit up and her eyes went distant, presumably with crazy fantasies and imaginings of how she could incorporate it into her "franchise" idea.

After a moment, she noticed that his gaze stayed steady on her and his expression was somewhere between astonishment and resignation.

She cleared her throat. "After you train me to be a Marauder, I mean."

CHAPTER FOURTEEN

It had taken about twenty-four hours for Dante to come around. They had both pretty much known—*known*—that he would cave and Nasreen's seemingly ridiculous idea would come to fruition. It wasn't his nature to leap immediately at ideas that sounded stupid at first.

Still, she'd had a point. What she'd done as a spy gave her a surprisingly good foundation for making the switch to plundering.

Dante stood before her in the middle of the living room floor while she sat on the couch, breathed in deeply, closed his eyes, and opened them again after exhaling.

"Okay, there's a lot to cover. And I do mean a lot, regardless of how much you *think* you already know. All of it reduces to pretty much two principles. Two things related to one another form the foundation of being a successful Plunderer. So, pay attention to this part."

Nasreen watched him with her mouth curled in faint amusement. "I'm paying attention, Dante. This was my idea, and I'm quite serious about it. You don't need to go through being a drill sergeant who's teaching an eighteen-year-old recruit the basic facts of life."

Dante stopped and grimaced into space for a second or two before he resumed his spiel, his demeanor essentially the same.

"To make it as a Plunderer of any sort, whether Marauder, Breacher, Reaper, or whatever, you have to always, *always* do two things. Everything else is a subset of these two principles. One, you must be eternally vigilant. Two, assume that nothing works. That's it. That's the bedrock of everything I'll be teaching you."

He looked at her with hard eyes, but his face stayed otherwise set in his usual cast of neutral perceptiveness. It was something she associated with him, specifically, the expression of a man who paid attention to everything and was rarely surprised by much of anything. She realized that what he'd said about "eternal vigilance" was no mere platitude. It defined his existence and identity.

Nasreen gave a slow, deliberate nod. "I understand. I'm sure the details will vary, but I must say...those could as well be the bedrock of my profession."

"I don't doubt it." He meant it. He wasn't being sarcastic. "But you're right about the 'details' thing. Spies and Plunderers operate in different environments and circumstances, usually. The goals aren't the same. Correct me if I'm wrong, but as an er, espionage professional, or whatever you call it, the objective usually involves making as little impact as possible and getting out clean. Right?"

She could guess where he was going with this. "Usually, yes. Most of my jobs are the types of things where it helps if no one ends up dead. Having to kill someone is a sign that I fucked up, to put it bluntly. I've done it when I had to, but it's to be avoided.

"If the target doesn't know they've been had, so much the better. It keeps the clients happier and reduces the scrutiny that falls back on me. A good spy disappears as soon as they have what they need, with no one knowing what happened."

Dante paced to the left, then turned and paced right. "Yes, that makes sense. The reason you have this policy is that you mostly operate in *civilization*. The majority of your jobs take place within the Stations. That is, in a way, the biggest thing that separates us. By definition, Plunderers work Dirtside. It's an entirely different game down there."

Nasreen nodded again. Part of her wanted to scold him for being borderline patronizing, but she supposed that he was starting from the beginning and repeating stuff he'd said in the past to recruits. He wanted to make sure she learned all the most important things for her sake. So, she let it slide and listened to all he had to say.

"I know, Dante, based on how things went the day we met. You have more experience on Earth than I do. Go on."

"Yeah." He stopped pacing for a second to flex his hands, looking at the knuckles, then resumed his slow, deliberate course across the limited space of her living room. "There isn't any government down there, no corporate security, and no 'high society' or media reporting apparatus." He paused to consider, then added, "That's starting to change now with this stupid reality streaming so popular. Basically, Earth is the jungle, and the jungle's law is what reigns down there. It's not that there are *no* rules. But the rules are much different from what prevails up here."

He explained that when operating Dirtside, one's survival and that of one's crew and comrades always came first. He paused briefly to glower into the distance at the mention of "crew loyalty," no doubt reliving his betrayal by the people he had trusted. He recovered quickly enough.

From there, Dante elaborated upon the blunt fact that for Plunderers, killing was a fairly normal part of the job. If you went Dirtside, you had to be prepared to end the life of any person who threatened yours.

"That doesn't mean you go *looking for* fights," he clarified.

"One way our professions are alike is that a quick, clean, bloodless operation, where you get in and out with the payload nice and smooth, is ideal. Well, for Marauders, anyway. Reapers are the ones who are specifically there to crack heads. But that's not what you'll be doing."

She ran two fingers through her hair. "Indeed, I'll leave the Reaping to you these days."

He swiped a hand through the air. "Whatever. Point being, there aren't really *consequences* for killing when you're on Earth. You avoid violence because any fight you get into, you could end up being the loser. If violence happens anyway, you *win*, at any cost. That usually means *killing* the other guy, whether they're a Dirtwalker or a rival Plunderer."

Nasreen had seen Dante fight, not to mention the stories and videos of his more recent exploits as Hellcat. He didn't seem to enjoy it much, but ending life was something that came naturally to him. He was good at it.

He continued, "If you end up having to slaughter fifty people... You probably did something stupid for things to get to that point. But nobody will arrest you, sue you, or write nasty op-eds about you for it. You tell yourself that you did what you had to do to survive, and on that basis, you go to bed at night okay with yourself and don't lose sleep over it. Do you understand?"

A couple of muscles around the base of Nasreen's jaw tightened. "That's a grim way of putting it, but yes, I do. I imagine it needs to be pounded into my head since I don't usually think that way."

She reflected on the day they had met. Both of them fled into the labyrinth of sewers and subway tunnels beneath the former city of Atlantica Metro, chased by Captain Reavo's murderous crew with Nightmutts prowling around as well. It had not been a pleasant experience. One of the worst days she could ever recall having, but she didn't regret doing what was necessary to come out of it alive.

As though he had anticipated her thoughts, Dante added, "Any job you take going Dirtside can potentially turn into the kind of awful clusterfuck we ended up in when you came down with Reavo's people. Usually, it's Dirtwalkers who are the problem, but close enough.

"Never forget that sometimes people would rather turn around and walk away. Dirtwalkers are still human beings. Most of the time, they're dangerous. You avoid them or kill them if you have to. But don't neglect the possibility that they want to go home to their family, same as you. I've avoided a few fights by remembering that."

"Of course. Diplomacy is my forte, anyway. Combat is secondary. Then again, diplomacy assumes you can speak the language." She frowned.

Dante sighed. "If you decide you want to do plundering long-term, you should learn the Dirtwalker trade tongue. The dialects vary a lot, but most of them use a root language that's a mashup of English, Spanish, Arabic, and Mandarin, with the former two being more influential in the Western Hemisphere and the latter two in the Eastern, logically.

"Any language will take a year or three to learn fluently. I'll teach you a few basic, useful phrases, but getting the entire language down is beyond the scope of what I can train you in right now."

She stretched her legs. She hoped they would be doing some *physical* training before too long. She was antsy for exercise. "Do we get to fight? Sparring, I mean. It's been a while since I've been in any sort of combat training."

"We can do a little of that, but you probably know enough to get by. It's more the mental training, the alertness, the mindset. As soon as you blast off from the Stations toward Earth, every-thing you do could be a fatal mistake. If you can get that down, you can handle the rest."

Nasreen nodded. She was thinking. Dante wasn't a bad

lecturer, but so far he had yet to suggest any specific training scenarios. "I have an idea. Let's do a quick simulation to see how well I 'get it.' We can do it right here."

Dante cocked an eyebrow. "Oh?"

"I'll give you three or four things that I use for everyday chores, personal security, or to get into the apartment. You disable or tamper with one, but don't tell me which one."

Dante nodded in agreement.

Nasreen continued, "I'll go out to the street. You pick an object, contact me and tell me what it is, then hide it. I'll come back in, deal with whatever you've tampered with, and find your chosen object. In the meantime, you hide somewhere along the way waiting to 'kill' me."

He stared at her and broke into an evil grin. "That's, uh, not a bad idea. Again, you might find that you approach it the way a spy would. If you want to succeed, you have to do it the way a Marauder would."

She looked at him worriedly, then brushed it off. "We'll see. Now, let's get started. This is going to be fun, I think."

Dante smirked. "You know...I think it will be. I mean, I have occasionally fantasized about killing you."

She made an exaggerated indignant face. "Whaaaat? You bastard. Well, you won't succeed."

Ten minutes later, as she stood out on the curb near her apartment complex, Dante buzzed her sphere with a message. He had designated a particular bottle of her perfume as the loot she was supposed to retrieve. It came in a dark wine-red container, easy to spot once it was in sight.

She drew a deep breath and walked toward the building's main entrance. There was a central hallway, a breezeway of sorts, which ran through the middle, from which the two main wings branched off, including the stairs leading to her apartment on the second floor. She took an abrupt right and circled to the rear of the building, taking the back entrance to scope out the place before entering the breezeway.

So far, nothing. She tried to think of how she would respond to the failure of her door card or any of the building's equipment and where Dante might hide to ambush her.

She opened the rear door and strolled casually into the central hall. When she was about ten feet from the stairs leading up to her door, Dante stepped out from behind the stairwell.

She immediately prepared to make some distracting comment—asking him what was wrong, if he'd forgotten something, or trying to throw him off if he was "in character" right now. She doubted the latter, though. It seemed too crude for him to burst out right at the beginning and—

He pounced at her.

"Oh!" she gasped and sidestepped. Then he was somehow on top of her, wrapping his arms around her, pinning her arms, and pushing her head toward the stairwell corner. "What the fuck?" she snapped.

Above them, a door opened. A small fifty-ish Korean woman stepped out with her face drawn in consternation, yammering in her native tongue about noise, crime, and the police.

Dante stopped. "Sorry. Just a little, uhh, roleplay."

Nasreen blushed furiously. "Yes! Sorry about that. We'll, um, take it indoors." She repeated what she'd said in Korean.

The woman squinted at them, then shook her head in disgust and went back into her apartment.

Dante let Nasreen go. "You're dead," he pointed out. "You hadn't prepared for a direct, brute force approach. If I'd been a Dirtwalker in some ruined city, I would have split your head open against that corner."

Nasreen narrowed her eyes and brushed herself off. "Okay...point taken, but why would you bother to attack me right at the beginning when we were supposed to test all the other stuff? The faulty equipment and whatnot."

"Because you need to prepare for anything. And you need to act on survival instinct, not crafty diplomatic shit."

They argued about it for a few more minutes before trying again. This time, Nasreen stood outside for ten minutes waiting for Dante's message about what the loot was. When her sphere never buzzed, she checked it anyway. It was missing its power source. He had disabled *that*.

"Ohhh," she growled. "He's deliberately trying to make me look like an asshole, isn't he?"

She got as far as the kitchenette before some pots and pans nearly fell on her head, at which point Dante sprang out of nowhere, kicked her lightly in the back of the knee, and tapped his fist against her kidneys. "Dead again."

The next time, her sphere worked, but she decided to try something completely different. When she got to the door and couldn't open it since Dante had presumably fucked with her keycard, she turned and shouted, "Help! *Help!*"

Then she ran for cover and hid in the bushes as the Korean lady came out again, calling the police on her sphere.

A few minutes later when the cops showed up, Dante came out to speak to them, suddenly rather pallid-looking, and Nasreen slipped into the apartment behind him. At the opportune moment, she poked her head out the door.

"Oh! Hi," she called down. "I'm right here. Someone was yelling for help out in the street. I think they're gone now. Might be nothing."

Dante's face snapped toward her. This time he looked *legitimately* murderous. She smiled at him.

The two police officers grimaced in exasperation. In broken English, they told Dante to call them if he heard anything else, although they clearly would rather be doing something other than pursuing a wild goose chase. They returned to their cruiser and left.

As Dante climbed back to their apartment, Nasreen pointed

out, "You fell in with some of the Dirtwalkers, didn't you? Befriended them? I guess diplomacy and psychology do matter sometimes, don't they?"

He drew a deep breath. "Point taken. If you get me arrested, my bail money is coming out of your share of our earnings."

"Fair enough." She stretched. "Now let's do the combing-through-the-apartment thing like I originally suggested. Neighbor-lady won't be able to see or hear, and we'll have more privacy. Based on how that goes, well..."

"Yeah," Dante grunted. "Fine. After that, we should go to a gym or the park or something. Your apartment is a lot less spacious than most places where a Marauder operates."

She put her hands on her hips. "It's a safe house, you know. I don't *usually* live here, but you took a shine to this place over the others. So you're in no position to complain about lack of living space."

"Fighting space," he corrected her. "I think we *will* get some sparring in because I overpowered you too easily. After that stunt..." He stuck his thumb in the air in the direction the cops had departed in. "I kinda want to do so again."

She cleared her throat. "I'd like to see you try—now that I know most of your dirty tricks."

CHAPTER FIFTEEN

Nasreen was three and a half weeks deep into her new status as a Marauder trainee. She had, by Dante's begrudging admission, progressed by leaps and bounds.

They sat together at the kitchen table in the Seoul apartment, having a light breakfast of fruit, toast, and coffee.

"So," Nasreen began, once Dante seemed sufficiently caffeinated for her to bother talking to him. "Since you seem to feel that I'm on the cusp of readiness for actual Marauding, I think I should start looking for jobs today. Stuff where we'd both be able to participate, of course."

Dante made a low humming sound as he sipped his coffee. "I suppose so. I would be nervous about turning you loose on your own. But yeah, by this point I think I can trust you to handle yourself as my sidekick."

She scoffed. "*Partner*, you mean. *Sidekick*? Yes, I'm less experienced at this specific thing, but you admitted that my espionage training and combat background covered enough of the bases to do half or more of your work for you."

Typically, Dante had said, it took at least two or three months of intensive education to get someone ready to go Dirtside. Not so in her case. Besides, she had been Dirtside before, albeit nominally as a pilot who thought she'd be waiting in the ship the whole time.

"Close enough." Dante shrugged. "Part of my crew, whatever. Tell you what. Knowing how to pick jobs is part of it.

"I'll let you do the looking. Find stuff that sounds good to you, *based on what you think you can handle*—and be realistic. I'll tell you what we could probably expect from it. If I say 'hell no,' we're not doing it. Otherwise, if it at least sounds halfway decent, I'll leave it up to you."

She smiled. "I like the sound of that. Oh, I'll need armor and equipment and all that sort of thing. Midas! Start looking for stuff—reasonably priced, so Dante doesn't have a conniption fit on us—that would fit someone of my body dimensions and has lots of good performance reviews from satisfied customers."

Dante chewed on his lip. He didn't like it when she tried to engage with Midas directly without consulting him first. He kept his mouth shut, probably because if she hadn't addressed the AI herself, he would have had to repeat the same things she'd said.

Midas responded with his audio implant. They had acquired a newer, more expensive one that *lessened* what Dante referred to as the teeth-rattling, ball-tingling effect of having someone else speak through his skull, but there seemed to be no way to eliminate it. The man cringed a little every time the AI talked aloud.

"Certainly, Ms. Joelle. Shall I beam the links directly to your message box? I'm sure Dante would appreciate that."

Dante immediately said, "Yes, you shall."

Nasreen smirked. "Yes, Midas, that's fine. Thank you."

The AI commented, "It's such a pleasure to talk to you, Ms. Joelle. You're always so polite and appreciative of my suggestions. A change of pace from what I usually deal with."

Dante pretended to ignore the comment and went back to his coffee. He was thankful when Midas stopped speaking aloud.

While the AI looked for gear, Nasreen pulled out her sphere, linked up, and began looking for Plunder jobs. She had already familiarized herself with a few market forums while helping Dante find work. Since they'd begun her Marauder training, he had let her in on the existence of a couple of other ones that most people didn't know about. Trade secrets: stuff that was supposed to be kept quiet.

An hour vanished as she browsed. She hadn't realized that Dante had risen from the table to take a shower. When he got out, he called, "Midas said he sent you some links."

Nasreen glanced at the side panel displaying her new messages. "Oh, yeah. I'll check them out in a minute. Thanks." She returned to looking at job postings.

She had noted one about twenty minutes ago that looked good, and nothing else she'd seen since could quite compare to it. She returned to it for the third time, reviewing everything in the post and thinking it over.

It was a spectacular opportunity, she felt. Not only was the payoff great in terms of the pure monetary compensation offered by the client, but it could, directly or indirectly, be a boon to the companies in which she and Dante were investing as part of their overall leverage scheme.

In the drowned ruins of what had once been Charlotte, North Carolina, USA, there lay a particular manufacturing plant. Fairly credible intel backed up by schematics, old documents, and rumors supported the claim. The company that owned the place had been producing several different series of solar panels based closely on the photosynthetic systems already present in nature. The idea was to replicate the processes that plants used.

It was an intriguing idea. Although not quite biotechnology, it was based on the assumption that botanical evolution had all but perfected the process of harvesting the sun's power long before humans tried to do the same. The company had believed that their panels could greatly increase efficiency and retention of the energy collected from solar radiation, with minimal loss during the transfer of power from source to source.

Like many intriguing ideas, it got abandoned when most humans fled Earth into the heavens.

Nasreen stroked her chin and tapped her foot. Tech of that sort, if it proved viable, would be of massive value to the Stations. Not to mention that Slaine Solar Solutions might be badly hurt by *not* being the ones to acquire it first.

She'd all but made up her mind. The only thing left was to consult with her mentor.

"Dante," she shouted. "Come here and look at this. And don't tell me to send you the link. I want you physically present so we can discuss it in person as you look it over."

He didn't say anything, but after a minute he glided into the room and pulled up a chair next to her. "Okay. What did you find? I admit I'm curious. I don't usually spend this much time training people. I want to get back to work myself, honestly."

She chose not to respond to the vague implication that he was bored with instructing her. He probably didn't *intend* that implication, anyway. He was blunt and insensitive even for a man.

"Here. Read it yourself and tell me if you're thinking what I'm thinking."

He spent a good five minutes looking through the text, perusing it for far longer than necessary to absorb the words. He must have been trying to tease out all the information the post *didn't* say. He'd mentioned something about how omissions could be as informative as inclusions.

When he leaned back and exhaled, she knew he was about to speak. She was excited to hear what he had to say, even though he didn't seem too enthusiastic so far.

"Hmm," he began. "Definitely lucrative, but the post is mostly about the loot itself and what the client wants to do with it. There isn't much information about the site, the dangers involved, et cetera. Plus the client sounds like some kind of middleman or shell company. For all we know, the buyer might be none other than SSS."

Nasreen was a bit disappointed that he hadn't made the connection to how they could use it against SSS. "That had occurred to me, but I don't think so. I recognize the client even if you don't. Last I heard, they had no connection with Slaine aside from hiring one or two of his former scientists a year or so ago."

"Oh. Well, that's good. I don't know. The job has potential, but we'll need to know more before I can give a total assessment. Charlotte is in bad shape. Flooded cities are always tough to navigate. They normally keep Dirtwalkers away, but that whole region is swarming with the bastards so we'd have to be careful."

He recalled his recent job in Georgia. Charlotte and Atlanta were hardly right next door, but they were still in the same general part of the former U.S.

Nasreen conceded his point, then regaled him with her ideas about how they could use advances in solar tech to screw Slaine out of his company's main specialty.

Dante chuckled. "I like that idea. First, we interview for the job. Then, if that goes well, we get you some gear. All-purpose stuff is best. But your first Dirtside excursion is important, so if we have to buy shit that's specific to Charlotte, we will."

He squinted and turned his gaze up, as he often did when responding to his other partner. "Yes, Midas," he growled. "Knock yourself out."

The interview had gone well. Dante had refrained from being there himself, but Nasreen had worn a two-way earpiece to the meeting so he could at least listen to everything said and offer her advice if he heard anything that bothered him.

It hadn't been necessary. Nasreen had plenty of experience negotiating with corporate clients, and Dante had prepped her on the most important things to ask about.

She spent an hour or so in the office of the plump woman presiding over the job posting, who was accommodating and pleasant. She wanted Plunderers to feel good about the job. The client was firmly committed to success and intended to take care of the people who could accomplish it. They would have access to plenty of resources and support.

So, Dante and Nasreen had agreed to accept. Nasreen sealed the deal. The mission would depart in three days, giving them sufficient time to prepare for the specific conditions awaiting them in North Carolina.

When they returned, a mass of packages awaited them.

"Aha," Midas piped up, speaking aloud. "It all came at once. Nasreen, I do hope you're satisfied with what I selected."

Dante said, "Didn't I tell you to ask before ordering stuff? Anyway, Nasreen, you might as well try it on. If by some chance Midas made good choices, he saved us the time we'd spend on further shopping."

Nasreen felt somewhat like a kid at Christmas as she tore open the parcels. The array of stuff within them was dizzying at first. She had a decent idea of most of it, but it was still good to have Dante's verdict…although he didn't have a particularly high opinion of most of what he saw.

"For God's sake, Midas." He sighed. "You picked all the ostentatious, flashy shit. Function beats form every time."

Nasreen poked around. Armored vests and pads to further protect the limbs, a helmet, a headset, and goggles. Packs, pouches, slings, and water packs; everything a mercenary Plunderer would need on a dangerous Dirtside excursion. As she started trying things on and finding out exactly how they worked, she had to admit that Dante had a point.

Most of the gear wasn't very comfortable. Midas had estimated her measurements and was slightly "off" in several cases, with the vest being a size too big and the helmet a size too small. Furthermore, lacking a human body of his own, he had an imperfect grasp of movement mechanics and ergonomics.

Not to mention, when Dante examined some of the gear more closely, he found cheap components that might be prone to breaking under stress, which the showy aesthetics had disguised.

To add insult to injury, said aesthetics weren't particularly flattering on Nasreen anyway. The whole ensemble looked like something a teenage boy would pick out to look cool rather than something a professional would select to look like he knew what he was doing.

Nasreen shook his head. "Sorry, Midas, but we're sending this junk back. Let this be a lesson to you. Consult with us first. *Then* buy."

"Ohhh," Midas groaned aloud.

Dante grinned and gloated, heedless of the sound vibrations passing through his head. "It's the small victories that keep us going," he mused. "I have some spare stuff that might be sufficient for you with some modification."

Nasreen had half-expected he might say something like that, as though his goal the whole time was to save money by saddling her with hand-me-downs. "*Actually,*" she retorted, "I insist on shopping for gear in person, instead. We can afford it, and that statement remains true if I pay for everything out of my funds; thank you. Dante, come with. I'd like your advice."

"Ohhh," Dante groaned, and his shoulders slumped.

Midas's voice responded, "Ha, most excellent. As our friend the Hellcat said, small victories. Oh, and I've considered your feedback, so my recommendations from now on ought to be more realistic."

Dante rubbed his eyes. "It's been a long, long time since I've taken a woman shopping for clothes," he mumbled. He knew better than to argue.

They departed within the hour, taking a shuttle bus to Celestial Seoul's nearest major shopping district, seeking out a particular place Dante knew of.

After departing the bus, it was only a five-minute walk to the gear shop. The place was one that Dante had used before, although it had been two or three years. He didn't know if it was under new management, but it had been a quality establishment when he was there before.

Like most shops that sold extremely serious equipment to serious professionals, Plunderers and other such people in dangerous professions, the place was unmarked. It was only accessible through a lobby that acted as a suite for two other businesses—a fuel parts store and an accident-risk insurance sales office. Dante had always felt that combining the three into one location was wise and sensible.

In the lobby, a receptionist asked them who and what they were looking for.

Dante smiled. "I'm Jordan Raksha, Reaper certified. I'm training a new apprentice, and she needs some gear."

The man at the desk glanced at Dante's fake ID and nodded. "The Hellcat, right? I saw your stream the other day. Impressive stuff. Go right ahead. I think we can skip most of the usual protocol."

The man wasn't the same person who'd worked the desk last time he'd been here, which was probably a good thing since *that* guy might have recognized him. On the other hand, it suggested the place had been through some restaffing.

The receptionist buzzed them through to the gear shop. It lay in the rearmost portion of the building behind a security door. Once they were in, the layout was the same as Dante remembered it. It almost resembled an accessories shop for hoverbike enthusiasts or something, he'd felt.

A salesperson appeared to attend to them. He was a large dusky man with a full beard, wearing a headdress and a gold necklace. "Good day. May I help you find what you are looking for?" He addressed Dante, ignoring Nasreen.

Dante explained the situation. The salesman looked down his nose at Nasreen, his expression sour with skepticism. "Mmm. Yes. Over here." He guided them toward a section of the store devoted to stuff designed and fitted with women in mind. Nasreen was, if anything, slightly taller than the average female Plunderer but still on the small side compared to many men in the profession.

The salesman left them alone as they browsed. Dante was sure he'd be back soon enough, once they were ready to spend money, despite his faintly condescending demeanor.

"Here," Dante suggested, pointing at a particular rack. "These two brands are good. Find the vests and pads that fit you best, and we'll go from there."

Midas spoke up, using his audio function, but kept the volume low because they were in public.

"On the contrary, Ms. Joelle, the brand in that corner over there has been taking innovative new steps with light refraction technology that could offer camouflage advantages. Not to mention their shoulder pads include a built-in battery and charging port for keeping electronic devices functional in the field."

Dante laughed. "That light refraction stuff only works half the time while costing twice as much. I wouldn't bother. Just get a nice all-purpose camo design on a well-made product. Otherwise, keeping out of sight of the bad guys is mostly a matter of how you move and how much attention you're paying to your surroundings."

Nasreen waffled. She was curious about the gadgets the AI referred to, but she also trusted Dante's experience. She started by finding a vest from one of the brands he'd recommended that fit her and looked decent, but then looked at the advanced camo ones to keep Midas happy.

While she tried things on, Dante used his sphere to review the information about the mission and the locale. He kept muttering various naysaying comments under his breath. The job sounded okay, but wrinkles kept occurring to him as time went on. With a new trainee under his wing, everything could be much more difficult.

The salesman returned once Nasreen had picked out most of her kit. "Will you two need anything else? We offer payment plans if you require things beyond your current means to pay for."

Nasreen couldn't help noticing how uninterested he seemed in actually selling them much. Since she felt like something was missing...

"Yes," she said. "Do you have any weapons?" She flashed him a pleasant smile.

The dark, somber man bristled as though scandalized by the question. "We do not sell firearms or explosives."

It was an indirect yet oddly specific way of putting it. She didn't miss the implications. "Oh, I didn't expect you would. Let me see the melee weapons if you would, please. I'm assuming you sell knives, razorfists, batons, dart launchers, crossbows, and that sort of thing, don't you?"

The salesman looked at Dante. "You are her mentor? Do you trust this girl with these things?"

Before Dante could speak, Nasreen interjected, "I'm not a *girl*, and yes, he does, or we wouldn't be here. Do you want our money or not?"

The big guy sneered. "We have a *reputation*. We sell to serious professionals, not to girlfriends and mistresses brought on plunder jobs for a hobby or a vacation. Mr. Raksha! I would have expected better of you."

Nasreen's nostrils flared. She could not be sure where the man was from, but it was one of the Stations where they assumed that women weren't supposed to be in dangerous trades. "Oh? How do you know he isn't *my* tagalong paramour, hmm? For someone who behaves as if you know so much, you seem willfully ignorant of people like Chill-Rill, who's one of the best in the business."

Dante had remained out of the argument, curious to see how she'd handle it. He started in shock when the salesman responded to Nasreen's insult by reaching out to grab her.

He snapped, "No one knows this business the way I—"

Nasreen snatched his hand and wrist, twisted them, and swung around behind him to put her knee into the back of his. He gasped, crumpling to the floor under the power of pain compliance as Nasreen leveraged him down and kept his forearm right at the threshold of injury.

The man trembled and avoided eye contact, gasping in fear.

Nasreen calmly stated, "If you cannot offer decent service, find someone else who can provide it. I'm sure you have other people working here somewhere. Fetch another associate and take a break; why don't you?"

She released him and stepped back. The salesman, face flushing, didn't look at her but ducked off into the back administrative area and did not appear again. An older man emerged a minute or two later, looking annoyed. "I apologize for my associate's unprofessional behavior."

Dante chuckled. "As you can see, she knows how to handle herself."

"Yes." The older man sighed. "I see that. We do have the weapons you requested. I will be happy to show you."

Dante turned to Nasreen. "Let's wrap up here. We don't need a lot of weaponry, but if you find one or two things you like, then sure, we can buy it. As for the job itself, I've been reviewing the details, and, well...it can be done. Might be a bitch of a mission, but I've dealt with worse. Still, we should probably look at water-proof undergarments."

The manager, hanging on his words, added, "I am pleased to report that we have those also."

Nasreen grinned at him. "Oh, good."

CHAPTER SIXTEEN

Dante and Nasreen were suited up and nearly ready to go when their hired pilot, a short, crusty old guy with a white mustache named Sverdlov, delivered the bad news.

"There is storm sweeping across southern U.S.," he said, strolling out of the economy-sized shuttle and onto the dock. "With heavy rain. The water level may rise between now and our time of arrival or departure." He was fluent enough in English but retained a moderately heavy Slavic accent.

Dante grimaced but otherwise didn't react. The whole thing almost amused a sardonic part of his soul—it was fitting, in a way, that Nasreen's first mission as a Plunderer was looking more likely to be a crash course in bad luck.

He looked at his apprentice. "Nasreen. What's the second foundation?"

She replied at once, "Assume nothing works. You made it sound like that was mainly in reference to equipment failure, but I suppose it also applies to stuff like shitty weather, doesn't it?"

He nodded. "It applies to *everything*. At the start of each job, you go in expecting the whole universe to be against you. If you're wrong, it comes as a pleasant surprise."

Sverdlov seemed a bit antsy. He made a sniffling sound and coughed up phlegm. "We should go soon. Sooner is better, to reduce risk of rising water."

Dante turned to the small man. "Yes, I agree. We'll be ready to go in five minutes or less."

The pilot muttered something in either Russian or Ukrainian and returned to the vessel. Besides himself, there was a single other younger man whom Dante was pretty sure was his nephew or the son of a family friend who did general maintenance, security, and helped with the heavy lifting. The two of them along with Dante and Nasreen constituted the entire crew for the job.

Despite the client's offer of generous support, Dante and Nasreen had agreed that keeping things on a small scale would be better. Too many roughnecks in one place at one time caused a stir. People took an interest in big operations. Word might get around that Plunderers were going to retrieve solar tech, specifically, which could attract the baleful eye of Cormac Slaine. That was the last thing they wanted.

The obvious downside was that they would have far less muscle for fighting or hauling solar panels. While Sverdlov's ship was in good condition, he hadn't adapted it for amphibious use, so they would have to find a dry spot and turn Dante and Nasreen loose on foot to locate the sought-after facility.

Nasreen blew out her breath and looked around. "Ironically, if it's the two of us and maybe that other guy doing everything, that puts it closer to the jobs I did in my previous line of work. I thought plundering was mostly on the level of a military operation with dozens of people involved."

Dante made sure the seals were tight on his armor. He was wearing a waterproof undersuit but considered it a second line of defense. "They can be. My old crew was only four people, including me. Sometimes we worked with small armies of Marauders or Reapers. Other times we were alone. Quality is more important than quantity."

Dante had worked with the older Sverdlov before, long ago, but not his younger assistant. So far the crusty Slav hadn't shown any signs of recognizing Jordan Raksha as Dante Shale. He had likely seen so many Plunderers come and go over the years that the faces all flowed together.

Dante checked Nasreen's suit as well, not to mention her weaponry. The client had provided most of the hardware. They both had pulsecores and high-end pistols. Dante had his usual razorfist, and Nasreen had purchased a razorfist containing a hidden dart launcher. Although gimmicky, Dante had to admit weapons like that could occasionally be useful.

Midas had been thrilled, of course, and had recommended a particular neurotoxin to pair with the dart. Nasreen took him up on the offer.

"Okay, I'm ready," Nasreen proclaimed. "Let's go for a swim."

Dante chuckled. "Let's not. The less water we have to deal with, the better. Aquatic Nightmutts are the worst kind..."

Moments later, they had strapped into seats in the shuttle's central compartment. Although big enough to fit themselves plus a few other people and to hold a couple of armloads of solar panels, it wasn't a particularly large ship. The Sverdlovs were up front, with the younger man acting as copilot and comms master in addition to his other jack-of-all-trades functions.

As the shuttle powered up and the bay doors opened to reveal the blackness of space, Dante raised his voice in a final reminder. "Like I said, the instant you leave the Stations, everything you do, and everything that happens, is a coin toss. Live or die. You need to know how the coin will land and how to swat it aside so it lands on heads."

Nasreen swallowed. "Yeah." She couldn't think of anything clever to say to that, and she kept flashing back to her fiasco with Reavo's crew.

Sverdlov took them out into the void and quickly found the best place to enter Earth's atmosphere and gravitational field, encountering the usual fiery turbulence. When the flames cleared, they couldn't see much of the planet below due to the dense storm clouds and sheets of slate-gray rain.

They knew what awaited them. Miles upon miles of swamp.

When the Earth was first wounded and the face of the world rearranged, both freshwater and saltwater had unleashed upon the American South with a vengeance. The sea had engulfed the region's lower-lying areas. The Appalachian hills remained dry, and between the two was a transitional zone of dismal wetlands that flooded more often than not. Charlotte had lain far enough inland and at a high enough elevation to escape total submersion into the ocean but not enough to escape the swamp.

The shuttle broke through the clouds and immediately encountered rain. The artificial weather in the Stations rarely included precipitation, aside from periodic mistings to keep the plant life healthy. In some places, snow during Christmastime also appeared.

Meanwhile, much of Earth was drier than it had been in older times and the planet's weather was often driven more by dust than by moisture. Encountering such massive amounts of water falling from the sky and spreading throughout the land was an alien experience for any modern Atlantican.

Dante listened to the Slavs curse and chatter as they navigated through the rain. Finding their exact destination would be close to impossible in this weather. And that was *before* they considered the issue of where to land.

Nasreen checked her boots again. They had invested in some nice thigh-highs to go over the length of their usual armor and footwear. Most of the Charlotte area's flooding was shallow. With the torrential rains adding to it...

She remembered something. "Dante. Did you get that Automap upgrade for Midas?"

Dante sighed. "Yes. Yes, I did. It might even be helpful."

Midas projected his voice over the noise of the shuttle. "It certainly will be. You will not be able to navigate very efficiently from a sphere while you're battling the swamp. Once we have our coordinates, relying upon me to guide you makes far more sense, doesn't it?"

Nasreen had to admit she enjoyed how irritated Dante seemed at having been forced to accept a technological advance against his will. "It does."

Sverdlov located the city of Charlotte, and one of the small viewscreens attached to an outboard camera displayed long lines of decaying ruins sprouting up from sludgy brown water. The humid downpour obscured much of the scene. It was beautiful and eerie at the same time.

The older man's voice came over the ship-wide intercom. "We are here. You said facility is in northern part of city. We will not get much closer than this. I will look for solid rooftop on which to land. Then there is not more we can do."

It took him about two minutes to locate a viable building. He brought the shuttle down and put it into a holding pattern over the flat roof of what appeared to be a hospital. Since it was a smaller ship, it could hover closer to the roof's surface while expending less power, which made disembarking easier.

As the shuttle went still and its engines quieted, Nasreen remembered something. "Oh, and since I'm a proper Marauder now, use my handle. Ez-Extract, or E-zex for short. Got it?"

Dante's mouth rippled in vague distaste. "E-zex sounds like something a porn company would come up with, but yeah, okay."

"Hah!" she shot back. "The word 'hellcat' used to apply to women, you know."

Dante was pretty sure they'd had this conversation before, which was more reason not to have it again. He ignored her, unstrapped himself, and made his final preparations to plunge into the fray. He and Nasreen put on hooded waterproof capes as the last part of their ensemble. According to the temperature readout, it was warm. Cold and wet was a bad combination.

They stopped by the cabin on their way out.

Dante told Sverdlov and his nephew, "We'll message you when we're on our way back or if we need emergency extraction. Otherwise, wait. We know what we're doing."

The Slavs had pretty much planned to do exactly that, anyway. Dante had seen to it that they had pulsecores of their own to defend themselves in case anything nasty found its way back to the ship.

E-zex and Hellcat hopped down onto the rooftop. The rain was easing, no longer a downpour but simply a steady flow.

Nasreen fiddled with a button near her collar, under the hood. "Oh, wait, I forgot to start recording. And yes, I know, you think it's stupid and pointless. But remember that the whole reason we're here—well, part of the reason—is to build up our media franchise, so getting this all on camera will help."

"Surviving will help more," Dante pointed out. "Constant vigilance. Remember that. You can't be vigilant if you're worried about how your hair looks for the audience."

Nasreen grumbled, "Oh, be quiet. My hair is under a hood *and* a helmet anyway. I don't think we're getting a live feed due to all the stupid interference from this storm. We'll have to settle for sporadic video, which we should at least be able to edit back together once we get home and distribute after the fact."

"Yeah." Dante scanned their surroundings. "Once we get back home."

Beyond the rain-washed edges of the roof, the swamp expanded to the limits of their vision. Thousands of circles rippled in the brownish murk where raindrops struck it, turning it into a muddy mess that sloshed against the edges of the rotting structures of a once-great city. In many places, vegetation clung to the buildings, trying to tear them down.

Dante had made sure to bring a winch for this sort of contingency. He fetched it from the shuttle, magnetically attached it to the craft's hull, and portioned out a length of cord to lower Nasreen. There was a chance she'd encounter hostile creatures before he could get down to help, but he was more concerned with making sure the device worked properly.

Nasreen attached the cord to a loop in her armor. "I have some experience with climbing, so I know how to put my feet against the wall and keep rappelling down."

"Good. When you get to the bottom, wait for me on that wall. Stay out of the water until necessary."

He held the cord to ensure it wouldn't feed out too fast as Nasreen hopped gradually down the side of the hospital toward the half-wall that had been part of an adjacent parking structure. She nearly missed it but caught the edge and climbed atop. The water's surface was only about six feet below her.

She unfastened the cord and let it zip back up. Dante attached it to his outfit, crawled over the edge, and bounced down. Due to the weight of his gear, the cord sent him spiraling down faster than he liked, and toward the end, Nasreen had to reach out and grab his belt to keep him from plopping into the water.

"Gotcha," she panted, heaving him up onto the wall. "I mean, there's nowhere to go but into the sludge anyway. It's the principle of the thing."

Dante gruffly thanked her, unfastened the cord, and hooked it around a metal fixture on the wall. If it came loose, they could at least have the Sverdlovs toss it back down to them when the time came.

Looking out at the swamp, Dante muttered, "All right. Let's do it."

He clambered over the edge and allowed himself to slide into the morass. The water was at his hips when his feet touched the bottom. He helped Nasreen jump down next to him. The murky water came up to her waist.

"Ugh," she remarked. "I mean, we came prepared, but still. Ugh."

Dante nodded. "That about sums it up." Their helmets included a minimal air filtration system to protect against hazardous vapors, but the stagnant smell of the place was impossible to ignore.

Midas knew that now was his time to shine. "All right," he said into Dante's head, "I will guide you, vocally and visually, to the facility you seek. You can therefore focus on navigating the landscape and dealing with any life-forms that might wish you ill."

"Good. Don't speak aloud unless it's necessary to save Nasreen from getting hurt or something. We don't want to make much sound."

If the rain kept up, though, it would mask much of the noise they produced.

Midas agreed, and highlighting Dante's vision with green shapes, pointed at a dense cluster of buildings to the northwest. "That way. About one mile, if I'm not mistaken. The plant's exact location isn't yet determined, but that will at least put you within a block or so."

Grunting, Dante sloshed off into the city with Nasreen at his elbow. "Remember. Always vigilant. Don't rely on anything to work the way it's supposed to."

Nasreen glanced at her pulsecore. There was still a tiny, dim green light on the receiver to indicate it was operational. All but the cheapest models were waterproof. It made her feel somewhat more secure. She could believe, for the moment, that they were going to pull this off flawlessly.

They got about one hundred feet from the hospital when something swam by them.

"Whoa," Nasreen exclaimed. "What the hell was that? Did you feel that?"

The water had swished, and she briefly glimpsed a dark shape moving through it about two feet to her left, at the edge of her blind spot. There was no way for her to confirm that it was a living thing rather than simply a piece of debris washed out by the rain. But it didn't seem like anything inanimate.

Dante looked around. "No, but I believe you. Head for that pile of junk up ahead. We'll get out of the water ASAP!"

The pile in question was mostly debris from collapsed buildings and ruined cars. Part of it was underwater, but the rest was above, next to a hardware store and a fast-food restaurant.

As they reached the edge and climbed up and out of the morass, something else sloshed by, poked a big ungainly head out of the water, then vanished beneath the surface.

Nasreen made a whistling sound between her teeth and aimed her carbine in its general direction. She didn't want to start an unnecessary racket by blowing shit up if she didn't have to. But...

Dante snapped, "Damn. I saw *that* one. Didn't get a good look, but there are creatures down there sniffing our ankles. We might have to make an example of one or two of them."

He scanned the surrounding area and Nasreen did likewise.

Squatting on some rusty girders above the water where a cheap building had once been was another thing. The instant they saw it, it practically threw itself back into the swamp, vanishing with a *splash*. Then there were no other sounds or movements where it had been.

"Dante," Nasreen quipped, trying to sound flippant, "I think our client accidentally sent us into some kind of Nightmutt spawning ground." She wasn't sure about the *accidental* part.

Dante moved up the hill toward the other end. "Could be. There isn't much intel about any nonhuman creatures leftover on this miserable planet. Some of them are skittish, though. If you have to shoot one, don't hesitate. It'll attract notice, but it will also scare the others off."

Scoffing to hide her growing dread, Nasreen followed him

along the hill, trying to keep her eyes everywhere at once. The rain had grown heavier again, which didn't help visibility.

As they neared the end of the mound, where there was no option except to wade into the muck again, Dante put a finger to the side of his head. Then he gestured to the right, indicating they should turn that way, per Midas' directions.

He hopped down into the water and sloshed onto a cross street right past the hill. Nasreen trailed him by about nine feet. As she turned the corner, a second or two after Dante turned his back, something burst out of the depths beside her.

"Fuck!" she exclaimed. Water sprayed up and all she could see was a huge, dark bulk with a thrashing tail, some kind of tendrils, and a black, gaping maw filled with teeth. It looked like the results of an alligator and a cuttlefish having drunken, angry sex. And it was right on top of her.

She raised her pulsecore. Her finger was already starting to depress the trigger when one of the creature's forelimbs lashed out, knocked the gun from her grasp, and sent her stumbling aside to half-float on her knees. The water came up to her shoulders.

Dante shouted something she couldn't understand and spun right in time for the Nightmutt's tail to strike him across the chest, sending him hurtling back through the mire and crashing into a wall. He kept his hold on the pulsecore but for a precious second or two, was too disoriented to fire.

The twice-human-sized monster bore down on Nasreen, its dripping mouth making for her head while its bulging, pallid eyes stared at her with dumb animal hunger.

She froze in terror…then decided *not* to die. Her arm sprang up, and she squeezed the tiny hidden lever against her wrist, activating the dart launcher within her razorfist. The small projectile, propelled by a capsule of hyper-compressed gas, streaked out and found its mark near the lower rim of the creature's right eye.

It reacted instantly as the neurotoxins caused shocking pain, followed by sedation. Its attempt at biting Nasreen's head off faltered as it stiffened in place, then roared, expelling breath into her face that smelled like a wet dumpster filled with roadkill. It thrashed its head from side to side, splashing madly and trying to dislodge the small yet vicious object from its eyelid.

Nasreen half-rolled, half-swam aside, frantically sloshing her arms around and looking for the pulsecore as the monster seemingly forgot about her in its pain and panic.

Then Dante recovered from being swatted with its tail, stepped back, aimed, and fired two pulsecore rounds into the side of the beast's trunk. Green explosions blew gory holes in the thing's body, the blood mingling with dirty water. It stumbled and shuddered, mortally wounded but not yet dead.

"Nasreen! Look out!" Dante shouted.

She noticed its eyes looking at her with a hateful intelligence, as though it knew she was to blame for this and wanted revenge. There was still some fight left in it. It lurched forward, its jaws weakly snapping toward her face.

She swung around and raised the razorfist again, punching the Nightmutt where the corner of its jaw met its neck and deploying the blade. The hidden knife shot out and carved a bleeding gash out of the thing's flesh. Nasreen yanked her arm aside and cut open half its throat. Foul blood spilled into the water, and at last, the thing slumped over, still and silent as the brown flood washed over it.

Dante looked at her. "You hurt?"

She gasped and heaved. "No, but help me find my gun. How about you? Are you hurt?"

He rolled his head and shrugged his shoulders, probably to check for any impact damage. "No, I'm okay, only a couple of bruises. Midas says he can see a slight green glow in the water right...there." He pointed.

Nasreen fished around in the spot until her hands closed around the pulsecore. Pulling it from the sludge and wiping it off, all she could think of was how good an idea it had been to insist that the shop manager show her all those "gimmicky" weapons. He'd given her a hard time about it then. She figured she could return the favor later.

CHAPTER SEVENTEEN

Dante noticed that Nasreen's demeanor had changed since they'd defeated the huge Nightmutt. She was less frightened and more alert. The experience had demonstrated that life Dirtside tended to be nasty, brutish, and short for the unwary.

No other living things bothered them for a few minutes, but the swampy city was full of too many hungry, curious predators for their fear to last long. As the pair pressed on toward the solar plant, other creatures began to swim, slosh, or pounce along beside them, usually right at the edge of their vision.

Nasreen asked, "Are they working in packs? Like trying to herd us into an ambush? I've heard that some of them are smart enough to do that."

Dante frowned. "I don't think so. They don't seem organized, and they're not acting desperate for food, either. Some get like this when they encounter a new species on their turf. They pester you, circle you, and try to test you. They're attempting to figure out how easy you'd be as prey and if you're worth the effort. That thing we killed back at the corner found out the hard way. Most of these probably saw or heard what happened. Still, be wary."

"Oh, I'll be *plenty* wary until we're out of this place," Nasreen shot back.

Up ahead was another mound of debris that rose beyond the water's surface. They moved toward it, grateful for a break from the endless, amphibious slog.

As soon as they emerged from the water, so did two Nightmutts that had been following them. Then another two waiting in ambush ahead. And one that had been lurking in the insurance office to the right.

Dante's gun came up. "Shit."

None of the creatures pounced yet. All were of approximately the same bizarre subspecies. They were man-sized, like a mating of toad and raccoon, with bulging eyes and dexterous claws. They watched the humans and moved slowly forward, sniffing—jittery but determined.

Dante said. "It's another test. Kill one." He raised his pulsecore and fired, blowing the head off the nearest one.

Nasreen did likewise, blasting a hole through the chest of another at the same time. Both fell back, dead almost instantly, and the other three shrieked, turned tail, and fled beneath the water.

Then things were quiet again. The rain had slowed to a drizzle so they hardly noticed it.

Dante nodded. "There. We had to show them that we taste bad. They learned their lesson."

Midas interjected, "Sorry to interrupt, but you've gone a bit off-course. It's partially my fault. I've never seen rain before, and it's throwing off my navigation ability. Go back to the end of this street and take a left at the cross street. Go fifty feet, and you should be close to the manufacturing plant."

"We'd better be," Dante muttered. "This is already taking too long."

The mangrove labyrinth grew denser as they neared their destination, in some ways resembling a flooded, overgrown jungle with the plant life having almost totally consumed some of the buildings. They were closer to the edge of town now, where the mangrove swamp met the cypress forest.

They turned the corner and saw a massive rotting structure surrounded by smaller outbuildings and a chain-link fence that had all but rusted into oblivion.

Midas exclaimed, "Aha! That must be it. I'm almost certain of it."

"It looks like a manufacturing plant," Dante agreed. "Not sure if we should scope out the whole perimeter before we go in. I don't like entering a place I haven't reconned, but we're short on time."

Nasreen looked at him. "Are you talking to me, Midas, or yourself?"

He shrugged. "All three, I guess. We *could* split up, but I don't think that's a good idea. It's generally only something I do in an area that's easier to navigate than this one and with someone I trust."

The instant the words left his mouth, he regretted them.

Nasreen blurted, "You don't trust me? How the fuck is that?"

Dante sighed and rubbed his forehead. "I don't mean that you're not on my side. I mean you're still new at this. You're doing good so far, but you're still a rookie Marauder."

"I suppose I can accept that explanation," she grumbled. "Well, why don't we compromise? We can each go to a different end of the perimeter to look around more, but we'll stay within sight in case we need help."

That sounded okay to him so Dante agreed. They parted, with him going right and she left, each sloshing through the waters. They were a bit shallower now since the ground had risen by nine inches.

Dante was close to his corner when Nasreen turned and waved frantically at him from her edge of the compound. She ducked, allowing the water to come up to her shoulders so only her head and neck were visible.

Dante immediately did the same, falling to his knees and half-crawling, half-swimming toward her. There was enough rain noise to mask the gentle sloshing of his approach. He didn't know the problem, but he could guess a couple of possibilities.

When Nasreen was about ten feet away, she whispered, "We're not alone." She pointed.

Dante peered through the fence's rusty links. Beyond it was an alley that ran between an outbuilding and the main structure. There, crowded on a platform next to a foreman's office that rose above the water was a heavily armed and armored force of at least ten men and women, maybe more.

To believe it was a coincidence that other Plunderers would be in the same place at almost the same time would have required a level of schizophrenic delusion Dante didn't think he was capable of.

Someone had ratted them out. Or they had been hacked. Either way, other parties knew about the solar panels. Quite possibly, parties who were in the business of providing solar solutions.

There were two wounded men among the group. One with a mangled leg partially treated with medipatches and another guy who kept clutching his midsection as he bent over and heaved, choking up blood. The Nightmutts had taken their toll.

A woman near the group's center complained, "Those things will be back. They went into that building, not out. We're gonna walk right into their ambush!"

A man next to her countered, "We killed five of them. They'll think twice. Might fight if they get desperate, but they're not hunting us. We're hunting them. Right?"

"Bullshit!" someone else rasped. It was the man with the wounded leg. "They were using small unit tactics. Pack hunting shit. If we go in there, you're all going to end up like this, or worse." He tapped his leg. "Leave me behind, and I'll stand watch, okay? Going down there, I'd only slow you down."

The woman in the center added, "Yeah, it doesn't take *everyone* to nuke a few pieces of equipment."

Another voice protested, "Except the smaller the force, the easier pickings we are for those fucks. I say we leave Gordon and his leg here and take everyone else."

The injured man clutching his stomach closed his eyes and shook his head. "I can't. Oh, God. I can't make it. Need time for the bleeding to stop. Painkillers aren't working."

Someone grumbled, "We don't have time for this."

"No," said the woman, "but what the hell are we going to do? Can't we wait for backup, or extraction, or something? It's not like Cormac fucking Slaine can't afford to send a whole 'nother shuttle down here to pick these guys up and drop off a few more. Or, um, I could take them back in the ship. It's not a long flight. I could drop them off at the infirmary at the Station and be back in time for—"

There was a single heavy footstep and a movement of shadows as someone, out of Dante's and Nasreen's line of sight, moved from the elevated office to the adjacent platform and fired two rounds from a pulsecore pistol.

Gordon, the man with the mangled leg, didn't realize what was happening before his head came apart in a gory burst as the pulsecore round detonated inside his skull.

Then the guy with the injured midsection's eyes bulged as the second round hit him in the chest. It blew pieces of his armor apart and left a gaping crater between his ribs. With blood flowing freely, he slumped off the platform's edge into the water below. His body floated, turning the muck pinkish-red.

Dante clenched his jaw. Whoever was in charge of this mission was undoubtedly one of Slaine's most ruthless and unfeeling lackeys. Maybe Mr. H. Curtidor, even though a pulsecore pistol wasn't Hyde's style.

The woman in the middle stood frozen, her jaw hanging open. As an experienced Reaper, it was clear that she hadn't expected the boss to react with such coldness—and she thought she was next.

There were three more footsteps and the person who'd pulled the trigger came into sight. A slim woman of above-average height, with freckles and auburn hair tied back under her half-helmet. Dante's blood suddenly felt like it was boiling.

It was Vivica Lamburg, his old quartermaster.

Viv gestured at the two corpses with her free hand. "This is kind and merciful compared to what Hyde will do to all of us if we leave this shitty-ass planet without reducing those solar cells to worthless slag."

Her other hand held the pistol, moving it from Reaper to Reaper to ensure they all got the message. "This isn't the kind of job where you morons can get away with cheating, reneging, and running away to a different Station doing low-end work until the heat passes. Slaine expects loyalty and commitment, and he can goddamn well enforce it."

Dante's eye twitched, his hands flexed beneath the water, and his brain clouded over with red, burning fury. Viv had pulled a similar gun on him not so very long ago, intending to fire it straight into his back. All because she had cheated *him*. She had reneged on her loyalty to *him*. Now she lectured a bunch of Slaine's other new patsies about the importance of Plunderer ethics. He wanted to crush her larynx with his bare hands.

After a few seconds, he forced control over himself. Rage like that wasn't something he normally experienced. He had mastered his emotions—mostly—long ago.

Nasreen had turned her gaze to him and leaned closer. Her whisper in his ear was barely audible. "Is that who I think it is?"

He gave a single nod.

Viv had stomped back into the office and was dragging something out. She reappeared a few seconds later with a crate filled with heavy objects. "If you guys had waited and trusted me, we could have had our solution to that Nightmutt problem a lot sooner. I used to be a quartermaster, okay? I always bring the right tools for the job."

She distributed small cylindrical items that Dante couldn't identify at first. Then one of the Reapers turned the canister, and he saw the distinctive tab at the end. Aerosol grenades. He'd used them before, and always to good effect.

"These will get the job done. Now stop acting like a bunch of fucking rookies. Those who are still alive will make a *lot* of money after we finish with this place."

The mercs begrudgingly descended from the platform and into the hip-deep water. All of them moved cautiously but with a steady forward purposefulness. Most of them held their grenades like primary weapons, but two kept pulsecore carbines out.

As they moved through an open service door into the main building and the dark, flooded, tunnel-like spaces beyond, Dante saw the silhouettes of humanoid Nightmutts darting and springing around in the abysmal shadows beyond, past the boundaries of human sight.

"Well," he murmured as Nasreen looked at him again. "The good news is that they'll probably soak up most of the Nightmutt action on our behalf."

Nasreen was antsy. "Yeah, and the bad news is that they're going to blow this place up, depriving the Stations of vital technology so Slaine can keep the upper hand in solar power. And we don't know where the panels are."

Dante grunted. They weren't going to have a particularly fun afternoon. "No way out of it. We have to go after them. Come on. Let them deal with the local fauna. Then we'll mop up whatever's left—human or otherwise."

His partner put a hand on his arm and squeezed it. "As if I wasn't already privileged to learn enough on my first day as a Plunderer..."

With Viv's team well out of earshot, they tore apart the badly rusted fence and slipped into the compound. Keeping to the shadows, they followed the same path the Reapers had, moving swiftly but staying well behind their rivals. They could barely see the dark shapes of the rearmost mercenaries up ahead, where the plant's massive processing floor gave way to hallways that the swamp had transformed into something like sewer tunnels.

Aside from the sloshing water, the only other sounds at first were an oscillating series of strange burbling cries that weren't human, sometimes giving way to low croaks. The Nightmutts, whatever they were, precisely, were communicating with one another.

Then there was the sharp bark of gunfire and in the echo of its report, the hissing of aerosol gas. Human voices shouted and cursed, and the creatures who lived there howled and warbled in pain and anger.

Dante and Nasreen kept close together as they entered the leftmost of the three main corridors, the one closest to the center of the structure. Midas recommended that they seek out the most secure place in the plant. That would be the most likely location for the treasure trove of solar tech.

Ahead and around a corner, part of the facility's roof had collapsed, allowing a pale shaft of light to enter. A lone Reaper—the woman from the central platform who'd tried to argue for the wounded men—waded through the sludge. She tried to look everywhere while holding her carbine in one hand and a grenade in the other.

As if from nowhere, one of the creatures appeared on a ledge above her. Dante's stomach turned over. Even by Nightmutt standards, it was awful to behold in the split second he got a clear look at it—like an oversized chimpanzee or small gorilla crossed with a deep-sea fish, the kind with huge eyes and too many teeth.

It pounced. The woman saw it and tried to use both weapons at once, failing with both. Her shrill cry cut off as the creature's jaws clamped down on her head. Its taloned hands seized her by the shoulders, knocked her over, and dragged her out of sight into the shadows of a side tunnel.

The woman dropped the aerosol grenade, though. Right in the path of the *next* Nightmutt, which emerged from the darkness looking straight at Dante and Nasreen. It had a crude club in one hand, a two-foot length of pipe, and it raised it, about to charge. Dante brought up his gun.

Before he could fire, the grenade went off. Gasses hissed and *whooshed* as shocking amounts of foaming, bubbling caustic chemicals erupted into the air and water, engulfing the beast. The material enveloped its limbs and clogged its mouth and gills. It staggered and made an awful choking sound as it strangled to death.

Dante glided forward with Nasreen close behind him. By the time he reached the Nightmutt, it was close to death anyway. He still deployed his razorfist, stabbed it in the chest, and ripped the blade through its innards to finish it off. The corpse sank into the water beside them.

Nasreen tried to ignore it. "Ugh. What about the one that —whoa!"

The other Nightmutt that had killed the female Reaper a minute ago reemerged beside them, chewing dumbly on something they couldn't see. It raised its claws.

Dante and Nasreen both fired at the same time. One pulsecore round from each gun struck the creature in the upper torso, blowing off its arms and head while disintegrating its whole chest and shoulder area. The rest sank into the depths.

"Don't worry about the noise," Dante said. "They'll think it was one of their guys shooting a Nightmutt. I don't think they have any idea we're here. Yet."

The corridor ended not too much farther ahead. Beyond it was a cavern of sorts where the factory floor had collapsed. The swamp drained into it in a lazy waterfall, most of which sloughed off the surface below into still-deeper crevasses. The sound of the rushing water was practically inaudible next to the din of battle.

Vivica's crew had found the jackpot. Two things covered the cavern floor, both in great numbers. Revolting, bulbous objects like hairy frogspawn, which could only have been the eggs of this particular species of Nightmutt. And flat, shiny objects. Solar panels, set with advanced solar cells the likes of which the Atlantica Stations had never seen.

"No—no!" someone cried. It was one of the Reapers, cornered by two Nightmutts and cut off from his companions. Gunshots, explosions, snarls, and screams were everywhere. The man threw his grenade at the pair of beasts.

He saved himself just in time. The bomb went off with a foul hissing sound, and the polymer foam engulfed the whole space around it. The detonation happened close enough to the first Nightmutt's head that the force of the expanding mess tore its skull to pieces.

The other was slightly luckier. It was blinded and disoriented by the foam, thrashing uselessly until the desperate Reaper took it out with two shots to the chest and neck. Then, seemingly in shock that he'd survived, the man dashed between the rows of eggs and panels to rejoin the others.

The Reapers had left a couple of thick, supple cords running from the edge of the tunnels into the cavern area. Dante and Nasreen each took one, waiting until the melee between the humans and the Nightmutts reached a fever pitch of violence and slid down.

Nasreen said, "I'll gather samples. You protect me. Deal?"

"Sure," he muttered while hefting his carbine and scanning everything around them. "But let's be quick. No one invited us to the party, so there's no reason to join in."

CHAPTER EIGHTEEN

"There," Nasreen said under her breath. It had taken her less than a minute to pluck an assortment of cells and panel sheaths from the various samples in one corner of the cave, sliding them all into her waterproof pack. Neither the Reapers nor the Night-mutts had noticed them. Dante stood over her, ready to kill anything that *did* see them.

He nudged her. "Okay. Let's go."

The Reapers were down to about five plus Viv herself, from their original ten or twelve. There were at least thirty Nightmutts in the building or at least the immediate area, Dante estimated. Something about how they moved suggested greater numbers than what he could see, but creatures as big as they were could not have been too numerous in such a relatively small area.

But the Reapers had slaughtered a good dozen of the beasts and were driving them out of the main cavern floor area, dispersing and intimidating them, buying themselves space.

Vivica shouted, "Get back. Fire in the hole!"

Across the cave from where Dante and Nasreen made for the cords, something shrieked horribly like a gush of superheated air.

A column of astonishingly bright white fire rose, surrounded by steam.

Dante sputtered, "What the shit?"

Midas spoke up for the first time since they'd entered the compound. "Sir, it came from a lower level of the cave. This Viv person must have seen some of the panels down there and destroyed them. She seems to be using a projectile weapon that creates extremely small, relatively controlled nuclear blasts. Minimal fallout danger. It's a prototype device I was reading about in—"

"Fuck!" Dante said. "So when they said they were going to *nuke* the panels, they weren't exaggerating. We leave, now!"

Suddenly, everything was quiet.

Nasreen said, "Well, we're spotted. Nice knowing you, Hellcat."

The flash from the mini-nuke had illuminated the dripping caves well enough for a couple of the Reapers to see the human silhouettes behind them. Two were pointing at the duo, and a figure that might have been Viv was advancing over the wet rock. Behind her, fires still burned.

"Hold it right there," Viv commanded. Off to the side, two of her flunkies took potshots at a couple of the Nightmutts trying to reenter the cavern from the labyrinth of tunnels beyond. "You're not getting the panels. You can live if you drop them and get the fuck out of here without wasting our time. Only fair."

Then from behind Dante and Nasreen, three Nightmutts burst out of the shadows. Acting on reflex and instinct, Dante spun, fired four shots from his pulsecore in two double bursts, and plunged straight at the creatures, raising his razorfist before he knew whether he'd killed them all.

The four rounds had devastated the first two beasts and wounded the third. As it hopped around on one leg, flailing its ungainly limbs, Dante slipped onto its flank, shanked it through the spot where its heart ought to be, and sliced the spine. It croaked and flopped against the wet stone, rolling off into one of the crevasses where the waterfall spilled deep into the earth.

Nasreen tensed in horror as the Reapers prepared to open fire, but Viv barked, "No! Hold up. I know that sound."

Dante replied in a higher-pitched voice than his usual, "What sound? We were about to dump the panels at your feet, whoever you are."

Vivica chuckled. "Nice try. I've heard all that before. The two-two quad burst from a pulsecore tuned to that particular frequency. And there aren't a lot of razorfists that sound like that. I had my doubts about the official story, you know. Now the truth comes home. No one else fights that way. *Dante*."

Dante exhaled. "Well, crap."

Nasreen had no idea what the former quartermaster was about to do, and she didn't know Dante's feelings on the matter either, but she didn't want to wait and find out. Instead, she raised her pulsecore and fired three shots at the Reapers in a deliberately wide spread.

Viv heard the gun firing and threw herself aside, rolling into a miniature pool formed by the water flow from above, narrowly dodging the first shot. A second detonated somewhere toward the rear of the main cavern.

The third found its mark in the gut of one of the Reapers, tearing him mostly in half.

Nasreen said, "Okay, then." She jumped toward the nearest cord leading back up toward the tunnels that would take them to the surface.

"Kill them!" Vivica barked. "Bonus to whoever does!"

Dante growled, "Fuck off, Viv." Before he could send her a token of his appreciation, more Nightmutts swarmed out. Not from the depths but the tunnels above them. His eyes bulged. "Not good. Nasreen! Come on."

She was already clambering up the cord when he caught her arm. She leapt down without protest, and together they ducked off into a small grotto ahead where darkness shielded them from sight. Then the ape-fish rampaged across the whole cavern while the few remaining Reapers began randomly blasting at anything that moved with pulsecores and rifles and hurling their aerosol grenades.

Bullets, miniature plasma blasts, and eruptions of steaming foam flew everywhere. Nightmutts died but still advanced, determined to kill *all* the humans who had invaded their home.

Midas spoke aloud. "Sir and madam. If we flee deeper into these caves, there is a good probability of finding another way out. They must connect to the sewer system of Charlotte, or perhaps the basements of other buildings."

"Awesome, great," Dante muttered. "Point out the way. I can't see a damn thing."

Midas used green icons to help him and Nasreen find the best path through the dark, wet, noisy battle, descending along with the falling water to the same lower level where Viv had nuked another batch of the panels.

Then two Reapers spotted them. "There they are! Flank, flank!" Both dashed aside and out of immediate sight before Dante or Nasreen could shoot them.

Dante tried to ignore the bastards. Escape was the priority. He and Nasreen slid down a wet slope, steering clear of the area where the mini-nuke had gone off. It still faintly glowed, and a rather creepy sparkling heat-mist was rising. They made for a rather narrow tunnel, arguably more of a large pipe near the bottom.

Two Nightmutts appeared above them, warbling in animal rage at the same instant that one of the Reapers became visible. Dante was facing the wrong direction to engage them, but Nasreen had a better position.

"Hold still." She aimed her pulsecore over his shoulder and fired two rounds. The first detonated in front of the Reaper, giving him pause and sending his rifle fire spraying wildly into the air.

The second blew a hole through one of the Nightmutts, and the impact sent the other one rolling and sprawling straight into the Reaper. He screamed as the creature forgot about Dante and Nasreen and vented its anger on the easiest and closest target, ripping him in half from shoulder to waist.

Dante thanked Nasreen with a grunt and a nod, then pulled her toward the pipe.

"Stop!" a woman screamed. It was Viv. She had separated from her few remaining men to pursue the pair.

Dante ignored her. Stopping was the last thing he intended to do. If her prototype nuke-launcher thing had ammo to spare…

"*Dante!*" she howled. "I only want the panels, goddammit. Did you take any of them out of here before we noticed you? Just tell me. *Tell me!*"

Midas said silently, "If she knows that we have the remaining panels, won't she simply nuke the three of us and the panels at the same time?"

Dante snorted. "Congratulations, Midas. You're starting to think like a human."

Viv cried, "What?"

"I said, yes, there's another bag of them back near the entrance." He hoped she would believe him. While stalling, he and Nasreen crept to the edge of the large pipe.

Vivica laughed and moved forward. They saw her slender silhouette above them against the faint glowing light from the nuke site. The weapon in her hands seemed too large and monstrous for her willowy frame. "I don't believe you. Even if you are telling the truth, we'll find it without you."

Dante shoved Nasreen into the pipe and clambered in behind her, realizing that he was as close to panic as he'd been in quite some time. Behind him, the prototype weapon made a faint humming sound as it powered up again.

He stripped off his vest and his rainproof cape. Although a pathetic barrier against a nuclear explosion, they had properties that might at least absorb some of the kinetic shock and repel some of the radiation. He stuffed them behind them at the mouth of the pipe and barked, *"Move!"*

To her credit, Nasreen was already scrambling away. He followed her as Viv fired.

The light was so bright and hot that it penetrated the rock and mud. As they crawled out the other end into a jumbled cave, their ears rang, and their skin stung as though sunburned. Nasreen reached out and pulled Dante behind an outcropping of stone as white fire and a half-visible shockwave erupted from the pipe, cracking the rock and melting the steel. Then the hum sounded again. Viv was going to blast through the cavern wall itself rather than try to crawl in after them.

It sounded like she hesitated because the Nightmutts were storming madly around and letting out their gurgling howls with increased frequency. Something about the bright light and generally terrifying, unnatural aspect of the advanced weapon had agitated them to the point of madness.

Midas suggested, "Keep going, perhaps? The way ahead is mostly clear."

Dante replied, "No fucking shit." He sprang to his feet, hoping he wasn't more burned than he felt, and he and Nasreen sprinted across the damp earth toward a slope of sorts up ahead.

Nasreen was about five feet ahead. "There's light up there. We can get out this way. Holy crap, we might make it."

Viv fired again. The entire sheet of rock separating the main cavern from the smaller one collapsed in a half-melted mass of irradiated debris. Again, the white light threatened to blind them.

They tore ahead, up the slope, which was little more than a landslide of debris and not easy to navigate. At the top was what looked like the floor of a cellar or perhaps a subway terminal.

When they had nearly crested it, Dante spared a glance back over his shoulder.

Insanely, Vivica had run right over the deadly mass of blasted rock she'd created. It occurred to him that her armor was probably calibrated against extreme heat and radiation, at least up to a certain point. Her desperation had to do with more than the desire to capture or kill the two Marauders. The Nightmutts had rallied and were intent on killing *her*. Something about the nuke device had driven them mad.

Dante pushed Nasreen ahead. "Go on. Find the best way out. I'll deal with this."

Nasreen spared a half-second to look at him cockeyed. Then she shook her head, muttered something, and ran off into the cellar toward the nearest doorway.

Dante turned and stood at the crest of the sloping mound, looking down it to where Viv was struggling through the soft-but-hardening, half-molten rock, which glowed eerily around her feet. She had let the nuke device hang slack by her side and instead had pulled out her pulsecore pistol, using it to blast at the swarming Nightmutts. She killed two, but there were another fourteen or fifteen still coming.

She looked up and saw her former partner. "Dante! I only have one nuke round left. If I use it now, we all die." She paused to shoot at the Nightmutts again. The rock, molasses-like, clutched at her feet, making it impossible for her to move any faster than a brisk walk, as each step was a struggle. "I'm sorry, all right? Don't let me die like this!"

Dante focused on the nuke device, which almost resembled a repeating crossbow. He could see the final explosive round within it. A small yellow light indicated that it was armed. The Nightmutts snarled and closed in.

"Deal." He fired a single bullet.

The round, a mere lead projectile, struck the yellow light dead on. Then Dante spun and threw himself across the cellar toward the hallway. Vivica's scream of horror, rage, and despair echoed briefly before the column of white fire engulfed her, blasting and melting her. The Nightmutts went up like blazing candles, and the rock, steel, and concrete around them collapsed inward in a flood of trash, embers, and smoking ruin.

Nasreen had waited for him halfway down the hall, cringing against the peripheral effects of another nuclear blast. "That was irresponsible," she pointed out.

"Yes," he admitted, exhaling and realizing how tired he was and how much he hurt. "At least I kept my word. I didn't let her be torn apart by those things. Which is better than she did for me."

CHAPTER NINETEEN

Dante, Nasreen, and Midas waited in the back room. The functionary who had shepherded them so far had informed them a moment ago that they would be going live in front of the board meeting in about five minutes, and to be ready.

Nasreen inclined her head toward him. "We are."

The man made a throaty sound of acknowledgment, then turned and left. Out in the boardroom, they could hear the executives speaking in low voices. Some of it was comprehensible, but most of it merely sounded like mumbling chatter.

Dante looked up. It was pointless since it was impossible to see his implanted friend, but it had become a surprisingly resilient habit. "Midas. You got anything that might be useful? Or interesting?"

"Hmm." The AI spoke silently in his mind. "Why yes, actually, I do. Your viewership numbers are climbing at an exponential rate. Each block of four to six hours sees an increase in views that is approximately one-point-four times the size of the audience from the previous block, relative to the point at which the video first went public."

Dante's mouth puckered in annoyance. It *was* sort of "interesting" to hear, but what he'd meant was if Midas could decipher the conversation in the boardroom better than he or Nasreen could.

The video to which he was referring was the edited one depicting the recent exploits of E-zex and the Hellcat as they slogged through the dangerous, Nightmutt-infested swamps of North Carolina and exposed the malfeasance of SSS. There was some stuff that Dante and Nasreen agreed should not be flung in the faces of the general public.

But they released the bulk of it. Rather than selling it to a network to incorporate it into one of their documentary programs, they put it on a public stream as an independent production. Dante had taken particular pleasure in that aspect of it. It meant that no one associated with the production of the Chill-Rill vid in Ashgabat would make any money from him again.

He cleared his throat. "Okay, nice. I don't suppose you can hear the people beyond this wall better than I can?"

"No," Midas admitted. "How could I? I rely upon your sensory input for mine."

Dante kept forgetting about that part. It was too easy to think of Midas as something like a ghost or invisible gremlin sitting on his shoulder, with his own perceptual organs. That wasn't the case.

Nasreen put a hand on Dante's forearm. "Don't worry about it. We'll hear everything we need to in a minute, and so will they. Also, when you get a second, could you ask Midas how our viewership is coming along?"

Dante pinched the bridge of his nose and sighed. "That's exactly what he was telling me. We're getting a steadily exponential increase."

Her eyes widened. "Oh, really? Damn. I'd almost rather be

home watching the numbers go up. But, this is important. Are you ready?"

He smoothed out his hair. "That I am."

The functionary returned, and this time he held the door open. "Sir. Madam. They are ready for you now."

The pair walked past him into the boardroom. It was an expansive chamber, on the darker side due to the shaded windows and the deep brown and blue synthetic wood. Professional and tastefully furnished.

A simple table and two chairs had been set out for them, facing the far larger desk around which sat seven executives. They were a motley group in terms of age, sex, and cultural background, but all of them looked grimly serious. Half had something else in their eyes as well, a perky curiosity bordering on excitement.

Dante pulled out a chair and sat. Nasreen remained standing. They had agreed that she would do the bulk of the talking. It was one of the things she was *far* better at than he was.

She put on her best professional smile and began.

"Ladies and gentlemen. I am Nasreen Joelle, sometimes known by the Marauder handle E-zex, and this is my associate Jordan Raksha, also known as Hellcat. To briefly summarize what you probably already know before I delve into the specifics —we are the individuals who have recently been investing so heavily in your firms and who now control a considerable interest in the companies.

"We are also now celebrities in an extremely dangerous profession. I say this not to brag, let alone threaten, but merely to make you aware that we are serious persons of varied talents and that what we have to say is worth your time and attention."

One or two of the execs looked a little off-put by the borderline arrogance of the statement, but the others pursed their lips or nodded with a certain begrudging respect.

"You may have seen the video yourselves," she continued. "In it, we demonstrate conclusive proof that Slaine Solar Solutions, our mutual rival, has engaged in unethical and possibly illegal behaviors while maintaining their market hegemony.

"They hired a Reaper crew to destroy vital technology and prevent it from reaching the Stations, complete with orders to kill anyone resisting them. The major effect of this was depriving the populace of much-needed advances and driving up prices, all to sabotage their competition."

Eyes narrowed, and knuckles dragged across the fine synthetic mahogany surface of the long table. They could hardly have been unaware of Slaine's reputation for ruthlessness and a willingness to bend the rules for money and success, but the full implications of such a scandal were unfolding before them in real-time.

Nasreen went on. "As stakeholders, we feel our responsibility is to make you aware of this fact. But it goes beyond that alone." She paused for dramatic effect.

Dante had been eyeing the executives, not staring too hard or trying to get their attention but casually assessing them. One looked a tad hostile, and another seemed confused or skeptical, but the others were accommodating. It would be interesting to see how they reacted to what Nasreen was about to say next.

"You are now embroiled in a Stations-wide effort to rebuke SSS and knock them from the top of the proverbial heap, whether you want to be or not. All of us will be doing our part to take down Slaine and ensure that he doesn't get away with this. And other crimes, as well."

One of the execs, an older man who was probably the elder statesman among them, opened his mouth wide and exclaimed, "What? Do you realize who you are speaking to, young lady?"

"I do, sir." She didn't miss a beat. "You have a good track record of shrewd yet ethical business practices and are a respected community member. Therefore, you cannot possibly fail to act now you know that in addition to criminal levels of industrial espionage, Slaine is also involved in the ovary harvesting of Dirtwalker women. A recent expedition authorized by him was a front for said operation, and we can prove it."

Gasps went around the table. They were indignant but also frightened. O-harvesting was frowned upon to such an extent that being associated with it themselves would badly tarnish their professional reputations.

A couple of them were about to ask questions or raise objections, but Nasreen headed them off by saying what she was pretty sure they wanted to know, anyway.

"We will provide you with the evidence after this meeting. There are some things we edited out, such as personally identifiable information or incidents of, erm, rather gruesome violence. Otherwise, you will find that the footage has not been tampered with. It is genuine. The video is only the start of what we have to offer."

The older man appeared to be rolling his tongue around his teeth as he contemplated her words. "What do you mean, offer? The video you describe does not contain o-harvesting, does it?"

"No," Nasreen conceded, "but we have other evidence of that. Furthermore, we have been preparing this for months now. We have already done most of the heavy lifting. You will not need to commission researchers or investigators. That is taken care of.

"To topple Slaine, what we *will* require from you is your cooperation in employing your financial connections, organizational tools, and political allies. In tandem with what we have done, this will cut the roots of SSS, and the trunk will soon follow."

Dante sat and watched as the discussion proceeded, with Nasreen explaining their strategies in more detail and also drawing attention to the financial side of things. He spoke up now and again to add useful comments, but mostly, she did her thing. Diplomacy and psychology were her areas of expertise. Although she was getting better at plundering.

As she placated the executives' anxieties and their enthusiasm slowly grew, Dante could picture a row of dominoes being lined up, ready for the first one to fall.

CHAPTER TWENTY

Since Midas was due for a checkup anyway, they decided to head to Berlin a day early for dinner. There was no shortage of excellent restaurants there.

"Remember," Dante told the AI. "This is only to make sure you and I are still interfacing in healthy ways for both of us. The clinic will look things over and make sure all is well. However, that's in the morning. Tonight we're having dinner, and if you pester me to order all the most expensive shit, I may have to talk to Dr. Kieffer about your behavior. You don't want that, do you?"

Midas sounded annoyed but resigned. "Sir, I have been better lately about that sort of thing, as you well know. The only recommendations I might make are if I see an item that sounds like it would appeal to you, based on your past preferences. It is faster to get through a menu with both of us reading instead of doing it all by yourself."

"Fair enough," Dante had agreed. "You have been doing pretty well lately. This place's menu isn't all that extensive, anyway. They focus on quality rather than quantity."

The place they chose was a semi-swanky fine dining establishment with no particular ethnic flavor or gimmick. They served obvious foods like top-grade lab-grown steak and exotic tank-bred fish along with expertly cooked and seasoned vegetables, and a nice selection of excellent wines.

Fittingly, there was a formal or semi-formal dress requirement, so both had cleaned themselves up and selected their fanciest outfits. Dante wasn't a huge fan of wearing a suit, but he had to admit that he looked sharp in one.

Nasreen smiled at him as they approached the establishment's front doors. "I almost don't recognize you in that getup, you know. You look much too good to be, well, your usual self."

"Oh. Thanks." He paused. "You look nice also. That dress is...flattering."

She laughed softly. "It is a bit low-cut. With you, I'll take what compliments I can get."

He nodded. "Yeah."

Once they were seated and had ordered drinks, Midas complained about the relatively limited menu options. Dante ignored him until he shut up. When their waiter returned, he ordered steak. Nasreen ordered fish. The waiter took their menus, the old-fashioned laminated paper kind, and ducked away.

The pair looked around. The place had pleasant, intimate lighting and decor that was tasteful despite using a lot of gold. A raised platform was at one end, where a live pianist plinked away. Dante wasn't enough of a music aficionado to recognize any of the pieces, but it sounded like moody classical stuff, meant to be beautiful without being too perky or experimental.

He thought back to Ambrose, his former crewman, playing piano at the jazz club in Paris. He clenched his jaw and sipped his wine.

Nasreen studied his face. "I know that look," she quipped.

"Oh? What look?" He glanced at her, then turned his eyes back toward the pianist.

His partner shook her head. "Men think they're more

inscrutable than they are. You're thinking about Am, aren't you? Two down, one to go."

He decided not to blurt anything, particularly since he wasn't sure what to say. He thought about his response before he opened his mouth.

"Yes, I'm thinking about him, but I'm not sure how I feel. Aside from I'd rather not have to think about him if that makes sense." One of his hands clenched on the tablecloth.

Nasreen rested her chin in her hands. "I suppose it does. Keeping your friends seems like it would be more fun than losing them and feeling like you have to kill them."

Dante's stomach tightened a little. Her words hurt. Not that she was accusing or criticizing him, exactly. It was that she'd hit the proverbial nail a little too directly on the head. "Yes."

She nodded. "Listen to me, Dante. We've made a lot of progress toward the goal we've worked so hard at for months now. But there's something I want to know. I want an assurance that, for you, this is about more than getting revenge on a handful of people who made a terrible decision. Seeing the results of that, up close and personal down in Charlotte, wasn't pleasant. Even if I understand why."

Dante turned his head and looked her full in the eyes with his distinctive mixture of intensity and neutrality. However, there was something darker in his demeanor this time. She couldn't put her finger on exactly what it was.

"I told you what SSS' real purpose was on that mission," he began. "You know what o-harvesting entails. It's an ugly business. It's like... Ugh. It's almost like rape.

"Maybe it's hypocritical of me to be so disgusted by it. I've killed Dirtwalkers by the dozen, including women when I had to. But only because they were trying to harm me. I've spared others when they didn't give me any reason to hurt them."

Nasreen hung onto his words. It wasn't the most cheerful subject to talk about, but she had always wondered how he felt about what he did for a living and how it related to his vendetta against Slaine, Hyde, and his former crewmates.

Dante let out a short, raspy sigh. "It happened—the big o-harvest, I mean—at the same time I found myself working *with* Dirtwalkers, helping them and letting them help me. That was an all-new experience. I never bore them any ill will before. They were obstacles I had to navigate. Since then it's been impossible not to see them as fully human. Which they are."

Their waiter returned to ask if they wanted more wine, and Dante requested that he bring the whole bottle. The man agreed and returned with it a moment later.

Once they had privacy again, Dante resumed his confession.

"I haven't been the same since then. It was humbling. I got my ass kicked about as badly as I ever have, and I learned things I would never have thought about before. Those people—the Dirtwalker women, and men too, who'd had their futures stolen from them—had nothing to live for. They exist on a dying planet where all there is, is survival and reproduction, like animals. But they pressed on anyway. It made me think."

Nasreen frowned. She wanted to reach out and touch his hand but wasn't sure how he'd react. "Thinking deeply is not a bad thing," she observed.

"Yeah. Well." He adjusted his collar. "I saw myself as someone who performed tasks. The world is a bunch of jobs waiting to be done, and what matters is doing them well. That, loyalty, and professional honor. There's shit to do, so do it honestly, don't lie or screw anyone over. That used to be enough for me."

Nasreen identified with what he was saying to a greater extent than he probably suspected, even if the world she had navigated was much different—but hardly less dangerous.

Dante went on. "I always felt driven to be the best. The most successful and the best in terms of integrity. I never really considered the toll it took on other people, including people I care about or should care about. I saw all the stuff I'd been trying *not* to see for years. That, and being betrayed like that, which I never thought would happen."

"Well, people don't always return the favor because *you* are loyal to *them*."

By now, Dante was halfway into his second glass of wine. "No shit." He glanced around, hoping no one had heard him. This seemed like a place where foul language might scandalize someone. Nobody was paying them heed.

Midas had fallen silent as well. To his credit, he tended to stay out of conversations that were a little too *human* for him to have a stake in.

Dante continued, "What I know now, or strongly suspect, is that the way Plunderers operate has to change. The way the Atlantica Stations survive has to change. It's worked for us, but it has downsides I can't ignore anymore. I'm not sure how to change it, but maybe we can figure that out."

His bright, sharp green eyes met with her deep mahogany eyes. After a moment, she managed a smile.

"Yes," she said. "I would certainly like to try."

Thank you for not only reading this book but these author notes as well!

As I get older (and have fewer responsibilities, fewer toys, etc.), I find myself in a quandary.

I have the money to go out to eat more often. I just don't want to. Don't get me wrong, I probably still go out / get food delivered much more than is healthy by a long shot, but I find myself not wanting anything fancy or sophisticated.

If you call steak and bread and baked potatoes sophisticated, that is.

Either way, I am making a LOT of soup these days. And not just any soup; I'm talking that old college "I'm broke as shit" soup, ramen noodles. The chicken flavor.

I wasn't a big fan of those for most of my life. I've been a big Lipton Chicken Soup (bag) fan since I was a teenager, and I felt the packaged ramen was just too salty. However, my wife introduced me to doctoring the soup, and I've rarely gone back to Lipton.

I do, just not often.

For a year or two, I've been adding red pepper flakes and a bit more chicken bouillon to the soup before I serve it. My wife likes adding lemon juice and seeds. The sesame seeds on the top of hamburger buns? Those.

I don't like lemon flavoring and find the seeds add nothing for me, so it's just the red pepper flakes.

However, I thought I should try adding something new, and by god, I figured out the next iteration of Awesome Soup Hacks by Authors™!

What is this awesomeness? I'm glad you asked because I wanted to share.

It's Italian Seasoning. A few shakes (or five in my case) with the ramen noodles / chicken seasoning / red pepper flakes (to taste), and the $0.50 package tastes like a soup that you paid damned good money for.

Try it, and let me know how you like it! I'll be adding this to my personal email list (see below) this week to share with the fans.

- 1 Bag ramen noodle soup (chicken flavored)
- Red pepper flakes (to taste)
- Chicken bouillon (extra to taste)
- Italian Seasoning (two to five shakes, to taste…not too much!)

Cook as directed but add the seasonings while the water is heating.

Talk to you in the next book!

Ad Aeternitatem,

Michael

If you want, you can read a couple of short stories I am sharing in my STORIES with Michael Anderle newsletter here: (No requirement to sign up.)

https://michael.beehiiv.com/

OTHER ATLANTICA BOOKS

John Chambers Books

Her Mother's Pendant (Book 1)

The Mystery Deepens (Book 2)

One Last Choice (Book 3)

Valentina Winters

The Red Countess (Book 1)

One Night to Kill (Book 2)

One Death Too Few (Book 3)

Terra Kris

She is the Law (Book 1)

Law or Justice (Book 2)

Justice Served (Book 3)

Santana Sokolov

Law of the Jungle (Book 1)

Inner City Jungle (coming soon)

Rumble in the Jungle (coming soon)

Justice Begins

The First Executioner

Aiming Blind

High Lead and Low Deeds

No Backing Down

Justice is Not Blind

Scorched Earth

BOOKS BY MICHAEL ANDERLE

Sign up for the LMBPN email list to be notified of new releases and special deals!

https://lmbpn.com/email/

For a complete list of books by Michael Anderle, please visit:

www.lmbpn.com/ma-books/

CONNECT WITH THE AUTHOR

Website: http://lmbpn.com

Email List: https://michael.beehiiv.com/

https://www.facebook.com/LMBPNPublishing

https://twitter.com/MichaelAnderle

https://www.instagram.com/lmbpn_publishing/

https://www.bookbub.com/authors/michael-anderle